The Last World War

Volume 2: Attempted Liquidation

By

Timothy Imholt, Michael Garst

I0556250

Also by Timothy Imholt

1) *The Forest of Assassins*
2) *Toddler Art*
3) *The Layman's United States Constitution*
4) *China Bones Book 1 – China Side*
5) *China Bones Book 2 – The Bamboo Caress*
6) *China Bones Book 3 – The Red Pagoda*
7) *China Bones – The Complete Series*
8) *The Layman's Articles of Confederation*
9) *A Collection of Mother Goose Tongue Twisters*
10) *A Study in Scarlet with Annotations*
11) *The Sign of the Four with Annotations*
12) *Laughing at a Military Enlistment*
13) *The Hound of the Baskervilles (Annotated)*
14) *The Last World War Volume 1: Trial by Fission*
15) *The Valley of Fear (Annotated)*
16) *Degrees Book 1: Saving the Earth*
17) *The Adventures of Sherlock Holmes (Annotated)*
18) *The Memoirs of Sherlock Holmes (Annotated)*
19) *Boston, Sort of Legal Part 1 – Win Some, Lose Some*
20) *The Return of Sherlock Holmes (Annotated)*
21) *Concusstitution: Welcome to Football*
22) *A Princess of Mars (Annotated)*
23) *Fighting Spirit*

Forward by Timothy Imholt

1) *Warbots*
2) *Warbots: #2 Operation Steel Band*
3) *Warbots: #3 The Bastaard Rebellion*
4) *Warbots: #4 Sierra Madre*
5) *Warbots: #5 Operation High Dragon*
6) *Warbots: #6 The Lost Battalion*

Also by Michael Garst

Forward

It has been a few years since the first in this series came out, and for that, dear reader, we do apologize. It wasn't that we didn't care for it or wanted to abandon the story line. Far from it. Between the two of us we (and our wives who we couldn't do things without) we have five kids, three for Tim, two for Mike. Both of us also has one child with special needs of one sort or another. If that wasn't enough there have been a lot of other books published between then and now, just look at the list preceding this forward! Well, Tim got more published, Mike was continuing his graduate degrees and gave his career choice a hard-right turn and started over.

Then, of course there was the whole how do we make the entire world more chaotic than it was in the first story. Every single time we thought we had it figured out, the world around us went crazy, in some cases crazier than we put in the book (part 2). So, we had to amp it up a notch.

We go up a notch, the world gets nuttier, over and over.

We finally got it, we finally went a little nuttier than the world and at the same time we strove to keep it believable. One thing we made every attempt to do in the first book (right up until that last chapter) was to keep it in line with where the world is currently. Keep the technology similar, keep the threats things we really face today, in other words keep it kind of rational, something that could really happen.

If the year 2020 has taught us anything it is that sometimes the implausible, is actually plausible. As a result, we found a way to get this to work, and even have a really tight outline and series of ideas for the next one (already being furiously worked so there won't be another multi-year hiatus).

With that in mind, thank you for your attention, and I bring you, the Last World War Volume 2: Attempted Liquidation.

Timothy Imholt PhD and Michael Garst

P.S. (update from early 2024) This book was conceived and written before COVID-19 so all of that "how nutty are we" stuff got a little bit more odd in real life on occasion than we would have tried in a fictional setting. There are aspects of this book that involve a bioweapon that is much more deadly than COVID-19, and we could have (and maybe should have) made the public response to that far more extreme. Truth is always stranger than fiction.

Chapter One
The US Invaded

As Matt pulled up in front of Shelly's house, he couldn't get over the fact that it had been a year since they'd gotten serious about their relationship. They had known each other for years, growing up in a relatively small town made that just a natural part of life, but they had started dating at the end of their junior year of high school. As graduation approached it was hard to believe all that had happened in that relatively short period of time, and how it had altered their lives forever.

They watched together as the most recent in a long list of wars unfolded on television. It was a driving factor in the series of events that made them grow emotionally bonded more quickly and deeply than either of them had anticipated. Even though multiple nuclear weapons had been detonated on American soil the fighting had taken place overseas. Yes, two of the nuclear attacks were inside the U.S., but those bombs had hit far from their small town, making it abstract in some ways, but hit home in others. They had personally felt safe, but it was strange to watch. At times it had seemed like it was a work of fiction.

Wars were things that happened elsewhere in the world. They didn't result in the complete devastation of American cities. That was the way it had been for so long that almost nothing but black and white photos existed of the last organized military attack to cause any damage on American soil. Those ancient events served to pull the United States into World War 2. It was considered unthinkable for any military to be able to hit the American Homeland given the advancements in military technology the United States had achieved since that ancient attack in Hawaii.

That was, until these recent attacks, but at least there had been no follow-on invasion of troops. Everyone had feared that was inevitable at the time.

Most people could remember the 9/11 terrorist attacks in New York and Washington DC that marked the start of an active war on terror, but this had been different. Those attacks had tragically destroyed some massive office buildings and killed more than twenty-five hundred people, but that was small-time by comparison to this new insanity.

Nukes going off on U.S. soil had always been a threat, petty dictators loved to make public claims that they would one day do such a thing, but the threat had always seemed empty. It was the kind of thing they used to fill airtime on a slow news day. No rational person even considered it a real possibility since the Cuban missile crisis way back in the 1960's.

Watching the news coverage of the attacks, with all the dead and injured civilians had changed their young world forever. It made it all that much worse considering Matt had lost his brother in one of those hellish fireballs. At first it was abstract, like his brother was away on vacation, or on a semester abroad and would still return home for a semester break. It took a little bit of time, but reality finally set in.

It made him angry in ways he had never experienced, and even angrier that his brother had insisted on going to a University so far from home. If he had stayed closer, like Matt had wanted him to, he would most likely still be alive.

Now it was Matt's turn to get ready to go to college. Shelly and he were going to attend the same University. The idea came about because of all they had watched unfold, after all that the world had been through, they were sure that this love they shared was the one and only love they needed for the rest of their lives, and they didn't want to be apart for four years. That would seem like an eternity. They intended to use this past year of loss, danger, and recovery as the basis for a lifetime they intended to spend together. That long-term plan was their secret for the moment because they knew their parents, and even their friends would be against it. They would all say they were too young.

Matt felt he owed Shelly his life. She had pulled him out of a downward spiral.

After the loss of Matt's brother, Chad, in the attack on Detroit, Shelly had helped him as he mourned the loss. That support meant a lot to him. He would miss his brother for the rest of his life, but the thought of Shelly in his life made it easier to cope with the loss. Matt had been on the verge of trying some very foolish things to dull the pain when she came along and stopped him.

Despite the challenges, the United States had fought back and quickly won the War. The other side had suffered staggering military losses. Unlike the sneak attacking assholes, the US military made every attempt to spare their civilian populations any physical danger whenever possible. Ultimately the enemy had unconditionally surrendered, and even agreed to nuclear disarmament.

Matt had thrown a party to celebrate the victory. With that victory it was like he could claim his brother had died for a reason. Now, perhaps, there could be peace in the world, and terrorist attacks, as well as the resulting wars, could become a subject for historians to ponder.

Matt got out of the car and headed for the door. Shelly came bounding out of the house before he was halfway up the walkway.

She threw her arms around his neck, "A year, can you believe it?" she asked, hugging him with her eyes closed and a huge smile.

Matt took a step back to look at the young woman he loved. Her blonde hair was shining in the late afternoon light, her athletic build, and tonight of all nights, wearing her "comfy jeans" as she always called her favorite pair of threadbare cutoffs. They were accompanied by a bare midriff t-shirt that may as well have been custom designed to shift his teenage hormones into overdrive.

"So much has happened. I feel like I have known you my whole life, and I guess I have really known you a long time, but not in this new way. You somehow managed to keep me sane through it all. I have a special surprise planned to celebrate our anniversary. You ready to go?" he asked with a devilish grin.

"Oh, I like surprises," she said with a flirtatious smile, and a wiggle of her eyebrows.

While hiking with some friends Matt found an excellent spot where they could park, take a walk in the woods and watch the airplanes take off out of Bangor airport on their way to someplace better than the middle of nowhere Maine. Seasonal tourists might love this place for the scenery, and the two of them enjoyed that as much as anyone but growing up here made it not seem all that special. However, all of the leaf covered scenery would offer some privacy for a romantic night, and that was what they both really wanted.

Matt always loved it when his dad let him borrow the convertible. There weren't a lot of months that option was useful in Maine, but he enjoyed it given the opportunity. With the top down Shelly's long hair was blowing in the wind. It made her look even sexier than normal.

Once they made it to the surprise destination, they parked the car and headed into the woods for their walk, hand in hand.

Matt had managed to time things perfectly. Just as they were finishing their walk, the sun was just starting to disappear over the horizon.

They got into the backseat and were sitting side by side talking about graduation while doing nothing more than holding hands.

Slowly their talking stopped, and the kissing began. Matt didn't know when, and didn't really care how, but Shelly wound up straddling his waist and he felt like he was about to explode. The hormones were raging, and he wasn't sure he could keep his bodily functions under control long enough to get to the finish line he hoped they were both thinking about.

Shelly abruptly stopped. Matt was confused.

She eagerly looked down at him, knowing this break in activity was a total tease, and slowly removed her shirt, then her bra, exposing herself. The sight of her in this position, and in a state of undress was what he had been looking forward to all day.

Matt had been so distracted by the sight of her bare breasts that he failed to notice the man in jeans and a black t-shirt with military gear strapped to his body coming out of the tree line.

The bastard grabbed Shelly by the hair and dragged her from the car as she screamed wildly, as much from pain as surprise, shock and fear.

Matt watched in disbelief as the man threw her to the ground and kicked her in the stomach while shouting in guttural tones.

Matt launched himself at the man.

"Who the *fuck* are you?" he shouted and got no answer he could understand.

The man had two partners who grabbed Matt by the arms and brutally dragged him down onto the dirt road. He landed hard on his back with a huge rock digging into his spine as the three men started to kick him in the face, back, chest, in any exposed area until his head was spinning from pain.

He felt some bones cracked in his chest. The favorite target of their savage assaults.

It was all Matt could do to get out a few words between blows, "Shelly, *RUN!*"

Matt was on the ground half naked and bleeding from more places than he could count. Blood had run into his eyes and mouth. Finally, the kicks stopped. Every time he tried to move there was a searing pain in his chest, left arm and right leg.

He made a huge mistake by looking at his arm, then realized it probably would have been better to not know. It looked like a white stick was poking out of his forearm. Blood was streaming down his arm to finally fall to the ground when it got to his fingertips. It took a minute for him to realize that the "stick" was one of his bones coming through the skin. At first, he couldn't believe it, then he panicked and was certain he was going to die...then he thought of Shelly and regained focus.

He watched helplessly as the largest of them stalked back to where Shelly was trying to crawl away, screaming hysterically. The men laughed as one of them grabbed a handful of her hair and pulled her head back as the young woman kicked and screamed. The man started working her around to the front of the car.

The largest of the assholes picked her up and threw her onto the hood of the car hard enough to dent the thing into a rumpled outline of her body. Another one of them pulled a huge knife that had been dangling from his belt and cut her shorts until he could easily rip them off, throwing them to the side. Shelly kept screaming, "Help! Help!"

The shouts grew louder and more desperate as he slid the cold metallic blade along the skin of her legs, then stomach.

Matt wanted to help, but every time he tried to move his vision got fuzzy and it felt like he was going to lose consciousness.

The largest of them unbuckled his pants as the other two moved to the sides of the car to hold her down on the hood. Knowing what was about to happen, Shelly bucked wildly trying to break free from their vice-like grips. She did not want him to put that thing sticking out from the massive mound of bushy black hair into her.

They were too strong for her. She was quickly becoming exhausted by the struggle, but she continued to kick, getting weaker and weaker with each attempt at striking or breaking free from her attackers. With a little luck, she managed to get an arm free and connect with some soft part of one of the men. He let out a surprised howl. She had no idea where she hit him, but the yelp of pain gave her some semblance of hope.

She redoubled her efforts, lashing out even more furiously, with renewed energy. The injured man stumbled back and fell to the ground. One of the others laughed and grabbed a handful of her hair, then slammed her head against the hood of the car a few times until blood ran from multiple cuts to the back of her head and she stopped struggling.

They shoved her to the center of the car hood. Two of the men took up proper position and held her left arm straight out. The third asshole, who had finally recovered from the lucky shot, kicked the elbow, causing bones to shatter and the joint to dislocate. In the process he rendered her arm completely useless as a weapon.

The man who had fallen to the ground after Shelly kicked him picked up a large rock and returned to the struggling young woman. He bashed her in the leg with the rock causing her leg to emit a snapping sound as the knee bent backward, becoming dislocated, likely breaking ligaments free from where they had been connected since birth.

Shelly lay, barely conscious, across the hood of the car.

They kept shouting in a language Matt didn't understand. He vowed to someday learn what they were saying and find a way to make them pay for what they were doing, if he lived through this.

Their words, in whatever language it was, would be burned into his brain forever. Death would be too easy for them. He wanted them to suffer.

The largest of the attackers flipped Shelly over, so she was face down. With no consideration, he pulled his dick out and shoved it into a body part of hers that was designed for an entirely different purpose.

Shelly could no longer offer any form of resistance.

She could barely manage painful groans as she tried to cling to consciousness. From what Matt could see from his vantage point it seemed like every inch of her body was bruised or bleeding. Blood seeped out of cuts from more areas of her body than anyone could count as she silently cried as the brutalization continued. She finally managed to turn her head to look at Matt and could see that even with his leg bent the wrong way and his arm obviously broken, he was trying to make his way to her.

She saw him stop crawling, vomit blood, and collapse to the ground. It was impossible to tell if he was alive or dead, it could have gone either way.

It was at that moment she began to realize she may die. She also knew she didn't want to go down without a fight.

The largest of the attackers picked her up and flipped her over again. He shoved her down on her back, denting hood of the car further.

She let out a primal scream.

With the little strength she had left she spat blood into his eye and yelled, "Fuck you, you goddamn pig!"

He reached down to the ground to pick something up.

In a fit of violent lust, he forced his dick into her, then bashed her face in with a rock so large that took two hands to lift. All three men laughed as her skull splintered, and dark, thick fluid came oozing out in every direction. Strange pieces of shredded tissue littered the windshield as her body went into death spasms.

Matt was in and out of consciousness and could only watch in horror, not exactly understanding or believing what he was seeing.

Through his blurred vision Matt saw what he thought were grains of rice on the ground, but then realized it was her teeth, making him even angrier and more scared than he had been before.

He vomited more blood. Barely able to move, he was drifting in and out of consciousness, there was just too much pain for his to maintain his senses. He had to lay there and watch as all three of them ravaged her lifeless body. She was dead and would feel no pain, but Matt's rage boiled. He was twenty feet away and could do nothing. He had done effectively nothing as the love of his life was killed. His ribs sent lightning bolts of pain through his chest every time he moved.

The men, having finished with the girl, walked back towards Matt's prone body. With one last blow to the head, everything turned black.

***

Matt faded in and out of consciousness. He was only half aware he was being sodomized. His mind was still trying to process everything.

He slowly became aware of the sounds of multiple

large truck engines starting. He heard a large group of people moving around somewhere down the hill. Apparently, this was not a couple of random guys wandering through the woods. Through the fog Matt's brain guessed that somehow the war wasn't as over as people thought.

***

Matt wasn't sure of the exact time he passed out, or what time it was when he woke up, but he knew that he had to stand up, had to move, and above all, he had to find some help. He looked around the area, realized it was dark, and his dad's car was gone. He was on his own, with a broken body, no transportation and deep in an isolated area, far from a heavily trafficked road. The grand slam of trouble.

Slowly the memory of what happened came back, bit by horrifying bit. He scanned the area for Shelly, hoping it had all been a dream. He found where her body had been. The outline in the dirt was unmistakable. There were some large paw prints and a blood trail. Some animal must of have taken her body off into the woods as a meal.

Matt couldn't believe any of this had happened.

Was he dreaming?

No, this was real.

Was the love of his life really being digested by some furry woodland creature at this very moment?

It couldn't be possible.

It was too much to think about. Hopefully he was wrong, and she was alive someplace. That had to be the case. Hopefully, she had crawled away and found help. He knew that was not likely, but he needed to believe in something. He needed a reason to endure the suffering that moving down the path on his quest for help would cause. Walking caused more pain than he ever thought possible to endure, and he knew he had at least a mile, if not more, to go.

He moved his feet, slowly, carefully. He had to get out of the area. He had to let someone know what happened. He needed to find someone to help him look for her.

Who would believe him? Who would believe it wasn't just the delusional rambling of an injured kid who got his ass kicked?

This sort of thing just didn't happen here, not in the United States, and certainly not in Maine. This was where people went on vacation, there was nothing of strategic military importance here, or anywhere within a hundred miles.

Three guys, come out of nowhere and brutally attack two teenagers, probably killing one and leaving the other for dead?

It just wasn't something that happened, it shouldn't happen.

How could this happen?

Why did this happen?

Why did it happen to them?

Maybe they had taken Shelly prisoner. That had to be it.

Matt started moving as fast as he could, which was a slow shuffle but at least he was on his feet and moving forward. He was making his way back to the road by remote control. Making matters worse, his shoes were missing. He was still bleeding from multiple wounds but had to find someone and tell them what happened.

He cradled one arm in the other and tried to move faster. He had to convince people of the danger, no matter what. The alarm *had* to go out.

No matter how much he wanted to lay down on the ground and sleep, Matt knew he could not. His injuries could wait. Someone had to know what was going on out here before someone else suffered like Shelly.

Someone had to help find her. She had to still be alive out there somewhere in the woods, just unconscious and in desperate need of help.

Barefoot and bleeding, with stunted unsteady steps, he kept making his way down the dirt road. He took no notice of the sharp pricks of the rocks and broken glass cutting into his abused feet. He was beyond feeling pain.

An hour later Matt was slowly limping his way up a country road. He was near exhaustion. He hoped someone would come along and stop. Then he hoped when it happened that it was the right person. There was no way he could survive another attack.

***

National Guardsmen Sgt. Greg Spoker and Sgt. Aaron Little had received the call to mount up into an armored Hummer and head off to a remote part of the countryside. Once there, they were to patrol and report any unusual activity. As they drove along the country road they talked about how they were glad that at least it was not another trip to Afghanistan or Iraq. Both had done several tours over there and did not relish the idea of going back.

Little had just popped open a soda can and was about to light up a smoke when something moving on the side of the road caught his attention.

"Hey, Sergeant Spoker," Little said, "slow down and load up. I see something up ahead about five hundred yards on the right."

The Sergeant slowed the vehicle to a crawl two hundred and fifty yards out from what looked like a zombie slowly shuffling along the road. Both men raised their weapons to the ready with their fingers off the trigger, but not far away, resting on the trigger guard. As they slowed down to understand the level of this potential "threat" they sarcastically hoped the zombie wasn't a real one.

They figured the whole thing had to be part of a training exercise, and this was one of the participants playing a role of some kind. It was the kind of thing that happened when you were trying to prep for a type of attack that only exists in the mind of some Army training "expert."

As they neared the person, zombie, or whatever it was, the zombie-person began to weakly wave them down. The other arm did not look right from a distance, somehow it looked different, misshapen.

"Stop where you are," Little shouted at the whatever it was, wondering what the hell was going on.

Sergeant Spokers got on the radio to call in the "unusual activity."

Sergeant Little looked through his rifle scope as he worked his way in closer to the potential threat and saw the frightening image of Matt, "*GET THE MED KIT, AND CALL A DAMN AMBULANCE!*" he screamed, jumping into action mode, almost in a panic.

"Aaron," Greg said, "What the fuck is it?"

"It's some kid. He is seriously messed up. Someone worked him over just like the Iraqis used to do to uncooperative local prisoners."

Sergeant Little grabbed the medical kit and ran to Matt. Sergeant Spoker was frantically talking on the radio looking for help, "Headhunter Base, this is Ghostrider three Alpha, over."

"Ghostrider three Alpha, this is Headhunter Base, go ahead, over," said the disembodied radio voice.

"Base, three Alpha, we need casualty evac at," looking over at the GPS on the dash he read the coordinates.

"Casualty is a teenage male, severe blunt trauma, broken bones and bleeding. First Aid initiated, but he will need higher care before we move him, over."

"Three Alpha, this is Headhunter six, say again your last. Do I understand you have a casualty, over?" came the confused reply.

"Six, this is three Alpha. Roger on last. One civilian casualty, priority evacuation is needed. First aid is started, but the kid has massive blunt force trauma, open fractures, and looks like he may lose a leg if you don't get that evac, preferably air evac, here right now, over."

There was a short pause before the reply.

"Air evac is on the way. Secure the area, treat the casualty to the best of your ability. Keep whoever it is alive, we need to know what the hell is going on. Intelligence reports coming our way from all over are confused at best, and contradictory at worst. It sounds like this person may know something, over."

"Six, Three, roger, out."

Sergeant Little slid to a stop as he ripped open a medical kit. Sergeant Spoker was moving the truck forward to shine more light on the scene so they could work on the injuries more easily.

"Shit, where the fuck is Doc when you need him? This kid is messed up. I can stop most of the bleeding, but he has so many broken bones I don't know where to start," Little said to no one in particular. He had already bandaged some of the head wounds and was working his way down the body trying to prioritize the worst injuries first. Looking at the open fracture, he just immobilized the arm as much as possible and moved on. Matt was such a mess it was hard to tell active bleeders from injuries that had managed to clot and still had blood flowing across them from somewhere else.

Sergeant Spoker was moving around, sweeping the area with his weapon at the ready, looking for any source of potential trouble when he saw the dragged footmark trail Matt had left on the side of the road. Kneeling down, he flipped on his tactical light and discovered the trail of blood.

"Aaron," he called out, "check the kid's feet and see if they are bleeding."

Little moved to Matt's feet and recoiled in horror. He had seen people, friends as well as enemies, blown up. Never in his life had he seen as much damage done to a human body part still attached to someone that had just been moving under their own power. The only thing his mind could think of was how much they resembled ground beef. The same kind of stuff he had made into burgers on the weekend countless times.

There were bits of twigs sticking out of Matt's feet. His heels were ground down to the bone in multiple places. There was torn flesh just dangling off in all directions. One toe was missing from what appeared to be the result of Matt dragging that foot behind him, like it had been sandpapered off.

He put tight bandages over both feet as fast as he

could and said, "Just save your energy man, stop trying to talk. We have more help on the way. You are massively dehydrated on top of everything else. I am going to start an IV drip and try to get your fluid levels back up. Don't worry, you are in good hands now. You will be just fine."

Sergeant Spoker kept patrolling the area while Sergeant Little worked on Matt. They could hear sirens in the distance, and a large helicopter thumping its way towards their position.

"I think we can say this isn't a training exercise," Sgt Little said, vocalizing for the first time what they both knew, but didn't want to say out loud.

What the hell had happened?

The War was supposed to be over.

<AP NEWS FLASH> There are unconfirmed reports of a foreign military invasion in the state of Maine. These reports are scattered and varied. There is no video, photographic, or audio evidence of these claims. The Governor of Maine has activated the National Guard, who are currently patrolling the regions of these reports looking for unusual activity. The thought right now is that there is some kind of widespread criminal activity going on that has evaded police departments until now. Residents in that part of the country are instructed to call local authorities if they see anything suspicious, but for their own safety they are urged to let first responders or National Guard deal with any threats. <STORY DEVELOPING>

<AP ECONOMIC NEWS FLASH> Upon initial, unconfirmed reports of a military invasion in the United States prices for oil and other commodities futures were driven much higher. As these are unconfirmed reports it is thought that this is the result of high-risk speculators attempting to take advantage of a small window of opportunity. Given that this event occurred late on Saturday afternoon, and the US markets are closed, it is expected these rumors can be put to rest before the markets open on Monday and will have little to no impact on the overall market averages and that these speculators may make some short-term profits but overall the market is expected to remain flat.

Chapter Two
Things Heat Up

Alex took a deep breath as he climbed into his car to start another long, traffic-filled commute so he could get a few things done on a beautiful late Saturday afternoon in downtown Los Angeles before heading over to work the night shift as a security guard on the Universal Studios lot. Once he made it to work his only stress would be keeping fans, or worse the corporate spies from the competing film companies, off the lot so work could continue on whatever television series or film happened to be shooting tonight. It would be a long day, and by the time he got to work he would be tired, but Los Angeles was an amazing place to experience.

People flocked to Southern California for vacations from all over the world. Others moved here for their chance at the "big time." The result was that downtown L.A. had become a difficult place to get to work on time because of all the traffic. He was growing envious of people with nice suburban office jobs.

The year-round fantastic weather *almost* made up for all the hassles. Adding in the fact that this was where he grew up made it nearly impossible for him to even consider leaving, despite the growing headaches involved in the daily grind.

He closed the driver's side door, started the engine

and took a sip of piping hot coffee from his thermal mug to help him gather some strength before putting the car into reverse to officially begin the day. The radio had the band Kansas singing *Dust in the Wind* as he glanced at the mirror and realized the sky had changed and kept quickly changing as he watched.

Whatever the cause, it appeared to come from somewhere behind him, and it was impossibly huge. He wasn't sure what it was, but whatever had happened it was not a typical occurrence. It was strange even for Los Angeles where there always seemed to be something new happening. It was probably some movie production with a bizarre scene they needed to catch on video and decided to do a practical shot rather than CGI. Some directors were purists. It was a little unusual for it to happen this close to the city, and it was really big for that sort of thing, but he supposed stranger things had happened.

Suddenly, and without warning, the car's engine shut off. He had almost enough time to fully turn back around to face the front before his car was thrown wildly into the air and through the roof of his single-story home like it was barely there. The blast was one thing, but the heat was even worse. It was so intense that the metal of the car's frame burst into flame.

Alex felt an intense burning sensation in his lungs and lost consciousness mere microseconds later.

It was more humane that way, half a second later everything from his clothing to his skin was on fire.

What remained of Alex was quickly turning to ash as the intense pressure wave came through. It disintegrated whatever parts of him were left of him into so many pieces he no longer resembled anything that had once been a living human being.

***

Just forty minutes after the detonation in Los Angeles, President Scott Press was sitting at the head of the conference table on Air Force One, not wanting to believe that they had to go through this…again.

His Presidency was still relatively new, and this was the second nuclear attack on U.S. soil. So far, this attack was only one city, but that was already one too many. They still hadn't finished cleaning up the previous wave of nuclear detonations or gotten things back to normal after the battle to save Israel, and yet here we go again. The war was supposed to be over. They had even signed a damn peace accord.

He had ordered the military to stand down and now realized the doubts he had at the time were not unfounded. He should have taken the opportunity to wipe the bastards out completely and totally. He *should* have eradicated them from the surface of the Earth. This new loss of American life was on *his* head, *his* head alone. No one else's.

He felt foolish for having believed the assholes were done trying to destroy the western nations of the world. He had stupidly believed that those bastards had finally changed their ways, that after thousands of years of fighting they had *finally* decided to change their ways. What a joke, damn he felt like such an idiot. He had wanted to believe they could change, but he should have been more logical and less emotional. Hope was not a strategy.

It was supposed to be his responsibility to keep the American people safe, and he was failing at it, miserably.

The public had wanted him to order the military to continue fighting until the enemy had not only been defeated, but decimated. Some people had even used the word exterminated.

After the war had been declared over, and the peace accord signed, there had been so many phone calls, so many pieces of regular mail, protestors, news interviews, emails, and whatever other form of communication people could figure out how to use in order to express their opinion, all of which seemed to agree that he hadn't gone far enough. People were pleased that we had won, but it wasn't enough to satisfy the national desire for and eye for an eye. He had ignorantly decided that when someone laid down their arms and quit fighting, they should be given the chance to live in peace. He still believed, or at least he still wanted to believe, that it was possible to survive in peace.

But they hadn't truly surrendered. They had only been taking some time to regroup and recover. The statements of peace that had been made were nothing but lies. No, that didn't go far enough, those statements were complete bullshit.

In hindsight he should have shown absolutely no mercy. Instead, he had allowed them to survive and even treated them honorably when they signed the "peace" agreement. Then, for reasons he couldn't fathom at the moment, he had gone to Congress and gotten them to offer fucking *humanitarian aid money* so that the parts of *their* civilian population who had been impacted in some negative way by the fighting could rebuild and recover more quickly.

The President continued to curse himself for being complacent and naive, and then grew even angrier with himself for allowing his mind to wander from the crisis unfolding in front of him.

Different groups in the Middle East had been fighting each other, and anyone else who happened to disagree with them, for thousands of years. Why should he or anyone else believe they would suddenly be prepared to stop now?

They were supposed to stop just because he was the guy in the Oval Office and had been the one who signed some scrap of paper with meaningless words?

What a waste of time.

This time would be different. He wouldn't make the same mistake again. Nope, not this time. This time, it was all or nothing. They had to be wiped from the face of the Earth with as much fury and speed as possible. Their ability to function militarily must be eradicated. Permanently.

Fueling the flames of his anger was the fact that none of the intelligence organizations at his disposal had managed to see this coming or even confirm anything about who was behind this attack. Given that there had been no warning of incoming missiles or aircraft, and it appeared to be a surface level detonation, the attack profile fit Iran's known strategy. Not only that, but logically thinking, who else would do this within a few months of the war, a war they started, "ending."

Their tactic was frustratingly simple, incredibly difficult to detect, and phenomenally effective.

All they had to do was sneak a few people willing to die for a cause into the target location, have them detonate the bomb, go up in flames along with the bomb, meet Allah, enter paradise, and get the promised seventy-two virgins or whatever the current promise for the afterlife happened to be this week, all the while killing millions of Americans in the process. They weren't even bothering to target militarily relevant sites this time. This was a purely civilian target with the intent to kill as many people as possible.

The city of Los Angeles had absolutely no military value. It did nothing to enhance the ability of the United States to conduct operations in the Middle East, or anywhere else in the world.

Why destroy a place that was primarily known for really nice weather and exporting American culture to the world?

That had to be the answer.

This was an attack on the American culture, on the American way of life. This was an attack on a way of thinking they disagree with.

The last time the U.S. had been attacked he had barely been able to hold back the public's blood lust and desire for a retaliatory nuclear strike. This time he was certain that this situation could spiral quickly out of everyone's control. Besides, it was difficult to disagree with such a retaliation at this point. How much of the world would be destroyed in the process, well, that was still to be determined. He wasn't even sure how much of the United States had been turned into a radiation filled wasteland yet. He was somehow convinced by a group of so-called experts, none of whom saw this coming, that the extent of the damage would take days to get any real data because this weapon was much more massive than last time.

Images of the nuclear devastation in Dallas and Detroit were running through his head. He had to respond now, right now, not in days. There was absolutely no time to spare, and he wasn't about to try to stop retaliatory unconventional attacks this time around once a reasonable target package was determined. The allies would understand. The enemy's entire population would just have to deal with what happened in the process of destroying the enemy's ability to project force.

Unfortunately, trying to solve problems from onboard an airplane was becoming second nature. This plane was so large that it had everything he needed to make that happen. It even had its own surgical suite, if that mattered.

The pilot was randomly moving around North American airspace to decrease the chance of a successful attack on the mobile command center, should such an attack be planned. Currently they didn't know of any such impending attack, but then the nuke in Los Angeles had come as a complete surprise, so what the fuck came next was anyone's guess. Two of the most advanced fighter planes in the world were flanking the giant aircraft to help with that problem, just in case the random flight pattern didn't serve the purpose.

The President was at the head of the table, flanked by the Chairman of the Joint Chiefs of Staff General Jackson, The Secretary of Defense Johnathon Martin. The National Security Advisor Brian Kentworthy was pacing around the table. On video screens mounted across the opposite wall were Vice President Frank Banner, along with anyone else who his leadership team decided had any sort of relevance or domain knowledge that might aid in solving the problem. Mainly they were from intelligence agencies, none of which saw this coming so their usefulness on what might happen next was questionable. Billions of dollars a year and they couldn't manage to track the supply and shipment of the world's known, highly regulated, relatively small supply of special nuclear material.

The National Security Advisor was doing his best to hastily inform the room of the very few facts that could be verified, and to his credit he was actively avoiding any kind of speculation. Speculation on something this big was too hard to undo later as it was generally taken as fact. That made it dangerous.

In the worst-case scenario, speculation could lead to

the wrong country being nuked if there was a critical error or rash over-reaction in their decision making. A retaliatory nuclear strike was the consensus, and very hard to argue against. That strike would be ordered just as soon as the identity of the perpetrators of the horrifying attack could be verified, and targets chosen. Everyone already knew who that would be, it was just a matter of verification, then target selection.

As the information on the screen changed, he forced himself to refocus on the briefing.

"As can be seen from these high-altitude images of Los Angeles, the damage radius is far greater than in the previous attacks. While this was certainly a nuclear attack, with almost absolute certainty we can say that this was a thermonuclear device," Mr. Kentworthy said. His voice sounded numb, as if he had intentionally emotionally shut down and was working out of some small part of his mind to avoid anything that might cause any type of negative emotion to rise to the surface. It was like he believed that if he allowed anything other than the cold logic centers of his brain to be in charge of his actions, he would not be able to continue to function in a useful fashion.

"What the hell is the difference between nuclear and thermonuclear, in simple terms?" the President asked while rubbing the bridge of his nose.

"Well, Mr. President, it means a few things. First, technologically speaking, it is a giant leap forward for their nuclear program. The bombs they used the last time were crude and very basic by comparison.

They were comparable to what we had in our inventory at the end of World War 2. They were nothing more than very basic uranium devices. To get that type to go nuclear you simply take two properly sized chunks of weapons-grade Uranium and smash them into each other fast enough, hard enough, and the result is a nuclear detonation," the National Security Advisor explained to the room.

Mr. Kentworthy took a deep breath to gather his thoughts, or perhaps he was looking for emotional strength before continuing, it was difficult to tell, "This device is far more complex. It is a three-stage bomb. It has a small amount of hydrogen at the center, surrounding that is an implosion-type fission device driven by a core of plutonium and a high-end chemical explosive shaped and timed exactly right to achieve the reaction goal. When the chemical explosive is detonated it causes the plutonium to implode and enter a fission runway reaction state and very quickly a nuclear explosion occurs. That fission explosion releases enough energy, in a short enough period of time, that due to the intense heat, sets off a fusion reaction of the hydrogen isotope inside the thermonuclear reaction set. This leads to us having a much different problem than we had previously. Such as a device can be built with a much larger yield, which means a far greater destructive capability than even the modern fission devices, and much more so than the older designs they previously used in Israel, Dallas and Detroit.

"To put it bluntly Mr. President, the devices they used previously were relatively small yield by comparison to this attack. As I said that older, crude design has an upper limit on how large you can make the yield, and typically they will not have yields higher than a few tens of kilotons. The thermonuclear designs can be made arbitrarily large. These are the massive bombs. This is the type of weapon we, and most of the known nuclear states have in our arsenal.

"We do have some early estimates based on the blast radius that this was ten megatons or so. That puts it at around one hundred times larger than anything that was used in the previous wave of attacks.

"In short Mr. President, Los Angeles has vanished. That is potentially as many as three million nine hundred thousand residents, plus anyone who was in town on vacation or business. We could have as many as four million dead, and no idea how many injured. One thing we are sure of is that the situation could strain the medical response capability of the entire region, if not the nation well beyond the breaking point. There are so many people in the surrounding area there will be enormous suffering from secondary injuries. As we all remember from last time those will range from lacerations, to broken bones to radiation poisoning. All of which come with an associated cost in time of treatment, medical supplies, and in some cases long term issues like rise in cancer rates, and increased rate of birth defects."

The President interrupted, "Do we have any indication that another device has, or is about to be detonated anywhere else on the planet?"

"No, we do not have any indication, at least not yet of another device having been, or a detonation being prepared anywhere in the world. But we are diligently watching and digging into every intelligence source we have that might have information on this or any future attack, Mr. President," concluded the National Security Advisor, nervously.

The President took a deep breath as he gathered his thoughts, "Couple of things. We didn't know they could build this type of weapon, and we didn't know an attack was coming. Honestly, I'm not very confident in the assessment that more of this shit isn't about to happen. Also, when you say that these can be made arbitrarily large, does anyone here know what that really means, and if so can they explain it to me in a way that I can understand?" he asked of everyone present, the stress of the situation clearly coming through in his voice.

"Back when the world routinely tested nuclear weapons, the Russians managed to make one so large that it completely erased an island in the South Pacific from the map. Mr. President, that island no longer exists above water. If I understand what the people from Los Alamos have said correctly, they could build one large enough that it could crack a large land mass, even flatten a mountain, or any of the other wrath of God images you can dream up. This is pure conjecture, but this device being detonated where it was in California just might have been an attempt to use a nuclear weapon in order to get a natural geological fault to start letting loose. In the process it could have kicked off a massive earthquake, thereby increasing the resulting devastation with no additional effort on their part.

We have no indication of earthquakes, but if they put one directly on a fault line that could amplify the overall problems we face," answered the Chairman of the Joint Chiefs.

"Wonderful," the President said with an eye roll. "I want everyone here to realize that since we didn't know they had this one, we can't be sure that they have any more or not. Therefore, in my mind, this implies we could get hit in a similar fashion again at any moment." the President stated.

"We can't be sure, that much I agree with Mr. President. However, the last time we were attacked it was a highly coordinated attack at five locations across the globe at practically the same instant. We can't be certain if they have more of these weapons or not, but we can make an educated guess that most likely they would have coordinated something this large if they could do more than one. Any nuclear strategy we have ever worked up since the final days of World War Two, when these devices were first invented, called for every target in the package to be hit as close to at once as possible. It is widely considered necessary to maintain the element of surprise in these scenarios. However, at this point, we have a problem of much greater importance, Mr. President," responded Secretary of Defense Martin.

"Mr. Secretary, we need to stick with facts, and not unconfirmed rumors," the television image of the Vice President warned, obviously aware of the direction the conversation was about to turn and was not pleased with it.

"With all due respect, Mr. Vice President, everything

I am about to say has now been confirmed. I know you saw some very preliminary data that was rather inconsistent and fragmented, but we are now beyond that level of confidence in the intelligence coming out of the area from multiple sources," rebutted the Secretary of Defense.

SecDef turned his attention away from the VP, "Mr. President, we have multiple confirmed reports of an armed invasion of an infantry division sized element of enemy combatants in Maine. We can also confirm that more troops are rapidly approaching our coastline in two flotillas of converted luxury cruise liners, along with some small escort fighting ships."

"How do we know if this is real? I have heard a lot of crazy things coming out of that area, and it could be people jumping at shadows," stated the VP. It was almost as if the man was trying to find a way to believe it wasn't true and couldn't be possible. A ground invasion was the nightmare scenario among all nightmare scenarios for anyone whose career choice involved protecting the nation.

"We have seen video footage confirming the reports on CNN, Fox, BBC, and even Al Jazeera America. In addition to that, there are a variety of sources we have on the ground as well as all the posts on social media coming from that area. By comparing all these pictures showing the same events from independent sources, not to mention different angles, our intelligence services have been able to confirm this footage is not fake," disclosed the SecDef.

The Vice President sighed deeply and rubbed the bridge of his nose, obviously wishing the data was not solid.

"At some point we will have an unpleasant discussion about why the hell we are getting our intel from cable news and fucking *social media*. Then there is the question of where the hell were our satellite people with some kind of early warning. General Jackson, we have to respond immediately! If they are here, we must stop them, and we can't, no… that's not right, we won't do that part with our own nuclear weapons. That would kill our own people in massive numbers. We need to keep Americans safe in their own homes," demanded the President as he pounded his fist on the table.

"Mr. President, at the present time the *only* way we can respond rapidly is with National Guard and Reserves. This is caused by where in the country the reports indicate the enemy troops are operating. They knew where to enter the Continental United States to establish a beach head. Just like last their nuclear strikes on Dallas and Detroit they thought this through. In order to facilitate a rapid response, the National Guard has already been activated and will be mobilizing in waves across the next day and a half. In addition to this, I recommend we send word out right now to get the entirety of the Military Reserves in motion from coast to coast. We don't know if they will try to land troops anywhere else. If I were them, I'd land where I have already secured some land positions. We will be disseminating as much intelligence as we can to those commanders on the ground, that is so we can try to avoid any civilian casualties that might be caused by anyone being caught in the crossfire," reported Chairman of the

Joint Chiefs Jackson.

"I agree, we must immediately call up the reserves and work with all fifty governors on the National Guard activations. How is the public panic situation so far?" inquired President Press.

He couldn't imagine how bad an impact it would have when some child was riding a bike to school or to meet a friend and encountered a column of armed infantrymen, or worse a long line of tanks moving down the street. The psychological scars that would occur to children as fighting took place in their front yards were so terrible, he could barely let himself think about it.

"In Los Angeles it is pretty bad, people in the area are clogging the highways. They are trying to get out of the region. I'm not sure anyone believes the invasion stories yet, so there hasn't been any resulting public panic in that area, or anywhere else that we are aware of. I am, however very concerned about Los Angeles as there are multiple reports of gun fights due to road rage, and people are heading east which will cause some of the gas stations people will need to get through the desert area meaning some will run out of gas," informed the Secretary of Homeland Security.

"Well, that won't last but we need to deal with it, and I can't say that I would act any differently if it were my family that I was trying to get out of the area to safety. Now, with regard to what we are going to do about these additional hostile troops coming to our shore. What Naval assets are in the area that can either turn them back or destroy them while they are still at sea? Preferably the latter," the President asked, clearly ready to engage and unleash as much military might as was necessary to decimate the enemy's warfighting capabilities.

"Almost nothing, all of our surface assets are still returning either from combat operations or are currently on peacekeeping missions in the Middle East or are undergoing maintenance and are not in any condition to put to sea. Based on what happened here we have already ordered the troops in that region of the world to prepare for wartime operations immediately, however that order takes time to execute," explained General Jackson.

"Anything we can send in from the air?" asked the President, obviously growing frustrated, and still searching for a solution, any solution.

"Nothing currently within range. If you recall, we sent almost every air asset we had into the Middle East to support the ground war over there, and still have not finished repositioning much of it back where it belongs. The air assets that are back here are barely flight worthy. Just like with our Naval assets, most of those that have been pulled back home already have been torn apart to perform repairs and maintenance, it will be at least a day or more before we can do much of anything from the air, and likely much longer if any of their escort ships have anti-aircraft capabilities," the Chairman reported, clearly unhappy with the current situation.

"So, what the *hell* can we do to stop them?" shouted the President.

"The enemy flotillas are spread out across a very large area at sea, and unfortunately Mr. President, the only thing…the only immediate option I see, is we either do a massive conventional cruise missile strike, which will deplete our missile inventory to dangerously low levels which would take the defense industry months if not years to replace, or we could do a coordinated nuclear strike of our own on their assets at sea," answered Chairman Jackson, to the silent, yet unreluctantly nodding heads of everyone at the table.

"Mr. Vice President, Frank, is this what we are left with?" asked the President, from his voice it was obvious he was growing tired, if not physically then certainly emotionally. He had been hoping for an easier answer, but this one would work just fine if it must.

The Vice President, a former special operations combat soldier, knew the military's capabilities as well as anyone. He had been relatively mid-level in rank, but his experience had been recent, and his opinion was as well respected as anyone's in the command structure.

"It we take into consideration the depleted nature of our troops and equipment, how many of our missiles in inventory were used in recent combat operations leaving our on hand stock already depleted below comfort levels, how spread-out we are, and everything else we have experienced due to the prolonged war on terror; I agree this is the best course of action if we are going to act fast.

"I think it is obvious that we need to act now. It is

true that we could take these ships out with conventional munitions which would take a massive strike to accomplish the damage we need to do. However, and I can't believe I am about to say this, I think we need to not only destroy them, but we also must send a message. We need to let these bastards know that enough, is enough. They need to be stopped dead in their tracks, and we don't know for certain that the ships at sea are not armed with more nuclear, or some sort of biological or chemical weapons for that matter. They could be planning more large-scale suicide attacks.

"The only way to know we destroyed and fully eliminated this threat is nuclear. Given where they are at sea, how far they are from a land mass, we know we will only kill the military members and ship's crew, which I am sure are either military or conscripted jihadis about to invade us. There isn't really a huge downside to nuclear weapon use in this case. Now, when it comes to dealing with the troops they already have on the ground, the 82nd Airborne can be there pretty quick, Special Operations a little faster but perhaps not in the numbers we need, and yes, the Reserves and National Guard can get there even faster," explained the Vice President soberly. "The one concern that I have about the people in the area is the so-called militia groups, which may very well consist of more than a few veterans. While they will be incredibly determined, they will be uncontrolled by our leadership and this can cause huge problems when an accidental friendly fire incident occurs, and they will."

The President was convinced. They had to stop this

once and for all. He had to launch nuclear missiles, and he had to send the active-duty military members into United States cities and towns on search and destroy missions. People would be frightened, some even killed, but there was no alternative.

There was no real decision to be made, President Press leaned back in his chair, closed his eyes for a moment, and saw the mental images of World War II European cities after fighting had passed through the area. In that case, fighting would sometimes involve using people's homes as bunkers. Total destruction of many homes, and even entire neighborhoods. Starvation, diseases and breakdown of civilization were commonplace in the areas that were most heavily impacted. In some areas on the eastern front, it was so bad it had resulted in people so close to starvation that they had resorted to cannibalism. That was one legitimate possibility for the future of the United States if this went the wrong way due to the distance between farming communities and bigger cities. Taking a deep breath, the President sat straighter and opened his eyes and looked at every single person at the table and then those online.

"Very well. Chairman Jackson, find a way to use as few warheads as possible, we may need others for future use the way things are looking. Only strike those vessels or clusters of them that are far enough from our shore so that our civilian population will not be harmed in any way even by fallout. While you are doing that, I want someone to inform the allies of our intentions. I am sure what we are doing won't come as a surprise to anyone, but better that they know up front.

"I also want to see a briefing on what else they are capable of doing, assuming this is Iran, and I think we can safely assume as much. I want a list of targets where we can use as few nuclear weapons of our own on their military ground force capabilities around the world to eliminate their capabilities of landing more troops here, or anywhere else, while minimizing civilian casualties. I know it goes against doctrine but let's get those ships taken care of as an opening salvo, then we'll worry about their land-based targets as we'll need absolute confirmation of who this is, where the most opportune military targets are, and some planning before we launch that strike. Let's see how they like it when we use our arsenal, only we will do it with more precision and destructive capability than they could possibly imagine.

"We need to get whatever conventional ground assets we can headed into New England. I am sure they won't stay isolated in Maine for very long. That is clearly just a start for whatever they have planned next. We need to turn back their damn invasion. While many people in the United States own firearms we are going to need a professional response instead of Jim Bob and Amy Sue with deer rifles acting as local militia. When this type of militia activity starts, and it will, I want it treated as friendly, and don't order them to stand down but try to use them in support capacity. When this cluster of shit is over, someone *will* explain to me how the fuck they moved on us with a conventional force this size, landing what is it like six thousand soldiers inside our borders, without any of our intelligence agencies getting a whiff of it. We *will* close whatever fucking capability gap exists. And damn it, recall able body veterans, or those who will volunteer to help out, my guess is we won't have to ask twice. Find them jobs before they find themselves something to do that will confuse matters. They will *not* be happy we have been invaded by Iranians. They will get very creative if left outside our command structure, so we need to get them brought into the fold as quickly as possible.

"We need to stop any additional threats from getting to our coastline. I don't give a shit if we do it with nuclear, conventional, or any other as yet unknown or untested form of weapon. I want this over, and I don't want any of those ships to find their way to our shoreline. The only place those ships will go is to the bottom of the ocean or evaporated in a ball of nuclear flame. Get that done! If *anything* else they have even starts to come this way it will meet the same fate this group is about to, at least as long as I am in this office," charged the President.

"Mr. President, what do you mean by other form of weapon?" asked the Chairman, slightly confused.

"General Jackson, when I was in Congress, I voted to approve the classified Department of Defense development budget for years, I know we have prototypes all over the nation. If we have to get some later stage technology out of a lab someplace, and we feel that now is the time to use those new capabilities on the battlefield, I want that done. Call it a field test if you want to, but I want these people stopped, even if it means using our most advanced experimental prototypes, or any of on unconventional weapons if nothing else is going to work, enough is enough," the President said as he stood and left the briefing room.

<AP NEWS FLASH> Multiple sources are confirming there has been a nuclear weapon detonated in Los Angeles, California. An invasion of foreign military in this State of Maine is now also confirmed. It appears that the War, just recently declared over and a win for the United States, has come back to our homeland in ways never imagined. No word from the White House on the response from the United States to counter this new wave of hostile activity.

While the United States has been bombed and suffered terrorist attacks in the recent history, it has not been invaded since the 1800s. This is a time for all of us to stick together. Official word from governors is to not attempt to engage the foreign military. They will be too well armed. This is something that the U.S. Military and Reserves must do. This is a statement that must be repeated, do not attempt to engage any foreign military on your own.

<AP ECONOMIC NEWS FLASH>The military assaults on the United States homeland have come as a complete surprise. These events are causing huge increases on the spot prices for precious metals and oil. It's expected that the various governing bodies will order financial markets to remain closed on Monday. This market closure likely to continue for several days until the exact status of the situation can be fully understood. The markets do not favor uncertainty, and in these uncertain times are likely to crash without some extraordinary measures. Investors are calling on the President to make a statement as soon as

possible.

Chapter Three
Some Bizarre Help

Every time he set foot on the massive airplane President Scott Press felt privileged to be on board Air Force One. This was the second time he did not care for the circumstance that put him on the aircraft, but that didn't change his sense of pride in his nation or how humbled he felt to be the person in the seat.

The weight of the office he held, which he never aspired to hold, was unlike anything he had ever experienced. It was unlike anything he could have ever imagined, and it was getting worse by the day. Well, he thought, that wasn't entirely true. There had been days when it lightened up. When they "surrendered," he had allowed himself to relax a bit. Now he felt stupid for having done so, and he was sure he would *never* relax like that again until he retired.

He was sitting in the cockpit watching the pilots work, and on the current flight vector he would be able to visually inspect the damage to Los Angeles, at least from the air. This sort of thing was done so that he could give assurances to the people of the United States, and really to the people of the world, that he had seen the damage for himself. Then he would have to convince people he would set things right. Unfortunately, he knew from experience that it actually would help him strike the right tone in what would be an upcoming global address.

Seeing the damage with your own eyes gives the situation a far less abstract meaning, and he knew it would piss him off even more than he already was, for whatever good that would do. The alternative was a stack of statistics and abstract statements along with some drone video. The hope was that he would be able to give confidence to the American populace that this would be something that they could survive, and that the nation would thrive once again. Advisors said he couldn't hope to instill such confidence without the firsthand visualization. He wasn't sure he agreed with them, but he had a challenge understanding how any detonation could cause more widespread damage than the last attack, yet the claim of the intelligence agencies who failed to see the attack coming was that this was indeed the case.

He wasn't sure what survival was going to look like this time. The other side of this conflict would be a very changed world because, without a doubt, there would be more nuclear strikes. Hopefully there would be no more of them inside the United States borders, but there would be more. The next one would just destroy a few ships at sea, but the one after that would impact civilians located near the ground targets, and once a target package had been identified he was ready to give the order.

The issue he struggled with was that he could not admit that he honestly didn't know how things would be once this was over to anyone, that was a secret he had to keep. A nation with a leader that has no solution, no confidence, no plan and no hope would almost certainly lose the upcoming fight. That leader would absolutely end up with a nation full of people who would have challenges rising to meet the bumpy road ahead due to lack of inspiration from the top.

The President knew that someplace there was some sort of briefing people wanted him in. He also knew that so little information was actually known for certain that it was best for him to step away for a few minutes and let the intelligence teams get prepared. With a little time, they could filter out the facts from the bullshit, and then he wouldn't have to worry about which was which later. Besides, it would offer a few moments in which he could gather his own thoughts. Making a hasty decision right now could be tragic in ways he didn't want to let himself think about.

The pilot quickly placed, then took his finger away from his ear, "Mr. President, we have several calls stacked up for you. The operator is going to push them through to your desk one at a time. I will be sure someone comes back and lets you know when we are getting close to Los Angeles."

"Thanks, General," The President said, clapping the man on the shoulder.

He made his way to his desk and took phone calls for half an hour. They were all the same. It was a long line of world leaders offering some variation of an apology he had already heard from someone else, followed by a courtesy offer of assistance. He wasn't sure what help was needed, or where to send that help if he knew. One thing was consistent, no one had any useful information, at least none that they were willing to share.

What he really needed was some time to figure out the next move. What he felt he could not really ask for at the moment was help from Allied Navies. With the plans in motion to fire nuclear missiles at the incoming converted troop ships he knew he would not risk asking for naval help from nearby Canada or even the English Royal Navy, for fear of destroying their ships during the attack as collateral damage. He knew the scientists had told him the exact blast radius that would be impacted, but he also knew that was a calculation done by some computer program and that the United States had not detonated a real one of these devices in decades. He hoped they were right with their calculations but, as they say, seeing is believing. Maybe they had their calculations correct, but if Canada had a naval vessel too close, and did so at his urging, he wasn't sure how he could cope with that decision, or how they would react to the sinking of their ships as a result of a miscalculation concerning the performance of US nuclear weapons.

He had allowed himself to become lost in thought for a moment and had been staring out a window. A small but rare bit of turbulence in the large aircraft brought him back to reality and he looked down at his desk. He had to get his mind wrapped around the fact that very soon he would be watching a satellite feed of a nuclear strike as it took place. Then there would be the follow-on nuclear strike against land targets, once those targets could be identified. Then he briefly daydreamed what it would be like to be a peacetime President. One where his only concern would be arguing with the other political party, job creation, rebuilding infrastructure and growing the economy. That seemed so much easier by comparison.

With no warning the engine pitch changed and Air Force One started to descend in a slow, controlled fashion, suggesting this was expected and not part of some new radical emergency maneuver resulting from an imminent attack. Pressing the intercom button the President called his Chief of Staff, "Les, aren't we descending a bit early? I thought we were further out and had more time before we got to Los Angeles."

Lester replied, "Mr. President, the pilots indicated that this is an approved departure from the schedule that has a Presidential security priority. He knows nothing more than he is supposed to land at White Sands Missile Base, and that he is to keep everyone except you and a small security contingent inside the plane and remain prepared for immediate departure."

"Ok Les, thanks for the update, also please pass along to the pilot that I would like to speak with him when he gets a free moment," the President said. He wanted to leave the man alone to land. Bringing a plane this large down safely may seem routine from the outside, but it was a bit more complex than most people realized, especially given that this one was heavier than most thanks to all the specialized equipment and there would be no automated landing system used given the identity of the passengers. Those landing systems were commonplace on commercial aircraft, but with even a fraction of a percentage chance of someone hacking the system in order to crash the airplane carrying the President of the United States, they were not installed on Air Force One.

As the aircraft descended into the desert landscape, he pondered what the hell was going on. The day had already contained enough surprises, and one more security protocol getting in the way of what came next was not what he needed at the moment.

The phone buzzed, and the President punched the button to connect the incoming call. "Mr. President," voiced the pilot on the other end, "concerning your question of why we are landing here, we don't necessarily have a standing non-theoretical protocol on how to handle part of the current situation. However, we do have a high priority message indicating a covert trip to White Sands, which is where we are about to land. Mister President, I do not know what is here, who, or why your presence is required at this point in time, but it appears to be vital. All I have been told is that it is for some classified meeting, the subject matter is unknown to me, and apparently, I am not cleared. These orders have passed all verification checks, and this is therefore considered to be a legitimate message. We have been instructed that we are to land, and have you considered as being in briefings for the next several hours, but that we are to remain ready to get back in the air at any point in time, on little or no notice."

"Thanks for filling me in. Just one more question," the President replied. "How do you keep people from wondering what happened to Air Force One when someone sees us landing here, especially when we are doing so without some pre-announced and planned out reason?" He was glad no press had gotten on the plane with them. That would have led to additional issues to consider. However, thanks to the ever increasing use of social media someone was likely to get a photo of the aircraft and post it online along with the location for all to see.

With a slight chuckle, the pilot answered, "That's the easy part Mister President, we tell them the truth, or at least a version of the truth. We are landing for some mandatory preventative maintenance on the avionics, which have gone slightly past their regular inspection schedule. While we are on the ground, some mechanics will come out and inspect the plane to ensure they are good to go. By the way, the maintenance schedule isn't truly up, but no one will know any better as those maintenance files are classified. And since actual mechanics will come out and do actual maintenance checks we can push back the next routine inspection and maintenance schedule."

"Good to know that's all covered. Anything else you can tell me, unofficially?" the President queried.

"No Mr. President, sorry, but for safety and security reasons the pilots are never allowed to exit the aircraft when we do these strange and off-the-record things like waiting for you at some meeting in an out-of-the way place. It doesn't happen often, but it has happened before. I believe it was three times that I am personally aware of with your predecessor," the pilot added.

"Ok, thanks. If possible, I will get your crew off the plane for a bit, but I can't promise anything until I know the details of what's going on. Now, I will stop bugging you so that you can land this monster." The President signed off so that the pilot could concentrate, and he could ponder what the hell might actually be going on. Who had the authority, not to mention the audacity to distract him while responding to a nuclear strike was a question that needed an answer.

A short time later, after a perfect landing, Air Force One rolled to a stop on a well-hidden taxiway, or perhaps it was a reception area. It was tough to tell which one it really was. Perhaps it could be said that it was both, depending on the need. This one looked like it was designed specifically for Air Force One, or other aircraft of equally substantial size.

As they came to a gentle stop, several things happened at once. A limousine approached the giant jumbo jet, heavily armored tanks, infantry vehicles, and blast shields, appeared as if from nowhere to provide security for the plane and whomever might be coming down those steps.

It was either a massive level of protection or the most elaborate kidnapping ever devised of a world leader. The President assumed it was just overkill.

Mechanics and fuel trucks came rushing out to deal with the aircraft's needs. All the standard preparations for a jumbo jet to be ready to fly again began at a brisk pace.

The President stood up, grabbed his jacket, and made for the front of the plane where the stairs were being moved into place. It was at that moment when the floor came out from under him, and he fell from his feet, landing with his butt on the floor right in front of the now open exit door. It was only after he got back on his feet that the President looked on in amazement as the entire reception area was slowly sinking into an enormous, obviously man-made cavern under the desert.

He wondered what kind of hydraulic system it would take to support all this weight. It had to be massive.

Standing at the bottom of the stairs was a lone figure dressed in a military combat uniform. The man somehow seemed to express that this entire scenario was completely ordinary through his relaxed demeanor. It was as if in his world, airplanes always fell through the ground while surrounded by heavily armored vehicles. He seemed calm to the point of being bored until he saw the President coming down the stairs. Then the figure straightened up to salute his Commander in Chief and stood waiting for the return salute at the bottom of the stairs.

As members of the President's Secret Service detail started to descend, the figure reached for his rifle where it hung from the tactical sling and in a loud, commanding voice bellowed, "Ladies and Gentlemen, the President and *only* the President is authorized to leave this aircraft. You should all return to your seats, and someone will come by shortly with instructions. This is not negotiable. Please folks, for your safety return to the inside of the aircraft now. The exceptions to that are the head of his Secret Service detail, and the Chairman of the Joint Chiefs, and only those persons."

The President looked towards the head of his security detachment and gave the nod for them to do as they were instructed. While nothing was normal today, he was inside a secure underground facility which, until twenty minutes ago he did not know anything about. Given the scale of the facility, which he had only just begun to see, it had to be a government operation and not some massive enemy conspiracy. He would have his head of security as well as the Chairman of the Joint Chiefs with him, and that was some comfort. He pulled his detail head over and quietly instructed him to get the Chairman and to make sure both of them were armed with a small machine pistol from the plane's arms locker before coming back down the steps.

Everyone else slowly made their way back up the stairs, bewildered by this development, while the President waited to be rejoined by the Chairman and the head of the security detail before continuing his way down the last few steps.

Looking at the soldiers surrounding him, President Press noticed that the typical decorations, rank, and even the name tags were missing from the uniforms. He lifted an eyebrow in a silent inquiry as to why they were missing, then he decided he didn't have time to care about such things. Anything that could divert Air Force One in the hours following a nuclear strike had to be more important than his curiosity concerning some missing insignia.

With a slight chuckle at the President's bewilderment, the waiting man smiled and said, "Not that this will clear anything up, but they call me Mr. Smith, Mr. President, as I have no official name right now, nor do I have any documented past at the moment that existed prior to me coming to work at this location. What I am is the head of security for this facility. That is something I take very seriously. I will not tolerate any security breaches while I still in charge. You three are allowed off because we must brief you on what goes on within this facility. The others are not allowed off that plane because many of them do not need to know what goes on here, even if they have top secret clearance, at least not until the President decides they do. If anyone else attempts to come down the stairs, or tries to sneak off the plane, Mr. President, that person, or persons will not see the light of day for a long time. At least not until I am ordered by higher authority to release them, and that is *only* after a very thorough and rigorous interrogation and a background check that would make your head spin. That person or persons will have *absolutely no* legal rights until I am certain they do not pose a security threat to this facility, or our nation. If you will accept the pleasure of our company for a short time, you will learn things that might help you with the challenges being faced by our great Nation today. Believe it or not, some of what you are going to see in this facility just might help us survive the war someone else has decided to continue."

"Well, Mr. Smith, I am going to ask a few questions before we proceed," the President requested.

"Go ahead Mr. President, I will answer all the questions I can, or if I don't know the correct response, I may ask you to kindly wait for the full briefing where they can be answered in detail by the real experts," came the reply.

"How long have you been the chief here, and you say you won't tolerate any security breaches, but has there ever been a breach at this facility while you have been in your current position?" President Press asked.

"Mr. President, I have been security chief here for almost a decade, and in that time, there has not been one single security breach of any kind. The staff here has all undergone the same type of deep investigations I went through to get here. What you are going to find here will shake you to your core, but it will give you hope for our future, especially if people are going to keep popping off nukes like they are part of the festivities on the Fourth of July."

"Okay Mr. Smith I will take your word for that, and if you could have someone go back to direct the people in the plane to stay put or risk being locked away. If you let them know that request comes from me, I would appreciate it. Now, can you escort me to wherever it is I am supposed to go? I assume the flight crew, and anyone else left onboard will be taken care of for however long I am here. Also, please remember we are in the middle of a crisis, and

I have work to do so I am hoping that this briefing is vitally important to helping us get through said crisis."

"Mr. President, those on the plane will be cared for, they will have monitored network access, meaning they can't transmit any details about your location, but they can monitor the external situation, and any mechanical service that needs to be done will be performed, or if any supplies are needed on board of Air Force One that will be taken care of as well. We will even send information to the Vice President that you will be out of communication for a short time, and for him to transmit to us any specific decision that must come from you. If I know the type of man he is, he will understand and make sure as much as possible is taken care of, and only bother you if absolutely necessary."

With a quick series of hand signals, another uniformed man sprinted to the plane to relay the information. The President followed Mr. Smith to a small hatch which reminded him of the armored door on the old infantry vehicles, or maybe of blast doors from the holocaust movies that survivors hid behind. He couldn't decide which. As they moved further and further into the complex, President Press started to wonder where the hell they were going and why was his Vice President not being brought into this same briefing if it was so important. Even the Chairman of the Joint Chiefs seemed to look very confused about the situation yet remained silent.

Just as the President was going to ask where they were going to end up Mr. Smith paused at an ordinary door with no markings on it, "Mr. President, through this door is your briefing. I am not allowed in there as I don't have a need to know everything that goes on in this facility. Myself, or one of my deputies, will be here just outside the door when the briefing and tour have concluded."

"I am granting my security chief and the Chairman instant clearance, as I am the ultimate classification authority, and as my closest advisors certainly have a need to know," the President instructed.

"That is your prerogative Mr. President, would you gentlemen please go inside?" the strange man asked politely.

Mr. Smith turned and walked away, leaving President Press standing there as a deputy security agent took up position outside the door. With a sigh the President opened the door and walked in to see an older gentleman with steel gray hair, glasses and wearing a white lab coat over what looked like hospital scrubs. Silently he made a gesture towards the only other chairs in the well fitted room.

The man extended his hand and said, "I am Dr. Jonathan Gross. I am the head of Research and Development of this and two other similar facilities. Over the next hour I will brief you gentlemen on what these facilities are about, what we have in them, and some capabilities I can give you immediately that will be applicable to the crisis facing our nation. I will say, Mr. President, Mr. Chairman, that much of this will sound farfetched or even outright crazy. But I assure you gentlemen, it is all absolutely one hundred percent true, and everything I am going to show you functions precisely as described."

"Now, I will begin with faster than light travel, and handheld plasma weapons. Perhaps some of this will come in handy during the ongoing conflict."

<AP NEWS FLASH>The world has been shaken to the core. The United States has been hit with the largest single nuclear strike ever witnessed outside of test detonations. In addition to this tragedy there are confirmed reports of a military invasion in Maine that appears to be working its way south along the East Coast. There are now unconfirmed reports of nerve agents being used in the southern part of the United States. There has been no official release from the White House on any of these matters, and neither the President nor the Vice President have been seen or heard from since the renewal of hostilities. There is now speculation that the President and Vice President have been killed, and the United States may find itself leaderless for the moment, or at least we don't know exactly who is in charge. We can only hope that is not the case.

We in the news business would like to urge people not to panic. We learned in the last nuclear attack that we can survive. The invasion is of unknown size and currently believed by our military experts to be the greater danger than a nuclear strike that has likely already ended. The alleged biological agent, we simply do not know enough about to gauge the danger level yet and are working to confirm.

<AP ECONOMICS NEWS FLASH>With the news coming out of the United States the prices of precious metals have almost doubled in the span of a few hours. OPEC nations have announced that they will not be increasing production which has caused oil prices to break through the 100% increase line and are continuing to rise.

Chapter Four
Complete Devastation

Mark Long had been a national news anchor for so many years he barely remembered them in any way outside of the massive improvement in teleprompters. He was sitting at the pinnacle of the industry and had his own show simply called "The M.L. Review." It was frequently used as a reference for many other, less highly rated news and commentary broadcasts all over the nation and was occasionally picked up and discussed by foreign news outlets.

For him, the days that stood out were never the good news days. It was always the tragic stories the seemed to find a way to become burned into his brain. He had hoped to never have another day as horrible as the nuclear strike strikes in Texas and Michigan, but you don't always get what you wish for in life.

Today was turning out to be another one of those types of days. Mark watched as the timer above the camera counted down and braced himself for the segment to come. He wondered why the network was bothering with commercials on a day like this. No one would pay the least bit of attention to whatever company was trying to sell the latest whiz bang whatever it was.

"I would say welcome back, but on a day like today there are no words which seem appropriate to welcome anyone into viewing what we are about to share. Earlier today we reported that there has been another detonation of a nuclear weapon within our borders, and that device has devastated another part of our great nation. The city targeted this time was Los Angeles, California. This represents a pure civilian target, with no military value whatsoever. That fact makes this an attack on our way of life, not just our ability to defend ourselves as well as our allies militarily, and the early reports we are getting indicate this attack is far worse, far more devastating than the previous wave of nuclear detonations in Dallas and Detroit.

"Here in the newsroom, we have been tapping into every possible source we can in an effort to find some way of getting images from the area. We were searching for anything that can tell us if there are any survivors in that densely populated city, and as we learned last time these first images will help us understand what needs to be sent into the area for assistance for those who have survived. But as we also know from the last time this happened that there is an electromagnetic pulse released along with these sorts of weapons. Any permanently fixed camera, or any piece of electronic equipment that was not destroyed in the blast but were in the surrounding area will have been rendered useless as a result of that pulse. As I speak there is a privately owned, small, recreational airplane flying towards the area that has some sort of onboard video capability, and we should have a live feed coming in soon. We don't know what the quality of the images we will be able to get are going to be, but we will be giving our audience whatever we can, live, as soon as it comes in. We will not be doing any editing, nor will we be degrading the image in any way."

The broadcast screen split into two pictures with the host on one side and a color barcode on the other. After a few seconds the barcode disappeared, and a wobbly, somewhat grainy live feed from a small propeller airplane appeared. The camera showed the underside of a wing for a second, then it slowly panned downward.

The devastation was massive, far more so than in the previous attacks, far more so than Mark had prepared himself to witness. It was so much worse that upon first seeing the feed he cursed on air, "fuck me," and no one bleeped him. Everything, as far as the camera could see was charred, steaming, on fire, or flattened. In the previous round of attacks there had been some structures that remained standing to the point where you could at least tell they had recently been buildings. That was not the case this time. This looked more like the wood of a fireplace that had been burning for a long period of time. Nothing remained, except the minimal ghostly remains of substructures of buildings that had been broken into smaller pieces and thrown around, finally coming to rest at bizarre angles. Many of these broken structures were still on fire, sending smoke into the air. Even the steel substructures were burning, red to their core, indicating just how intense the heat in that area had to be.

The pilot could be heard saying that he was having challenges keeping their altitude steady. There were thermal updrafts coming from all the fires trying to push the aircraft higher.

"In some ways I want to be higher, but we need to find survivors, so we have to stay low to get decent video with the equipment we have on board," the pilot said.

The airplane was flying around the area in a search pattern. The pilot was trying to find something that looked alive, but there was very little that looked like it had ever been touched by human hands, much less as though it could possibly contain anything still living. The pilot could be heard talking about what landmarks he thought used to be where they were, then he was just going on and on about the level of damage, and the lack of anything alive. "About the only good thing we can say is that anyone who had been in the area had to be instantly turned into ash and didn't suffer, or even realize what was happening," the pilot was obvious in shock and trying to make himself feel better as much as reporting to the audience.

"We have flown across the entire diameter of the blast area, and it is hot, noticeably hotter than where we took off in the westernmost part of Arizona. My God, there are at least ten miles of complete and total devastation. There is absolutely no way there is anything left alive inside this part of the blast area. It just isn't possible, the heat coming up from the detonation zone is so intense it is hard for us to get too close. I don't know what the radiation levels are, and I hope we're going to be ok but someone has to look," voiced the worried static filled transmission of the pilot, obviously terrified and stressed near the breaking point.

"We are nearing the edge of the main blast area now, we came in from the Arizona side and we didn't follow a major traffic route, I'm not sure where the line of possible survival is but from where we are, in the distance, some living people can be seen. We are coming up on their position now. They aren't moving as people normally would, the only way to describe what they are doing is that they are writhing in pain. Some of those poor people are so badly burned. I can't imagine what they are going through. Some, oh Jesus, I can see bones sticking out of their limbs, where the flesh seems to have just burned away, if what I am seeing can be believed. It...it...almost doesn't look real, in my entire life I could never have imagined seeing something like this. It is horrific. I can't fathom what these poor souls went through. If they are still alive, and the movement I see isn't my eyes playing tricks on me because of the heat, or some leftover nervous system twinges causing involuntary muscle spasms. If they are still alive, I can't see how they will be for very much longer. I'm not even sure how they could have survived this long. My God, that man is definitely alive, and he is somehow pulling himself along with his arms, dragging his legs which are burned down to the bone from the knees down to his feet."

"Can he hear us in the plane?" Mark asked the production crew, touching the earpiece that was always present while he was on air.

"Yes, I can hear you," came the static filled response from the pilot.

"Can you see any first responders anywhere, anyone trying to help? Is there someone, anyone trying to get through to help those people in pain? Perhaps a *few* lives can be saved," the host said frantically, obviously in shock because of what he was seeing, hoping that it was just a microcosm in the confusion and that elsewhere people were being helped in large numbers.

"No, not at this point, at least not where we are. We can see some flashing lights a few miles out. I think that is as close as first responders can get due to the debris, not to mention the fires that are all over the roadways. I swear the heat is so intense in a few places we saw roadways, paved concrete roadways, spewing flames into the air. Could the tires on their vehicles even withstand the kind of heat it takes for that to happen? Even if the humans in the vehicles could tolerate it. Wouldn't that level of heat in the air damage their lungs?" the pilot asked rhetorically.

Whomever was operating the camera tried to show how far away those first responders were by adjusting the telephoto lens to a wider area view. They then made an attempt to highlight the maze of debris any first responders would have to go through to get to the people far below the circling plane.

"So, there are a few miles of devastation with potential survivors that can't get any help? Those people are just going to be left to die?" M.L. asked, timidly, not wanting it to be true, but slowly starting to realize that was indeed the case.

"That is the way it seems to be from here. Even if anyone wanted to do so, I don't see any way first responders, or anyone for that matter, could get to them and live to talk about it. I'm not sure what the radiation level is here, but I don't feel comfortable staying this close to where the blast was centered any longer than we already have," the pilot replied, almost apologetically.

The host took over the narration, "I want to remind the viewers that Los Angeles and its outlying areas are some of the most densely populated parts of California.

"We are obviously looking at a new type of attack. During the last nuclear attack there was a relatively small geographic region destroyed, but this time it is much larger. The center of the attacked area is completely gone. In Dallas and Detroit there were at least some structures remaining. This time, well, there is nothing. The flying camera team had to get several miles out before we could see any kind of structural remains that we could positively identify.

"We have not seen or heard from the President of the United States about this attack. Last time the attack was highly organized, and we aren't sure if the President is alive or dead. There was no nuclear attack in Washington DC or anywhere else in the nation that we are aware of, however there could have been non-nuclear hits we have not been informed of yet. There is fragmented information coming in from all over the nation that is just too confusing to report yet. We just don't know much of anything right now, and logic dictates something this big would not be an isolated incident, this had to be part of a larger plan. We are obviously still at war. The peace accord we all celebrated was a meaningless pile of paper. May God have mercy on those who lost their lives, and may He protect those of us who remain," Mark said as the camera faded off.

***

The Vice President sat at his desk on Air Force Two with a camera in front of him, the only two other people in the room were the cameraman and a midlevel intelligence officer from the CIA. Frank had been on television a few times before, but he was still not used to it. This time, the whole world would be watching. To make matters worse, he didn't know where the President was at the moment, but the staff with him on the Air Force Two was correct, someone needed to go on television and let the world know that the full, and intact leadership of the United States was still in place and working on this problem.

The news anchors were starting to speculate that something had happened to various members of the nation's leadership, and the government was covering it up. He needed to get the word out that the leadership of the nation was intact, that they weren't running away and hiding out, or worse that they were trying to save only themselves. If people started to believe such things it would make a bad situation worse.

The cameraman signaled that they would be going on air in 3, 2, 1.

"My fellow Americans, I will not sugarcoat this. We have been attacked. We have been attacked in a way even larger than ever before. We were attacked in a way I know that we had all hoped, that we all prayed, would never happen again.

"In recent history we had two nuclear bombs go off inside our borders, and it was a tragedy from which we thought we would never recover.

"We did.

"This latest attack is indeed nuclear, and even larger than the other two. It was a device known as a thermonuclear bomb. It is a type of nuclear weapon, but it is even greater in destructive capability than the original weapons used in World War II, which were similar to those that hit us not so long ago.

"We don't yet know the true extent of the damage, but we do know who was responsible. Rest assured, we will respond, but there is something everyone needs to know that is new this time around.

"There is an enemy invasion force in Maine. I assure you that we can and will eliminate the enemy soldiers who have invaded our great nation. I won't speak to the size of this force, and I won't speak to how we plan to respond, as these are matters of national security, and to tell you is to tell the invaders. We will respond to and beat back this invasion. We will not be defeated. Not on our home field.

"Rest assured the President has not been seen publicly because he is meeting with our military leadership and determining the best way to quickly respond to both threats. We will respond, we will make the world safe again, we will protect our citizenry, and we will continue to function as a nation on this Earth.

"My fellow Americans, thank you for the time, the President will be speaking to you as soon as is practical. He will give you more information at that time. May God Bless the United States of America."

The camera turned off, and the Vice President wished he could think of more to say that might comfort people.

He took a moment to stretch as he stood up, he wanted to walk around the plane. He needed to think.

***

Approximately ninety minutes later the Vice President was flipping through a pile of briefing papers.

He had another pile to read after this one, and by then people would bring him even more piles to look through. He simply couldn't read another page, not without taking a moment. There was so much information coming in, being prepared for him and the President, by so many people, finding its way to his desk so quickly that he wasn't sure how anyone could retain, much less make sense out of a meaningful amount of it.

Not to mention it was so filtered by people trying to cut out things he "may not want" that it was frustratingly short on any useful details. But understanding a major portion of it was necessary before trying to figure out how to connect the dots to draw some conclusion that might help those planning a meaningful response to what amounted to uncharted military waters. Hopefully that response would make a permanent strategic difference, and not be some symbolic event meant to appease people's desire for revenge, but not really accomplishing the larger goal.

He reached for the remote control, half hidden under some papers and turned on the television. Occasionally it helped him to have a distraction, or at least some measure of background noise. He also felt that by figuring out how those people who were not looking at mounds of classified intel with streams of filtered data about the current situation were thinking, he might be able to get a clearer understanding of how those he was supposed to be defending were hoping their leaders would respond.

Were they enraged?

Were they frightened?

Were they preparing to fight back without waiting for the military?

Maybe watching the television news would help him figure some of that out. How they felt wouldn't necessarily influence military decisions meant to keep them safe, but it might help inform him on ways to better put people's mind at ease the next time he or someone else in the administration was called upon to do a live broadcast.

The current news anchor looked exhausted. Frank's mood improved knowing he wasn't alone in that feeling. His eyes shifted to a picture of his fiancé that was sitting on his desk.

She was currently fast asleep a few doors away. It still amazed him that Air Force Two, which was labeled as an older aircraft, but had previously used as Air Force One had a bedroom that included a shower, much less an office with hundreds of television channels available at the touch of a few buttons.

He wondered how long it would take for the technology to be available that would enable him to never have to see another commercial. Why that thought had occurred to him given the current crisis he didn't understand. It was probably a sign of how tired he was.

"Ladies and Gentlemen," the news anchor said as they came back from a commercial break. "We have all seen the video from the last time this great nation was hit with nuclear weapons. Hell, virtually every person on the planet has seen it at this point.

"By now we have all seen the early video from this recent attack. This time, well, the only way to describe it is bigger. When I say bigger, it is like the difference in the size of the stadium for a high school football game from a small school district, and one of the most modern facilities constructed for the NFL. When we finally add up the numbers I am, unfortunately, confident in saying that we will find that the loss of life to be far greater or, put another way, that it will dwarf the previous attack.

"We will continue to work diligently to get more information from inside the blast zone. It has been hours, but this device was so large it is proving challenging to get anything other than distant aerial shots. We have had only one limited feed from a private pilot, but even they had to break off due to intense heat and radiation fears. Very few pilots are willing to make an attempt at getting into the area and really, who can blame them.

"Unfortunately, believe it or not, this may not be the worst news we have to report today. We have a breaking story out of the northern part of New England. Before now we have only seen one dashboard camera video of their troops slaughtering local law enforcement, and that was leaked out on social media and had not been confirmed until just moments ago. We are unable to confirm the invaders have been mostly leaving civilian populations unharmed. Those reports are coming in from social media, so there is concern these may be originating overseas, from propaganda accounts rather than from local residents.

"We can confirm what the Vice President told us, and this comes from multiple sources that we have been invaded. We can add to that, from what we are being told by inside sources that the enemy is about to engage with one of our National Guard units."

The screen behind the well-dressed newsman changed to show a quintessential, peaceful, New England town square. At the far end of it, furthest from the camera, heavy military style trucks could be seen, painted with jungle camouflage pattern, complete with some strange writing. They were clearly not American vehicles.

The Vice President started to get angry and made a mental note to figure out how to get the news media to *not* show an ambush that was *about* to happen. If he was watching what he thought he was watching, and he could see it happen live on network television, the enemy could see the same thing, and it could help them with their battle plans. How to get the media to agree was beyond him at the moment. All he could do was sit and watch, getting angrier by the second, hoping his assumption would be proven wrong.

Something told him that the National Guard had taken up position in the buildings making up the town square. It just didn't look exactly right, almost like it had been prepped for battle. There were no people on the street, no lights anywhere on the streets, in the stores, in the bars, and what he could see of the store window displays just didn't seem right. That had to be for a reason and was obviously done without thinking through the camouflage necessary to pull off an ambush. There were items clumped up, then wide empty spaces in the displays. It was not the optimal use of retail space he would expect from experienced shop owners.

Once five of what looked like the thirty or so trucks

entered the area, the windows from all over the square blew out as the scene erupted with heavy automatic weapons fire. The trucks were immediately riddled with holes. The screams of the occupants being cut to pieces could be heard as the rifle fire subsided. There was almost no return fire from the trucks that had been in the square.

The remaining trucks were turning around and leaving the area as fast as they could.

Multiple questions were running through Frank's mind. Where the hell the newsfeed was coming from, whose camera was it, most of all he wanted to know whose spectacularly bad idea it was to cover this live, and not knowing was pissing him off. Whomever was operating the camera had things perfectly framed to give the enemy everything they needed to know. That could mean the friendlies would be sitting ducks if the enemy was monitoring this, and if they had enough troops in reserve to mount any kind of response to what amounted to a very small loss of troops.

Frank picked up his phone and started pushing buttons, "Get me whoever from the Joint Chiefs is available, *NOW!*"

The newscaster continued to talk the entire time the firefight was taking place, seeming to not take a breath, "It looks like the Maine National Guard has begun to fight back. This is live video, which is normally not something we would bring directly to you, but given the extraordinary times we live in, our policy has changed. We are a nation at war, and I want everyone to know that we have not edited these video feeds in any way. This is an attack on our soil, and we all need to see this for ourselves. I do want to warn viewers of the gruesome nature of these images you going to continue to witness. Our military consultant warns that it will get worse as things continue to unfold."

"General, it's Frank," The Vice President said. "Can we cut this damn news feed? Does whatever hair brained news jockey sending out this live broadcast realize the damage they are doing?" He was letting more anger show than he wanted to, but he knew what would happen if something didn't change quickly.

He looked back at the high-def television. Blood could be seen dripping down and pooling under the trucks. Bullet holes had filled the sides, more had filled the canvas covered back. Fire was coming from under the hood of one of the trucks. The screaming and cries of the few survivors could be heard in the background.

What was left of the five trucks that had been in the front of the convoy stood as a symbol to both sides of destruction yet to come in the conflict, if not this battle.

The VP turned the volume up so he could hear the feed.

"There, look on the left side of your screen, we can see some of the Guard members coming out from their concealed position. I suppose this is so that they can finish off the enemy, or perhaps take prisoners. Let's see how this unfolds," the news anchor said.

Frank hit the mute button. He saw what was about to happen. Even if the newsman missed it, his trained military eye couldn't help itself.

In the sky, a mile or so back, two helicopters could be seen rapidly approaching, staying precariously close to the ground. At that altitude, they would barely appear on any RADAR, military or civilian, that was operating in the area.

These were too large to be civilian craft, and he knew them not to be of an American design. These had to be enemy military helicopters, and to those men on the ground celebrating a minor victory they would be flying death machines.

The first weapon to open fire from the airborne gunships were the rocket pods strapped to the winglets on the sides. They would not be the last. Frank knew that the National Guard was not likely to have any weapons on the ground that would have any hope of bringing those monstrous aircraft down, they were too big, and they could accurately hit a target from too far away for any of the typical National Guard weapons to have any meaningful result.

The rockets flew.

The attack was turning the National Guardsman into red vapor at one extreme end of the spectrum, and screaming, bleeding piles of pain that would not live very long at the other. Chunks of meat ripped from body parts flew in all directions, and it all went out live in high definition for all to see.

Flesh splattered onto the sides of vehicles, like a

congealed sticky red gel. The entire population of the world was going to see a United States National Guard unit get its ass kicked over and over. It would be repeated for all to see until the end of time on every video streaming service. It would make an amazing recruiting tool for the enemies of the Unites States.

It was going to require DNA testing to identify which body part belonged to which person. There would be no other way. Heads were separated from bodies, arms flew in one direction, legs in another, and it all happened fast, mere minutes.

To say that blood was everywhere was an understatement. It was forming a river in the street as it ran toward a storm sewer drain.

The rockets continued to rain down. The National Guardsmen who were left alive were being quickly turned into piles of unidentifiable meat. Clumps of someone's brain matter was clinging to the side of one of the trucks, forming a bizarre mosaic.

Frank had seen these types of things happen first-hand. At this point the news anchor was calling for a drone attack to fight back. The man had no clue what he was talking about.

No drone in the inventory was going to be of any help in this case, not to mention none were available in the immediate area. Why the fuck they decided to move every air asset the United States had to one place and had not quickly brought many of them home was now escaping him. Unfortunately, it had not been given a high priority to move them back from overseas quickly.

At the time it made sense, now it seemed to be the dumbest military move made in the history of mankind. Frank was sure there would be documentaries in the future which would dissect the blunder. Some would probably, at least in part, blame him. Hindsight was always 20/20.

It didn't matter, right now these National Guardsmen were paying the price for other people's poor planning and decision making.

Frank turned off the television, slammed down the remote, breaking it into pieces, picked up the phone and punched numbers quickly from memory. He shouted to the people standing outside his office, "Someone get the fucking President on the phone from wherever he is and do it right now!"

He realized while he was shouting that his phone call had been answered.

"Colonel Jacobs, Frank Banner here," the Vice President said into his phone.

"Mr. Vice President, what can I do for you?" asked Frank's former Commanding Officer, a career long Special Forces Soldier.

"I just saw a bunch of Guardsmen killed on American soil in a conventional attack. We both know it won't be long before people try to defend themselves militia style, and that won't go well. While those men and women live there and know the terrain around them, the reprisals for militia style attacks will be ugly, and God help anyone unlucky enough to be taken prisoner. Those poor bastards will end up on the Internet being set on fire or some other bullshit the bastards dream up for propaganda designed to make us look bad, and it *will* work. It will turn public sentiment in their part of the world in their favor, which leads to easier recruiting for them. I know in the long run even unorganized militia can attrition them out of existence if we can stop the flow of their troops into the nation, but I'm trying to think one step ahead of what is going on today. Do you have *any* useful intel on the situation on the ground over there? We need to know what the fuck is coming our way next." Frank pleaded.

"Mr. Vice President, I'm sure you have better intelligence sources than I do," the Colonel stated flatly.

"Colonel cut the shit. This is me you are talking to. For the sake of all that is Holy don't go all politically correct on me now. I know my job title has changed, but I know you have people on the ground over there you speak with directly. All I get is triple filtered high-level crap. I want to take actual, real, raw, timely intel forward to the President so we can plan something with a real and immediate impact.

"We have to end this shit, but the only way I can see us doing that is by eliminating their military capabilities before they get to our shores. From what I'm seeing this isn't a one-off attack meant to prove a point. They really think they can beat us, and in our home territory, or they wouldn't be here," Frank added. He was trying to keep his tone of voice professional and the emotions he was feeling at bay.

It was the only way his brain was going to think clearly and perhaps find a way to stop this entire threat from expanding and resulting in further, more widespread loss of American life.

"Ok, Frank, this jumps like thirty rungs on the chain of command but because this is you, and you did ask. Just don't let it be widely known where this is coming from.

"We actually know a lot, but much of it has come our way in the last few hours. While some of it is only double confirmed, those sources are solid. They have had leadership-level discussions, I'm talking in person meetings, involving people from multiple countries over there ever since the first round of nukes went off around here kicking off this whole fracas. That was long before the peace accord was signed. We couldn't ever nail down all the details of what was discussed. However, if you will let me speculate just a little, I suspect what they want to do, or what they may have actually achieved, is to combine military forces in a united front, under a single command, all of them allied against us. It is the only way they have the numbers and equipment to matter, unless we go unconventional. But, with our smart weapons I'm sure we can beat them, the only question is how long it will take given how out of position we are, and how messy that process going to be," the Colonel explained.

"Sure, and they all went after Israel last time, but they weren't terribly well organized, so you mean this goes beyond that sort of thing, they are actually coordinating now rather than just simultaneously attacking without any kind of cohesive strategy?" the Vice President questioned.

"Mister Vice President, Frank, this level of cooperation goes way beyond anything we have seen before. We are only finding out most of this stuff for certain in the last hour or so, but information is pouring in from all over the region. In the previous case, they merely had a common target, they wanted to destroy Israel while hurting us, and they didn't coordinate in any sort of way. That appears to have changed. Most of the leadership over there seems to have decided that if Iran can actually field the kind of power they did, and severely damage us, as they did, and have now done again, that perhaps they have earned the right to be the Islamic State leader. In other words, the doomsday scenario we all feared seems to have happened. They also appear to have decided that all branches of Islam are better than we are, and therefore should work together to destroy anyone and everyone who disagrees with them. I personally think if they can ever get us out of the way on a global scale, they would just go right back to fighting each other, but I hope it doesn't come to that," the Colonel explained.

"Fuck me," swore the Vice President. "Ok, let me guess, Israel has days before it is gone, and we can't help. They will then increase their focus on us before hitting Europe because we are weak at the moment, and they don't want to give us a chance to fix our problems and get organized. Not to mention most of Europe really depends on us for defense anyway and, well, let's face it, they are not much into helping us at the moment, even if they had the capability."

"I don't have any specific information on that, but I can dig into it if you'd like," the Colonel offered.

"Please do that, Colonel. Can you also let me know if any of their units get out in the open in preparation to move someplace? In other words, if they stop intermingling with civilians, and get someplace we can drop really big bombs on them?" the Vice President requested.

"Absolutely, Mister Vice President," assured the Colonel.

"Thank you," Frank said, then added, "and if you think you may have anything that will help the President, please don't hesitate to pick up the phone. My old alert phone is still active. Use it if you get actionable intel that way you don't have to go through a dozen different assistants to get to me. Don't worry, I will not breath a hint of where it came from, you have my word on that."

"I will, and be careful Mister Vice President, they could attempt to specifically target you the way this thing is going," the Colonel warned.

"I will, and thanks," he answered as he disconnected the line.

Frank started to compile data on joint military capabilities for the region and hoped the President would surface from whatever hole he was in soon. Nukes were going to launch in the next hour, coordinates were plugged in, and allies notified. They could have been launched faster, but there was some civilian air traffic that had to be discreetly redirected before detonation. Once that was accomplished, the resulting strike would wipe out the enemy ships currently at sea and closing in on the New England shoreline.

***

Sam turned off his television and picked up his phone. "Phil, did you see the news?!?"

"Yeah, the National Guard got their ass kicked," Phil replied as he took a sip of coffee that could be heard on the phone.

"We need to get out there with our cameras and get whatever is left of the guard on our accounts, man," Sam prodded his friend.

"You really want to post this on social media?" Phil asked.

"Yeah, someone is going to, why can't we increase our followers and make some money before other people do? Cuz, you know if we don't, someone will."

"I wasn't complaining, just making sure I understand the plan. That attack wasn't more than ten minutes from your place. Pick you up at your front door in five?"

<AP NEWS FLASH> The first images out of Los Angeles have now been made public around the world. There are no

words to describe how bad the damage is. Once everything is counted, the number of lives lost will be a staggering total.

Images have come out of New England of a helicopter ambush against a Maine National Guard unit that appears to have been completely destroyed the Guard unit. The Vice President has given a brief address to the nation, and we are still awaiting word from the President.

The Governor of California has asked all residents living near the Los Angeles area to stay out of area. Even if your intention is to help, without the proper training more harm than good can come of the attempt. There is also a new quarantine zone extending twenty miles from Los Angeles outwards. If you live in that zone, please leave the area as quickly as possible. This zone may be reduced at some point, but currently this is the precautionary area while scientists and first responders work together to determine the minimum safe distance.

The Governor has also announced that stockpiling of food items will not be tolerated, and anyone who is doing this will have that stockpile seized.

<AP ECONOMIC NEWS FLASH> The United States financial markets have announced they will not be opening on Monday due to the attacks against our nation.

Prices on precious metals are rising on all international markets. Oil is on the rise as it is suspected that the Middle Eastern nations of the world will not be exporting, however domestic and Canadian producers say they can keep production high enough for this to be a non-factor. Speculators are continuing to drive up the prices.

Gasoline is in short supply around the area of attack. Food prices are spiking, and widespread shortages are expected in the near future.

Chapter Five
The United States Release of Nuclear Weapons

The Chairman of the Joint Chiefs had been listening to this scientist and wondering why, considering everything that had happened over the past year, he had never been briefed on any of these "experimental" weapons and unique capabilities. Then he looked down at his watch. He tapped the President on the shoulder, "Mr. President, we have a pending military operation set to take place, and we need to get back to Air Force One as we are necessary to be part of that process."

The scientist had been narrating a series of videos demonstrating some wild capabilities in weapons and transportation technology. Many of which he would have never dreamed possible. On any other day, he would have gladly stayed here until someone forced him to leave, but there were serious matters to see through to completion.

The President nodded, stood up and said, "Dr. Gross this technology of yours may just mean that we can bring this whole mess to a rapid close. For now, I must return to Air Force One, but I am going to have some members of the military leadership come down here so that you can tell them everything you just told me, along with whatever you were going to tell me next. They will have questions. Please do not hold anything secret from them. They have a need to know everything.

"This facility is not going to remain a secret much longer. With the crisis facing us we will need these, and any other new capabilities that exist around here in more ways than you may realize. I'm not sure of the best way to use any of this just yet, so we will have to bring in the experts on military strategy to meet with you, and I intend to start referring to you as my new advisor on exotic weaponry. In other words, you have just been effectively 'drafted' by this administration to serve as special advisor to the President of the United States for the duration of this war. Congratulations."

"Yes, Mister President," the strange man in the wrinkled lab coat said enthusiastically, beaming with pride.

As they exited the briefing room, they found that there was another nameless guard free of any type of uniform decorations waiting to lead the small Presidential party back through the maze of drab hallways. Just the same neutral color seemingly developed specifically to be difficult to identify and kind of landmark, making it impossible to remember where you turned last time.

"General, that has to have been the strangest ninety minutes of my life. How in the hell could they have gotten so far in front of everything else we have in the inventory, while simultaneously managing to keep this place a secret? Did you know about *any* of this?" the President asked.

"Only whispers. Those few things that the rumor mill has generated over the years. Before today I would have bet serious money that the people believing those things were insane. But after watching the demonstration videos that man has, well, now I can see that they weren't crazy, they probably didn't go far enough, and I only wish the people working here had come forward during the last nuclear attack. If they had we might not be in the position we are today," the General said, still trying to figure out the impact of what he just learned from deep inside the underground facility.

They were both in a state of disbelief that any of it was real but would operate under the assumption he had some new set of tricks to use in what could only be described as an escalating World War. The War was now being fought inside the Continental United States, a condition that must change.

They walked in silence for a few moments before the Chairman gathered enough thoughts to speak intelligently.

"Mr. President, honestly, I'm not one hundred percent certain how we can make the best use any of that equipment to our advantage yet. Two days ago, had you said we would be in a position where we authorized the use of nuclear weapons, I would not have believed it, but at least that notion I had considered, and knew it could someday be a possibility. This stuff is different. Now, I'm just hoping it works as advertised in real world conditions, rather than just in some lab experiment. If it does work the way I hope it does, we might just be in a position to end the crap we are dealing with for all time. Now my only question is how fast we can get it in the field, if we can do so at all," the General said.

The man was thinking out loud, as much as he was informing his Commander in Chief.

"General, I spent half of that briefing thinking I was in the middle of the most bazaar, fucked up dream I have ever had, and the other half hoping it wasn't. Given that we appear to have been thrust back into what we just need to give up and admit is World War III, maybe these new capabilities can help us bring this mess to a close, this time for real," the President said as they made their way to the boarding stairs of Air Force One.

They ran up the aircraft stairs, made their way to the cramped Air Force One briefing room and found that the area was at maximum human capacity with every single video screen already up and running showing different information streams. The only screen the President cared about at that moment was the one showing the grim, or was it pissed off, face of the Vice President.

"Frank, you will not believe what I have just learned, it might be exactly what we need given our current challenges," the President said to his Vice.

"Mister President, unfortunately I might be able to say the same, only my news isn't good, but we will discuss that in a minute. You need to know that I gave a very brief statement to the nation. First off, there was starting to be widespread speculation that you had been killed, and I needed to put those rumors to rest. There is a lot more you need to know, some of which I am still trying to get my head wrapped around what the potential impact of it will be, and how we deal with it," the VP lamented.

"Ok, we will get to that in a minute, once we get these nukes off the ground. You addressing the Nation is fine, and thanks for trying to bring some sanity to what is without a doubt an insane situation. We will be sure to get my face out there as soon as this is done, then we can inform people of what we have done to begin to beat these bastards back, along with whatever details we can pull together of what is actually going on, at least what we should release and not give away information to the enemy," the President said.

"This is a question for everyone. Is there anything I need to know immediately, or that might change our decision on the release of nuclear weapons?" the President said to Frank as he looked from monitor to monitor to figure out what information would be coming from where. Some held the digital presence of various Cabinet members, while two screens stood out from the rest. These two showed nuclear weapons in their tubes about to launch, complete with countdown timers.

"Yes sir, there is. Without our knowing it, in the brief time since they 'surrendered,' the entire Middle East has become, at least militarily, unified under the leadership of Iran. I compiled a two-page summary of those combined forces we are about to face. They have also engaged some of our national guard, and kicked the shit out of our guys, on live television. I have some people figuring out how we can immediately stop that crap," the floating video head of the Vice President said speaking very quickly.

"Wonderful, and with almost all of our military equipment that wasn't destroyed still in transport configuration, there isn't much our conventional forces can do about this at the moment? Do I have that sit-guess correct? As a result of that, we either need to buy ourselves some time, which we can't really do in a meaningful way with what we have on the ground or go unconventional?" the President voiced.

"That is the consensus among those I have spoken to so far, Mr. President," reported the VP.

"Well, Mr. President, Mr. Vice President, let's stop those bastards about to land on our shores. At least that prevents things from getting worse here at home, then we figure out the next most important task," said the Secretary of Defense who was difficult to hear over a loud computerized voice that had begun to fill the room.

"3...2...1...launch," the robotic, yet somehow feminine voice said. Flames erupted from the missiles as they lifted into the air. Within seconds they were at supersonic velocities and on their way to carry out their mission.

"How long before they are on target?" asked the President, gesturing to the video screens.

"Approximately nine minutes from launch Mr.

President," stated the Commander of the Nuclear Forces.

The room sat in eerie silence as the huge Minuteman III nuclear tipped missiles chewed up the miles. Two video screens showed maps with locations of the missiles as well as the flight paths to their targets. Then there was the all-important count-down timer. The displays had an uncanny resemblance to a navigation app used to guide an automobile driver to their destination.

The whole thing seemed very unreal. It was as if it was a video game, like you could push the reset button anytime you wanted if you missed your target.

An alarm went off filling the room with noise, everyone jumped in their seats, as if it were the last thing anyone expected to hear. Although no one here had ever launched an actual nuclear weapon they had all run the drills many times and never heard this alarm sound.

"What is that?" demanded the President, shouting to be heard over the noise.

"I'm not sure, Mr. President," General Jackson said as he picked up the nearest phone and punching buttons. He spoke to someone for a moment before wiping the sweat that had begun to form off his forehead as he slammed the phone down on the table so hard everything on the surface jumped.

"General, what do we need to know?" the President asked, speaking quickly, trying to remember the last time he heard someone, much less General Jackson say they didn't know an answer.

"Mr. President, we are being hit from multiple directions with the most sophisticated, largest scale cyber-attack ever seen. We have multiple viruses, and system penetrations that went active a moment before our missiles left their silos. They are infecting, or attacking every smart weapon, and communication system we have. I am not sure which systems will continue to work as designed. I am told multiple systems could begin going offline any second," the General reported, angrier than the President had ever seen him.

"Are the God Damn missiles we have in the air currently under our control?" the President asked, shouting his question, he was obviously angry, but not panicked.

"We assume so, but we aren't one hundred percent certain at this time," someone said from the back of the room causing everyone to freeze in place.

"If those missiles go off target, they could kill millions of Americans," some staffer said nervously, stating the obvious.

Suddenly, panic filled the room.

"We assume so?" the President asked rhetorically.

People started picking up phones, pounding away on keyboards, and even speaking loudly to one another, they were shouting commands or asking questions.

It was chaos. No one knew what to do, but they were trying whatever came to mind first. No manual existed for this situation, the data links in those missiles were supposed to be absolutely penetration proof, but today it was anyone's guess if that was true.

"How can we become one hundred percent certain that we are in control of our nuclear warheads and do so in the next thirty seconds?" the President shouted above the noise.

"The only thing we can do is to wait another few minutes and we will see if they veer off course. There really isn't any other way at this point," the Chairman of the Joint Chiefs explained. The expression on his face said he wished he had a better answer.

The General was known as a man completely dedicated to defending America, and right now his job was to sit calmly wait to determine if someone was about to take control of a nuclear weapon and try to use it to kill millions of people who he had devoted his life to defending. If that happened there were about to be lots of American's vaporized in a ball of fire resulting from one of their own military's weapons. A weapon that was meant to protect them. Everyone in the room wished there was another way, any other way.

"Fine," the President snapped. "People, focus on what matters."

Time appeared to stand still. Data was pouring in, people were speaking, now in more muted tones. Some of it would be helpful at some point, none of it was useful right then. People were naming off types of electronic systems being infected and slowing down, if not being completely stopped thanks to whatever hackers were hard at work.

The President barely noticed any of these distractions, he was laser focused on the video screens showing the trajectories of the nuclear warheads in flight. If those flight paths did not continue as planned, very little else in the room would matter.

"ATMs are down," someone shouted.

"Credit card transactions are no longer working anywhere in the country," someone else said, noting how big of a challenge that would cause for almost everyone attempting to buy anything, anywhere.

"Our economy will crater. How will people buy food? Who the hell keeps cash around anymore?" said someone on a video screen, their voice giving away that they were completely panicked and unable to function rationally.

The noise level started climbing again. Each person in the room had a different immediate concern. None of those things were important in the eyes of the President. None of which had anything to do with the missiles currently enroute to their final destination.

"Everyone be quiet unless you are reporting on the behavior of the missiles in flight. Right now, until we are confident where the nuclear weapons are going to strike that is the only thing that matters," the President shouted over the noise.

The room fell silent, it lasted for around thirty

seconds. One of the two displays showing the missile tracks turned its background to yellow, then quickly to red.

"Mister Chairman, can I assume that means we are no longer in positive control of that warhead?" asked the President, loudly.

"Yes, Mister President," the General answered, the tension obvious in his voice.

"If I remember the preparedness drills correctly, we can destroy it in flight without it going nuclear. Is that still something we can do given the current state of our networks?"

"Just say the word, Mister President, and we will find out," answered the Commander of the Nuclear Forces.

"Do it."

Someone in the back of the room could be heard relaying the order into a phone.

"It is going to self-destruct in 5...4...3...2...1," someone said.

The entire room watched as the screen showing the missile track in question went blank once the missile was destroyed. Everyone held their breath for the next thirty seconds, staring at the screen showing the other missile as it continued on its track to the target zone. It grew closer and closer until the two blips appeared as one.

The screen flashed, then froze.

"We hit our target, Mister President, we will have

satellite images in a few seconds, but we won't see much through the mushroom cloud at first. It will take approximately ten minutes before we know how much of the target we destroyed. The other flotilla, unfortunately, will continue on course and remain fully intact, unless you want to take a second shot at it," reported the Nuclear Forces Commander, Colonel Fisher.

"Negative on the second shot. Let's focus on the most important thing. First, get the damage assessment done, and more importantly, figure out how the hell we can be sure we will maintain absolute control of our damn nuclear missiles. We may not be able to quickly respond at the scale we need to in this situation without them. That is not a position that makes me very happy, I don't like using weapons of this type. If that's what we need, well, we have to do what is necessary but make sure those God Damn things are under our control. Let's go around the room while we are waiting for a clear view of the results from this strike. One at a time, tell me what the fuck is going on, and what other parts of our civilian population's day to day, or worse, military equipment are no longer functional," the President ordered.

"ATMs, credit cards, hell virtually all banking is currently offline. Given the number of transactions done with credit or debit cards daily this is a serious problem," the Chief of Staff reported, as calmly as he could.

"If we don't get that fixed our economy will tank in a matter of days and looting for food will start or at a minimum, those few with cash will begin stockpiling almost immediately," said the Treasure Secretary from a video screen.

"Noted," said the President, hoping things didn't get any worse in that regard. "Next item please."

"Hospital Emergency rooms all over the Southern parts of Texas and Louisiana are filling up. All of the increased influx are patients with symptoms fitting with a biological attack. Specifically, it appears to be some kind of advanced flu bug that presents quickly and violently," said the head of Health and Human Services.

"How the hell..." the President did not finish his thought as every piece of electronics in the room suddenly and simultaneously went dark.

"General, I think this just got harder," the President said, looking at General Jackson.

"Mr. President, the virus has now successfully penetrated, and shut down our most secure defense and intelligence communications networks," the Chairman of the Joint Chiefs said unnecessarily.

***

The Vice President was in his office on Air Force Two as the screens went blank. He leapt to the hallway and sprinted to the cockpit, "Colonel, get this thing on the ground. The United States is now under massive cyber-attack and this plane with all its electronics may be at risk. I do not want to fall out of the sky if they hit us and we lose positive control. We also need to get word to the FAA, if we can, to start getting whatever civilian and commercial aircraft that are in the air back on the damn ground as quickly as possible," the Vice President ordered.

"Yes, Mister Vice President," came the professional reply.

Frank made his way to where his fiancé was asleep. Before becoming his fiancé, she had been an emergency room nurse.

She had worked at one of the hospitals that had been overrun by patients suffering from injuries resulting from one of the original nuclear attacks. She knew as much about trauma patient care as anyone on the plane. She still suffered from nightmares about that day, and those patients, so he didn't like what he was about to do one bit, considering what she had been through. When word that there had been another nuclear strike, she suffered a massive panic-attack, and really needed to get some rest.

He gently shook her arm.

"What? What happened?" she asked, her eyes half open.

The only way she had gotten to sleep was with heavy sedation, so he was a little surprised he had gotten her to wake up at all.

"Sorry to wake you up honey. We are going to quickly land, but that's not why I woke you up. What do you know about a biological weapon that mimics a really bad case of influenza, and what we can do to treat people, or who do we call to figure out how to treat people who have been infected?" he asked.

"Oh God, what happened now?" she asked, brushing the hair out of her eyes as she got out of the reclined chair.

***

"Sam, to the left, I want to be sure the truck, or whatever is left of it is in the shot," Phil said to his friend.

"Are we doing this live?" Phil said as he stepped carefully on the blood-soaked slippery pavement.

"No, the cell networks aren't working, but I'm going to record everything, then we can upload to YouTube or wherever and link it to all our social media accounts. We are gonna be famous!"

"Just tell me when you are ready and be sure to get that head in the picture," Phil said hoping he wouldn't vomit. He had expected carnage but seeing it and smelling it in person was something he wasn't prepared for, at least not as much as he thought he had been. In places the blood, and other bodily fluids were so deep his shoes almost disappeared as he walked.

"Ready when you are man," Sam said.

Sam looked into the camera, took a deep breath, and

got started, "We came out here to tell the truth to the world. This isn't a Hollywood stage. This isn't fake news. I am surrounded by what is left of people I knew, people from my community that chose to serve. These were Patriots. They gave their lives, and we have to fight back against this bullshit, we, each and every one of us, have to take the fight to these asshats that invaded our country.

"I am standing in the middle of what used to be their soldiers, and ours, all mixed together in what I can only describe as a giant pile. Our guys kicked a little ass before those chicken shits brought in attack helicopters. They need to fight us on the ground like men. None of this attack helicopter crap, come down here on the ground like men. This is America, our women can kick their asses in a fair fight.

"We are going to get as much real information as possible out to you, our followers and subscribers, as fast as we can. If you are new, don't forget to subscribe and link us everywhere you can. Share this because the lame stream media won't have the guts to show the truth of what happened here. This is Sam and Phil, and we are just getting started.

Once Sam was sure he wasn't being recorded anymore, he vomited onto what he thought used to be someone's arm.

"We have to get the word out and help people get ready for what is coming, this is all out war man, if the President and the Army can't get here fast enough we have to do this shit ourselves," he said.

Some teenagers started to show up to the center of

town and first responders finally started to appear. Phil being ever present with his camera caught the tears, vomit, and rage of everyone, just certain that his Instagram following would be jumping as soon as he could get these pictures uploaded.

<AP NEWS FLASH>The world is still at war. There is an invasion in process, a nuclear strike has hit, and now we have confirmed reports a large number of very sick individuals across multiple states clogging hospital emergency rooms.

There are now food shortages in some of the areas surrounding Los Angeles as well as parts of New England.

The size of the invading force is unknown, however with Internet videos now going viral it is obvious there is some heavy equipment involved on the side of the invasion force.

The United States has been hit with a cyber-assault from some unknown foreign government The AP is unsure how long transmissions will conti

<AP ECONOMIC NEWS FLASH> There is a massive cyber-attack underway which has taken all banking offline. There is no information available concerning the origin of the att

Chapter Six
Can Israel Survive?

General Bijan Farwad walked through the compound admiring the size of the unified armored tank forces that had somehow been assembled in a short period of time. The first round of this new Great War had definitely gone to the Americans. But the second round had just begun, and now that the Islamic nations had decided to work together to destroy the large Satan rather than argue, and fight with one another, things would be different. It was believed that through this cooperation the tide would turn.

For so long the Christian and Jewish Nations of the world had been killing believers, for what appeared to be no other reason than they were followers of Islam. They would always use the defense of the so-called "Jewish State" as an excuse. That excuse allowed them to have a place to keep a military force in the area. Now there was a real opportunity to put the Americans into a losing military position.

As the internal meetings concerning this new plan began he had expressed his fears that there would be no tanks left after what the American fighter and bomber aircraft had managed to accomplish before the peace accord, but thankfully that fear had been misplaced. Without the machines lined up in this staging area, and the capabilities they brought to the battlefield destroying what was left of the Jews would be almost impossible. Even with this equipment it was going to be the most difficult, not to mention the bloodiest battle since those seen on the Eastern European Front during World War II.

The new military agreement between the Islamic nations of the world was going to be the key to final victory, even with that agreement it would still be difficult. Without this cooperation no single remaining military force among them could successfully face even the Israeli military, despite the enemy's weakened condition. Their aircraft and smart weapons were just too effective. He, and many of the Generals were of the opinion that the unification could not have happened had the enemy not won the last battle so decisively. If it had been just a minor loss, they would still be fighting each other. Instead they would be able to work together to fight the two enemies that really mattered.

The Unified Islamic State leadership told him those advanced enemy smart weapons would no longer pose a threat, in other words, theoretically, they had been taken out of commission. His faith was not supposed to permit him to question the word of the leadership, but he was a military commander in addition to being a man of faith, and had to know as much accurate information as possible in order to have a plan A and plan B. More than that, he was a commander who had faced the Americans in combat before, and personally he had his doubts about these instructions to consider those weapons neutralized based on his years of experience against this enemy.

The Americans were resourceful and seemed to

always find a way to win. He had to be ready for anything. He hoped those who had given him this information were not relying on prayers alone to make these things come true, not everything could be solved through prayer. The coming battles would take much more. They would require action, bravery, a little luck, equipment, soldiers, and a prayer or two would all be necessary.

As he continued making his way across the compound his admiration for the massive, armored vehicles became more and more obvious to those around him. He kept repeating that he had never imagined such a tank force would exist in one place at the same time in his life, not to mention that they would all be under his command.

As he made his way through the compound, he looked down row after row of tanks. Some, far too few, were the heaviest tanks he had hoped to see, but the numbers of medium and light tanks might just make up for the deficit. What they lacked in firepower they made up for in speed and agility. When coming across infantry soldiers they would be ideal, if it were a tank on tank battle, they could be rapidly destroyed in a ball of flame, one after another in short order.

He began his career in these vehicles. The destructive power they could deliver at the touch of a button amazed him to this day. While there were many of them present, this was all that was left in the entirety of the Unified Islamic State. If these vehicles were destroyed there was no stockpile to bring up from reserve. Even if somehow the enemy's smart weapons, including those in Israeli hands, no longer posed a threat, the Americans had another weapon that he greatly respected and feared as much as their infamous drone army that could assassinate someone with no warning while the pilots remained safe half a world away.

The A-10 Warthog was that weapon. It was commonly referred to as the flying cross of death, it was not a smart weapon, but if they entered the battle, it meant that these tanks, and his soldiers inside them would not survive very long. The Americans did not have many of those aircraft left, but it didn't take many of them to quickly tip the scales in favor of the enemy.

The only downside for the pilots of these A-10 nightmares was that in a dog fight it didn't stand much of a chance against almost any fighter aircraft on the planet. But the Americans always flew them with air cover from their more advanced fighter aircraft.

He had seen those aircraft destroy tanks with such efficiency in past conflicts that he prayed they would never appear in the sky above him again. Perhaps Allah would grant him that blessing, it was certainly a prayer worth making, it couldn't possibly make things worse. The fear he was feeling had been spawned in no small part by his knowledge that the main weapon on that aircraft did not depend on computer uplinks, satellite feeds, or even RADAR guided missiles, but on the cold, calculating eyes of the human pilot.

That primary weapon is a 30-millimeter Gatling

Cannon. That weapon was capable of firing depleted uranium armor piercing shells, and fire them rapidly enough that merely thinking about it would give him nightmares. It could fire those rounds at an astounding rate of 3,900 times per minute, and if any one of those rounds hit any of the tanks, even the larger ones, the armor would be penetrated, and that vehicle would probably not survive. Given how fast it fired, anytime an A-10 managed to hit a tank it would not be a single round, there would be more than could be counted. It was a weapon of pure fury, of pure tank killing hellfire, and it was to be avoided at all costs.

The A-10 wasn't his only concern. The Israeli Defense Force may have been wounded because of the nuclear strikes that started this War, but it was not completely destroyed, at least not yet. Israel may be a small country, but their mandatory military conscription of both men *and* women meant that everyone inside those borders over a certain age had military experience of one form or another. That was in addition to their entire nation having almost immediate access to military grade weaponry. Every adult had to be considered a threat to be taken seriously. It also meant that in order to avoid being surrounded as he and his troops moved deeper inside those borders, they would have no choice but to kill every single adult in their path. Being surrounded inside that tiny nation would mean death, no matter how superior his tactics, soldiers, or armored vehicles. Today was going to be bloody, but it was necessary to win the day. It also meant many Israeli children would perish in the fighting as they would be caught in the crossfire, but it was all for the greater cause of finally holding the lands that had been stolen from the followers of Islam. That certainly made it worth the sacrifice of some children of Jews.

The upcoming battle had to result in the absolute extermination of that Jewish threat. To be successful meant he and his men would leave a wave of destruction like no other in the history of mankind, and it would take place in a very small period of time. That was the only way the goal of capturing, and more importantly holding the Israeli capital city of Jerusalem was going to work. They had to kill everyone they came across. They could leave nothing in their wake but a large number of dead people. It wouldn't be enough to try to convince them to quit through massive losses, they must perish, it was the only way. History would call it the second holocaust, and that was fine. It would all be over quickly, he hoped.

He came to the massive vehicle he had assigned to himself and took his position. Being the Supreme Commander of these forces, he knew he should not be in a tank, not given his level of responsibility, but he did not care. He would be the first to cross into Israel. Leading from behind was not his style, and his men would respect him for it. He knew from experience that they would fight harder as a result of this type of active leadership.

The border was a mere twenty kilometers away from their current location. If things went as planned, he would be in their capital before sunset, if the plans were not successful, he might not live to see that sunset.

He got on the radio and gave the orders to follow him. Engines could be heard coming to life all over the compound. It was time to get things moving, there would be no turning back, it was success or death.

To just the crew of his vehicle, the crew he handpicked for this day he said, "At last, the time has come. FORWARD!"

***

It was a sight to behold, something that would be written about in history books and not just those specific to military history. Those books would be kind to the cause if his forces were victorious, and they would say he and his men were evil if they were defeated.

History books tended to be written by the victor.

The tank column ran for miles. Somehow no enemy aircraft had come upon their position. Not a single one. That should not have been possible. The Americans had their magical satellites that should have seen them moving by now. Normally even their intent to move would have been picked up the moment people started to climb into their vehicles and turn on their engines. Perhaps the intelligence reports had been correct, and his forces would be safe from the flying machines of death thanks to some miracle that had alleviated the threat of the smart weapons and intelligence gathering sensors on satellites and drones.

On the command communication channel he received reports of whatever aerial activity was in the region. The Islamic Air Forces had encountered no resistance thus far. Not a single enemy military aircraft had come up to counter them before they had completely destroyed the overwhelming majority of the relevant Israeli RADAR installations. This small miracle had allowed them to dominate the sky. If their positions were unknown to the enemy, the upcoming battle just became much easier. This shouldn't be possible, yet it was necessary for his plan to succeed, so he was relieved that it was proceeding as he had been promised, that it hadn't been wishful thinking n the part of the leadership. But this wasn't a situation he wanted to take for granted. He wished he knew more about whatever miracle it was that caused this to be possible. For the moment he would just take things on faith that it would continue long enough to achieve their goal.

With the RADAR sites out of commission, according to intelligence reports, his jets were effectively destroying ground targets at will. According to the most recent reports any Israeli aircraft on the ground were no longer able to take off, all the runways inside the Israeli borders had been rendered useless after being turned into crater filled wastelands by amazingly effective bombing runs. The entire nation was now incapable of getting any aircraft off the ground or landing any fixed wing aircraft for the foreseeable future. That left only the few American aircraft that had been in the air and on patrol that had to be deal with. Yet somehow, those planes had been easily shot down with every encounter.

Somehow their early warning systems had not alerted the American pilots to the threat.

It was almost too easy. It was as if the Israelis and the American's had not seen anything coming, but for that to be true their technology had to no longer be working as designed, and in the past it had never failed. While that shouldn't have been possible, he was not going to complain about it. Five days ago, he would not have believed it possible. He knew that part of what would make the day possible was that just as this attack was launched the Americans would have been hit hard inside their homeland in several ways and would be distracted as a result. They should have been watching for an attack from anywhere, but they weren't. He was pleased that whatever caused this situation to be possible had happened, but a year ago had someone told him even this alliance would have happened he would have laughed in their face. The mighty Allah was on their side. He admonished himself for his doubt in his faith.

The ease of damaging the Americans, along with the Israeli dogs in the air and the lack of response from anything on the ground could only mean one thing. Whatever new capability the cyber teams had developed in connection with the Chinese (if the rumors of their involvement were true) had to be what was responsible for this miracle.

He knew for certain that there was an American

aircraft carrier group in close enough range to his current position to hit his troops with any number of weapons. If the American satellites or high-altitude surveillance drones could see anything at all and communicate the Islamic troop movements as they normally would, they would have ensured that there would have been American jets pounding them hard, if not completely destroying them by now. So far there were no reports, not even a rumor, not a whisper of American Naval aircraft in the area.

He prayed this would continue until the operation was over. He had a small fear that the Americans were attempting to pull them into a trap and destroy them with some massive unconventional weapon, but that would have gone against their well-known doctrine.

The closer they came to the heavily populated city, the less likely that became. Unconventional weapons killed indiscriminately, and the Americans would never do that, even if there was no other option.

***

Less than an hour later General Farwad's tank was the first in a very long armored column to enter Jerusalem. He was told that the trail of dust left by the column could be seen for many kilometers, that would change as their progress would now be slower.

So far, they had encountered only minimal

resistance. Nothing more than local militia with light infantry weapons, and while it would have been tough for infantry to advance this far, this fast, they were nothing a tank couldn't handle quickly, easily and very accurately. There had barely been a case when they had to slow down their forward progress. If he were forced to report the types of contacts in some formal fashion, he might very well have said that there were days when taking target practice had held greater challenges.

This city was going to be another issue. This was the city the vermin referred to as their capital. All the Holy sites within should not be in the hands of the Jews but should be under the control and watchful eye of the Islamic nations of the world. The Jews misinterpreted most of them, and that must end.

They were finding that the assumptions made during planning were true and that there were militia as well as regular military everywhere in seemingly endless warrens of streets and alleys. Some groups of the enemy soldiers had equipment and explosives that could damage, and possibly destroy, even the heaviest of tanks in his arsenal. This was going to be a down and dirty fight. Every corner could be a trap, and the fighting would soon turn into a house to house struggle. His men would have to come out of their Tanks and Armored Personnel Carriers to ferret out those threats hiding in the buildings.

Tension was starting to build in between his shoulder blades. This was going to be extremely bloody before it was over, but it would mean the end of these people who had been the enemy his entire life, and his fathers before him.

They were three kilometers from the capital building. Between their current location and the ultimate destination were potentially thousands of enemy soldiers, hundreds of historic locations of significance, and dozens upon dozens of ancient religious sites which could not be destroyed. His orders, as well as his beliefs were very clear on that matter. While the Jewish bastards occupying this Holy City could, and in his opinion should, be exterminated from the face of the planet, these structures must remain intact for all time. Nothing could happen to them. Realistically, he knew there would be some damage done to the sites because of the massive exchange of weapons fire that would mark the day. Some stray shots could not be prevented. Deliberate damage had to be avoided at all costs, even if it meant the loss of some of his soldiers. These sites were to be protected as they were too important to the followers of Allah and had been coopted by the non-believers. They were certainly more meaningful than the lives of a few soldiers who would be going to paradise anyway.

It started, slowly at first. The sounds of single or small bursts of rifle rounds could be heard bouncing off the exterior of the vehicle. He always found it funny that people would shoot those weapons when battling against a tank like this without considering the result. Better to save the ammunition for when, and if it mattered. There was simply no way those small arms could even dent his tank.

Those meaningless impacts sounded like a gong

being struck. While the small bursts could be annoying, more impacts would start to cause problems with hearing and crew concentration on the tasks at hand, but no real physical harm would come to the vehicle or the soldiers inside.

Suddenly, without warning, there was an explosion large enough to be felt inside the multi-ton metallic cocoon.

It came from behind his tank and took him by complete surprise. He could not hear anything. His ears were ringing in ways they never had before. Whatever the round was that took the vehicle behind them out had not announced itself, but the explosion could not be mistaken. He looked to see the tank in position immediately behind his in the column had exploded and was billowing black smoke into the air. He could not tell if anyone had made it out, because if they had not, they would be burning alive, and certainly were not going to survive. Flames were leaping high into the air from the blow out panels and open hatches on top of the tank. Inside of the turret, rifle rounds could be heard starting to cook off. Nothing alive could survive the heat of that fire, much less the environment of flying metal objects taking place inside. The heat alone would be far too intense. Soon, the main gun rounds would start to cook off, and when that happened, he wanted the rest of his men and the surviving vehicles to be far away from this area.

Whatever it was that destroyed the tank had to have come from one of the multi-tenant structures standing four stories above both sides of the road.

There was no other alternative.

He got on the radio and ordered those troops in armored personnel carriers to dismount. They would have to begin going house to house, and quickly get themselves far away from the burning tank. He couldn't use the main guns on the tanks to destroy houses, they couldn't be sure they got everyone without a complete search of the area. Besides, there weren't enough tank rounds to destroy every single home in the area.

The cost for the infantry just got exponentially higher in terms of lives lost, as the house-to-house fighting would result in more face to face fighting than anticipated, and that always got men killed. It was exhausting, it would be bloody, but it was necessary to carry the day, win the battle, and meet the goals laid out by the political leadership.

His tank turned a corner, leaving the burning mass of metal behind them when the gates of hell opened up around him. Shoulder fired missiles came raining down from everywhere, and all at once, thankfully they had not been very well aimed, or something else was impacting their ability to hit the target. Word of their arrival was obviously spreading, and the locals were dug in and getting more prepared as the battle progressed.

The element of surprise had been nice, but it was now a thing of the past. Every inch of ground would become increasingly difficult to gain.

Down the street, on the right was a multistory building with several automatic weapons and occasional rocket propelled grenade raining down on his position, getting more accurate by the minute. From inside the belly of the tank, the machine gunner was firing back, but it was not making any damn difference in the amount of incoming fire. There were too many different firing positions spread too far apart for a single machine gunner to make a meaningful difference. His tank had been the first around the corner and was blocking the way for anyone to come up from behind and offer any backup covering fire and they would have trouble moving forward if things didn't change. Seeing the situation from his position in the turret, the main gunner took control of the turret. He quickly swiveled around, training the main gun on the building producing the most fire. The gunner took careful aim and fired a high explosive round. The tank rocked backward as the massive weapon let loose its awesome power, then it came to settle steadily on its tracks.

As the debris settled it became obvious the building was no more. It has been reduced from multiple stories of Israelis shooting at him and his men into a pile of fire, smoke, rubble and death. There could not be anything alive in that pile of garbage that would survive for long if they were not dead already.

Out of the corner of his eye from the right, a quick streak of flame came in and hit his tank over the engine compartment. The multi-ton vehicle jerked to a halt as the missile exploded. Fire and smoke began to rise from the devastated engine. It was a miracle the crew wasn't killed instantly, but he knew they didn't have long.

He checked the radio. It no longer worked. The tank was dead, and very soon the fuel tank would reach a critical temperature resulting in a massive explosion that would kill everyone inside.

"Everyone out," he ordered his crew with his ears still ringing. "We will fight on our feet. If we stay in here any longer, we will die. Grab your personal weapons, dismount and seek cover, *NOW!*"

They climbed out of the uppermost hatch and jumped to the ground. Automatic weapons fire was everywhere. Smoke from the burning buildings and destroyed vehicles mixed with dust and pieces of rock. Concrete was continuously chipped off the roadways by the massive amount of rifle fire flying in all directions. It was difficult to see, which was what kept the crew alive as they ran for the nearest building.

Screams of the wounded and shouted orders filled the air. Everything smelled of smoke, burning diesel fuel, and death.

Death had a very distinctive smell, and this much death magnified the odor beyond all imagination.

It was as confusing a situation as he had ever seen or could have possibly dreamed up. His troops were mixed in with the Israelis. There were no lines. Indiscriminate firing on the part of his men could lead to the death of their fellow soldiers instead of killing the Israelis. Given how confusing things were some of that had undoubtedly already occurred.

In his local microcosm of the battle, he could hear small arms fire inside every surrounding building. It would sometimes pause and all that could be heard were screams for help coming from the dying. The smell of fire and explosive residue filled the air. Heat seemed to be radiating from everything, from every surface, including his own rifle barrel. He realized that the overall amount of weapons fire was slowing, leaving increased periods with a strange set of noises. He would have never thought he would hear such sounds. It was not anything he had prepared himself or his soldiers for. He knew the sounds would haunt his dreams for the rest of his days, but that was a problem for tomorrow. He knew the sounds were coming from humans, but he would have never imagined hearing the overwhelming sounds of agony coming from so many dying people at once.

He walked down the street with his sidearm drawn, it was the only weapon he still had with ammunition. He bent down to pick up a rifle from the ground. The bloody pile of meat that was once one of his soldiers would no longer require its use.

Those men who had been in his vehicle flanked him with their weapons at the ready. Israelis would randomly pop out of a building, weapons drawn, and be mowed down before they had a chance to fire any kind of well-aimed shot. They always looked confused. He knew they had been told propogandist lies for so long about how this situation could not be possible due to their superior weapons, and they believed those lies so deeply that some seemed to think that their eyes were deceiving them. But extreme technological superiority could make an enemy arrogant, and arrogance could be an exploited.

Maybe there was something else to the confusion he was missing. It was as if they had no warning of these attacks. The battle so far had been completely one sided, and it was a slaughter. While his forces had continued to decimate the defenders, his troops had hardly been scratched by comparison. They had lost a few vehicles, and some men, but nothing compared to the Jews who needed to vacate the surface of the Earth immediately. He hoped the fight against the Americans in their homeland was finding as much success. If that was the case this war could be short lived. The homeland of the Great Satan was so vast that he didn't think that was possible to be progressing as quickly as this battle, but before today he would not have believed any of this could occur. Maybe his assumption was wrong. Perhaps the unimaginable had occurred.

Could the conventional military thinking be completely wrong due to some new capability on which he had not been briefed that had changed the game so extremely?

Some people even staggered from their homes in their sleeping attire. They were completely disorganized, some disarmed, and mostly seemed completely unsure of what was going on. Even those who were unarmed were being destroyed, his orders had been specific as an unarmed person can quickly become armed and therefore was still considered to be a combatant.

The few pockets of semi-organized resistance seemed to vanish. Now, all that happened was someone would stagger from a door and be shredded by so many Islamic soldiers firing at once that the blood being blown from the body would turn into a gory mist that spewed in all directions as the body fell to the ground with a sickening wet thud. Butchers slaughtering cows had never seen such terrible things done to a body. In the General's opinion, these Jewish bastards were finally getting what they had deserved for so long.

He was three feet from the next house when a young teenage boy, barely out of childhood stepped out with a rifle, "Stop, you fucking Islamic pig," the boy screamed as he raised the weapon preparing to fire.

The General did not think about it, he merely raised his recently acquired rifle and fired. The young boy went limp and dropped with a bullet hole in his forehead. It was not the first person he had killed that day and would not be the last. It was the first time he killed anyone so young, a mere child, but these people were barely human. He didn't really consider them his evolutionary equal. His conscience would let him sleep fine this night if he could get those bizarre sounds to leave his brain. He kept moving, stepping over the boy and the pool of blood expanding below the dead body with no further thought of what had just happened.

His personal radio reserved for calls from his deputy and a few key members of his leadership team came to life.

"General, where are you?" came the concerned voice of his deputy.

"I am around the corner, down from where my tank is on fire. You will see a huge plume of black smoke from my last known location, and any second there will be additional explosions when the magazine starts to cook off. This particular street was set up as a giant kill zone to wipe us out. We are battling hand to hand in several places, but their resistance is weakening," he replied calmly. "Give me a report."

"Sir, we will have a vehicle there for you in two minutes, hold tight. We have nearly reached the capital building from the south. We will get you there before anyone enters the building. This is about to end, and we have won the day," came the reply.

***

President Press had been sitting in the mobile command center on board Air Force One watching his people run around trying to get electronic equipment to come back to life in order to display some form of useful data when his phone rang.

The room fell silent.

"How did that work?" someone asked from the back of the room.

"Sir, all cell phones have been down coast to coast, and no one else here is getting any kind of signal," said Brian Kentworthy.

President Press looked at the caller ID before answering on speakerphone, "Yes, Mr. Prime

Minister," he said knowing it was the Prime Minister of Israel.

"Mr. President, I have been trying to reach you for an hour. Suddenly my phone rang, and it was you, thank you for reaching out. I don't know how your people got the phones to work, but we have had all electronic communication equipment rendered inoperable."

People around the room looked puzzled.

"I don't know how much you know about our situation. We have enemy soldiers at our door, a massive number of them. Their tanks are less than a block away from my position. I am about to surrender. We are finished here.

"I dare say, that Israel as a nation will cease to exist today. I wish you luck Mr. President. I think you are now facing a unified Islamic military consisting of soldiers from many if not every Islamic nation under a single flag. It is the only way to explain their numbers," the Israeli Prime Minister said, speaking more quickly than the President had ever heard anyone speak, obviously scared out of his mind.

"Oh, dear Lord, can you get out of there? We are officially offering you immediate asylum!" The President offered. He was confused, his mind was racing, how could this have happened and without warning. What did that mean for their level of intelligence of what was happening inside the Continental United States?

"I will not be able to take you up on your gracious offer. They are here for me, and I don't think I will live through the day," the man said, more calmly than he had been speaking, perhaps resigning himself to the inevitable. "I want you to do a few things for me, please let me speak without interruption as my time grows short. First, the ambassador of Israel to the United States is to become the Israeli Prime Minister in exile. Second, please harbor any Israelis who seek shelter from this storm. Before I announce my surrender, I am going to order all my surviving troops to disband and seek shelter with your troops, if at all possible. It is the only way they will survive the holocaust that is happening. Even as I speak to you those instructions are going out to commanders to order their units to make their way to U.S. bases to seek shelter. Mr. President…Scott…May God be with y…"

An explosion could be heard followed by machine gun fire.

The line went dead. Softly, the President tapped the phone with his index finger.

"Mr. Chairman, we have a problem. I had hoped that the Vice President's intelligence report had been an overstatement, but he appears to have been spot on, and he also appears to be in front of all of our intelligence agencies," the President said. He was unsure what to do next, wishing he could speak to the Vice President who seemed to somehow know as much or more than anyone in the room.

The intelligence personnel in the room started working with this new information. Having just lost one of their major allies in the Middle East was going to be a problem if some semblance of stability was going to be brought to that region.

"May God help us all," the President said.

The President's phone rang again. The caller ID simply said, "You know who," and displayed no numbers.

President Press pushed the speakerphone button.

"Mr. President. My name is General Bijan Farwad. I am the Supreme Military Commander of the Unified Islamic Forces," said the man in heavily accented English to the room full of people.

"What can I do for you General?"

"Mr. President keep him talking, we need to listen to the background noise as much as possible," someone quietly said from across the room, trying not to be picked up by the phone.

The President waved him off.

"Mr. President, I won't take up much of your time, as I personally have much to do. I have destroyed the government of Israel. What is left of their military is on the run. I suggest you get your troops out of my part of the world before they meet the same fate, and become food for dogs," the General said and disconnected the line.

"Mr. Chairman, who the fuck is Bijan Farwad and did he really just instruct us to run?" the President asked in disbelief.

No one responded.

"Now, can someone please figure out how the fuck they can call us, but I can't seem to call the Vice

President on this same phone? Someone else come up with a reason why the sitting Vice President seems to know more about what is going on in the world than anyone else around here including the leaders of our national intelligence organizations? Enough filtered shit, I need to know everything!" the President shouted.

<AP NEWS FLASH> Only intermittent communications are possible. The United States has been hit by a cyber-attack the likes of which has never been seen. Even consumer Internet access is being attacked. Authorities are urging calm, but without access to ATM machines or credit card transactions for even the most basic of food purchases the majority of American cities are experiencing rioting. The lack of consistent communication will make any kind of relief effort for the city of Los Angeles more complex than it already was. This problem may also doom anyone suffering as a result of what appears to be biological attack taking place in the southern United States at this very moment.

War has been brought to the United States Homeland. Something that hasn't happened since World War II with the Japanese attack on Pearl Harbor.

<AP ECONOMICS NEWS FLASH> Given the conflict between nations taking place at this moment, and the level of destruction expected to be the result inside the United States and Middle East it is considered by many financial experts that the economies of the world will experience a

deep recession if not outright depression. It may render certain currencies extinct and will certainly cause which nation will be the reserve currency for the world to be questioned. This may be a complete reboot of international economics. As a result, the futures markets are predicting massive downturns if not outright collapse in the immediate future.

Chapter Seven
From Bad to Worse

Alex sat down at his computer to do another financial model that would justify the "on paper" value of a small company to potential investors for their next round of raising capital. Financial Capital is the life blood of companies in the growth stage. This was the third one of these he had worked on this week. While it sounded like boring work to most people, to him there was a real beauty in those numbers. Those seemingly innocent little numbers represented people whose professional lives were on the line. Their hopes and dreams were wrapped into the companies those numbers represent and the people who founded them hoped would be the next Amazon sized company.

If he did the numbers the right way, these people could prosper. If he did them wrong, they could end up with a pile debt from which they might never recover. The numbers had to be done exactly right, there was no margin for error.

The people around him sat in their cubicles tapping on their keyboards doing similar tasks, and it looked like it would be a day much like any other. As he was just getting on a roll when out of the corner of his eye, he saw someone he didn't recognize drop a soda can in the trash and rush out the door. The rushing out the door was the oddest part of the whole affair.

No one in this office ever rushed like that. It wasn't an "I'm late for a meeting" rush it was more of a "I'm panicking and need to leave to get to the hospital" kind of rush. On top of that, he wondered why someone was drinking soda from a can instead of more environmentally friendly bottles, but he shook his head and just assumed it was just someone who preferred the coldness of the metal instead of the plastic, and maybe they had to go pickup their kid or something.

What Alex could not have noticed as he put his earbuds back in with music blasting out an 80s music was the louder than usual popping sound the can made when it hit the bottom of the waste bin. It was followed by a hissing noise that grew a bit louder every second until suddenly, twenty seconds later it abruptly stopped.

The news report he half listened to on the radio during his commute had said something about an "invasion," and some kind of military ground attack in New England. But that was a half a country away, did not directly affect him, and besides, he had important work to do.

Then there was some kind of unconfirmed report about an apparent biological attack. He figured that must just be a rumor that was bring spread as people panicked over what was really happening that could have just been a random rumor that got started on social media. Rumors should be ignored so he dismissed it.

Then there was something about a nationwide intermittent Internet failure. That was a concern, but he had all the research he needed stored on the hard drive on his computer, so for the moment he could be productive anyway. He could prioritize around things needing external access, at least for a while.

The news was something that he never put too much stock in anyway, since they had shown time and time again that they could not be trusted to actually report the news with any real accuracy. The "news" organizations were constantly reporting poorly researched information and then they always seemed to be retracting some part of a story, if not the whole thing. He figured it would be better to just wait it out and see what was true and what wasn't across the next few days.

The news reporter had said to be on the lookout and report anything unusual, but how weird was an aluminum soda can? It wasn't that strange, was it? Why was it so stuck in his brain? Certainly not something worth reporting to anyone.

He knew the attack in Los Angeles was real, but he still had to work. Getting paid by the hour served to focus the mind on things to get done for anyone who was a newlywed, even if that meant working with the weekend crew to get the models done for the executives to review on Monday, like he and half the rest of the office was doing today. He felt better that he was far from the only one who came in on a day when there appeared to be real things going on rather than staying home glued to the news, he couldn't do anything about any of that crap anyway.

Besides, if he didn't work, he didn't get paid, and last time there had been an attack in the United States it was over that same day. That had to be the case again, didn't it? Besides, that was California and, again, half a continent away.

On the other side of the office someone started coughing hard enough that it caught his attention. Normally it wasn't the kind of thing he would notice, but this was different. It was a wet and gurgley kind of noise. The coughing became harder than any person at work should cough. He hoped they wouldn't get everyone sick. He didn't have time for that, "Go home asshole," he mumbled to himself. If they had something that might be contagious, they should have just stayed home and not come in and risk infecting other people. Then, a second person, and a third started coughing the same sickly wet cough.

He took out his earbuds so he could listen more closely.

Someone vomited, then vomited again.

There was a scream.

This couldn't be an illness, maybe there was something in the air causing some people to have an allergic reaction.

People started standing up and rushing over to see what was going on or maybe they were going to try to help whoever was having the problem.

Alex stood up so he could see what was happening. From what he was hearing, the amount of spewed forth bodily fluid had to be enormous. He was fifty feet away and the smell was enough to make him want to join them and bring his breakfast back to the surface, all over his desk. He swallowed, hoping, trying to keep it down.

Alex was trying to figure out how large this disruption was going to be to his workflow. What he saw caused a strange, guttural sound to escape his throat. The people on the other side of the office were bent over coughing and projectile vomiting in a multihued stream of disgusting colors based on the contents of their most recent meal. He couldn't begin to imagine what made all of them start at once, but suddenly he realized there was no way there was anything normal about the situation, and this wasn't something caused by something in the air. Something was very wrong, and it had happened very quickly.

Looking around and realizing just how many of his coworkers were sick he began to panic. Fear set in, his eyes went wide, his breath was coming faster and faster with every beat of his heart. The sounds coming from the people around him was like nothing he had ever heard from a human, and the smell filling the room could have been coming from an old leaky cesspool after fresh rain.

His eyes found Angela. He knew she would be here today. She was a great friend and had been through so much lately that work had become her life. While she would never be a Victoria's Secret model, which wasn't a bad thing, she had an attractive presence driven by self-confidence that resulted in a sensuality about her. She was bent over on her hands and knees coughing and suffering from what looked like a nosebleed or was it blood coming from her eyes, there was so much of it that it was hard to tell. Despite the shock of it all and his instinct to run the fuck as far away from this as he could, he tried to rush over to her side of the room but, as he got closer, he got a tickle that quickly turned into a burning sensation in his throat and started coughing. He couldn't figure out why, he was healthy, and had just been to the doctor for an annual checkup and the doctor gave him a totally clean bill of health. He hadn't really been anywhere that he could have gotten sick since then.

He coughed harder and harder. His eyes became flooded with tears as if someone had turned on a salty faucet. Involuntarily stopping his advance towards Angela, he bent over, and all of his muscles tensed at once. He tried to fight back against whatever was happening but had somehow lost control over every part of his body.

He didn't understand any of it. Was this related to that thing in New England?

Here? In his office?

No way! That sort of thing just didn't happen. How could something like this happen to everyone in the entire office, all at once.

Violently, with no way to catch himself, he hit the ground hard, face first. He managed to lift his head just a little, and through an ocean of bloody tears freely flowing down his face he saw Angela on the ground about twenty feet away. She had foaming red drool coming down the side of her face and blood quickly flowing from of her nose, ears and her eyes seemed almost lifeless.

Then it dawned on him, he had the same problems.

But wait, that couldn't be right.

When did this happen?

How did this happen?

What the fuck *was* happening?

He could not focus on anything except Angela, hoping he didn't share the same future but some part of him knew he did. Her body continued to spasm out of control, she was just out of arm's reach he couldn't help her.

His eyes slammed shut against his will and concentrating as hard as he was still able, he could not open them. He tried, and tried again, but there was no way he could open them. That was stupid, opening your eyes is easy, he should be able to do that. He was growing more confused every minute.

His muscles started flexing, doing some crazy things, sending his body thrashing in all directions.

Without warning, every single muscle tensed, hard, all at once, and he could no longer move. He was stuck in one position. His lungs started to spasm. He was alternating between trying to draw breath into his now mostly destroyed lungs while projectile vomiting massive amounts of blood and liquified tissue. His colon was next to release its contents. A flood of bloody shit flowed into his pants, seeping out past his belt, while making its way toward his shoes and onto the floor emitting a smell that was the odor coming from rotting flesh, only in this case it was mixed with the reddish colored urine that his bladder had ejected into a pool on the floor.

His mind recognized the odor as the smell coming from the room when this whole thing started. The realization was enough to let him know that he wasn't the only one suffering.

What the hell was going on?

Why the hell was this happening?

His mind kept shifting, confused, going from one topic to another. He thought about his wife, his parents, his dog, his future, if one was still possible.

Some part of him was starting to realize there was no future, not for him.

How can everyone in the room go from healthy to whatever this was in such a short period of time?

It didn't make any sense.

As his mind shut down, his body continued to spew forth bodily fluids. Some of what escaped was once the lining of digestive organs, adding to the unique stench.

Alex's life ended in a puddle of oozing slime in intense pain and confusion.

***

Roughly twenty hours after the detonation in Los

Angeles the President stood at the head of the conference table, frustrated that he was still stuck on board Air Force One. He held his cell phone at chest level staring into space for a moment. Only some of the electronics gear was back up and running, with technicians and software people working furiously on the rest.

The experts wanted him to feel better that any computer files stored locally could be accessed. But, the data that anyone wanted to see wasn't local, it was new, and incoming.

Thankfully some of the cell phone networks were partially functional again, or they would have almost no updated information about what was going on outside the airplane, which was still on the ground and likely to stay that way for a while.

"Everyone quiet!" the President shouted.

The room fell eerily quiet, more so than the President had intended. He slowly put down his phone.

"Listen up, given that the Prime Minister of Israel was going to surrender and has now either done so or more likely has been killed, we have to quickly think this situation through. The only way that man would have agreed to lay down arms is if his citizenry were facing certain extermination," the President said, restating the obvious for himself as much as the people in the room.

"Mr. President, we have no other source, are we sure we can make the assumption that it is as bad as he made it out to be? Is it possible that the fighting was localized to just the capital?" Some unknown intelligence staff member asked.

"That was the Prime Minister himself, not some aid, and he was scared. Given that we had no cell access anywhere at the time, yet his call and that damn General somehow managed to get through, I feel safe saying that, I'm sure. Besides in a case like this we need to prepare for the worst, yet hope for the best," the President said. His tone of voice showing his rising anger.

"If that is true, and satellites gave us no warning, that implies some intelligence and even civilian sensor systems have been down longer than we realized and probably feeding us bogus data. Mr. President, I believe we may have the equivalent of a modern-day version of the D-Day invasion taking place, only we are on the defensive side this time, and we don't have massive defensive positions waiting on the beach. I think they are coming at us and possibly some, if not all, of our allies with everything they have available as fast as they can put it into the field, including their new offensive cyber capabilities which we didn't know anything about. If we don't have our networks, smart weapons, and sensor platforms functional this will be a war we are really not ready to fight without the use of unconventional weapons. The numbers are just not on our side," surmised the Chairman of the Joint Chiefs.

"General, we just launched two unconventional nuclear warheads and they took control of one of those. How do we know that the next time we launch one it won't be retargeted to hit one of our cities, and that they will take control of the self-destruct systems so we can't blow the thing up? Maybe it will be reprogrammed to hit one of our own military bases, or the capital city of one of our allies around the world, and how the hell would that be helpful?" the President's anger at the situation was coming through loud and clear.

"That is a possibility while those devices are on ICBMs. However, if we launch our attacks from bombers, we turn that back into dumb bombs and we can guarantee a hit thanks to the human pilots. However, we will have to turn off as much in the way of electronics, including navigation on our bombers, as we can just in case those aircraft are penetrated by this network attack. But honestly speaking, this may be the best pathway forward. We could also use one of those really fast point to point transport devices that research scientist guy just showed us, if it would work for the task. He said faster than light, and I while I don't know how fast that is, and I don't know how accurately you can choose the destination, if we can get our people into the right spot to be disruptive and get them back out quickly, that just might save our ass," the General was a professional in every way, and clearly was not ready to talk terms with the enemy. This was a time to beat them back, by any means possible.

"Ok. Let's go over the situation, just so we are sure everyone is on the same page. Israel is gone, and that is a huge problem for regional stability in that part of the world, which is a bad thing longer term, but let's figure out our overall status. Do we have word from any other of our allies around the world? Is anyone else under attack?" the President asked looking at his

Secretary of State, the nation's chief diplomat.

"Without access to our computer networks, or hell even television news, it is difficult to be certain. I'm going to have people light up the phone lines and do this the old-fashioned way, but it will take some time," the Secretary of State said.

"Get to work and let me know when you have something, and I'd like a better plan than watching the nightly news," the President ordered.

"General, where is our heavy combat gear? How much do we have in transport, and how hard will it be to make sure we bring everything we can home as quickly as we can? I have a feeling we may have no choice other than to become an isolationist nation for a while," the President said.

He clearly did not like these choices he was having to make, but it was obvious they were painted into a corner. Becoming isolationist could result in the rest of the world falling into an even greater level of chaos, but if they prevented global chaos and lost their own nation that would be unthinkable. That worldwide chaos might be possible to fix once things got under control domestically, but he couldn't very well protect the world while losing the homeland. The American leadership had to be able to protect its own citizens first before they could worry about any other nation's people.

"Mr. President, we have approximately forty percent of our hardware in the process of being repositioned. If you recall, we took a chance and sent almost every asset we had into the Middle East to try to bring an end to hostilities quickly. Most of it is still there, or in transit on the way back. If, and right now that's a big if based on our current cyber challenges, if we can find their staging area over there perhaps we can launch an attack on their military capabilities or leadership, before they make a move elsewhere in the world, or manage to get more of their forces here.

"We can issue an order for everything in motion to come home at best possible speed, fuel conservation be damned, and develop a reasonable plan to pull out of everywhere we are that isn't currently a war zone, but that will take time. I don't know how long, but at least weeks to months. The other problem is that there are many places around the world that if we pull out with the threat of global armed conflict spreading everywhere is going to go way up. It may not be the best course of action to just bring everything home. We may want to take a deep breath and wait for some form of intelligence information to start flowing while we defend ourselves here at home with what is in the ground, even at the National Guard depots. They can't have that much in the way of men and equipment on our shores yet," the Chairman said, clearly not happy with the timeframe any more than the President.

"Fine. Someone figure out where the Vice President is, and get him here to meet that scientist. Perhaps that crazy man can save us, if we can figure out how to properly use any of that stuff. He showed us that thing that apparently enables faster than light travel. Perhaps that can deliver our weapons, and people where they need to be without the need for huge amounts of air support. I can't believe I just said those words, but let's hope to Christ that the thing works.

"Also, we need a better understanding of what manpower the enemy has already managed to land on our shores. We still have active cyber-attacks taking place that may make matters worse, AND our smart weapons are fucked, so maybe, just MAYBE our scientists can pull our asses out of the fire," the President was shouting louder and louder as he finished his statement. He was also starting to ramble, the stress obviously taking its toll.

"Yes, Mr. President," said the Chairman.

More computers and video screens had been coming online during the exchange.

"Mr. President," the Vice President's voice said.

"Frank, I didn't realize your link was back up. Where the hell are you, and how soon can you get to wherever I am?" asked President Press.

"Somewhere in Texas, I think. However, I'd like to make a point that both of us being in the same place at the same time is a very bad idea, Mr. President," said Frank.

"Of course, and honestly, I'm not 100% certain where we are, just that there is some technology here that you have to see to believe and use that tactical military brain of yours to help us figure out how to use it to clean up this mess," said the President.

"I'm told the avionics in this plane are fine. Mr. President you need to get someplace safe and organize a response to the invasion making its way through New England, as well as a nerve agent or biological attack, we aren't really sure which just yet, that is at this very moment putting Americans into a horrifyingly painful death spiral in at least three cities that we are aware of so far, on top of all that we also had a massive nuclear strike. I suggest you go to Fort Bragg, and I go wherever you are," Frank said.

"Mr. Vice President, if I may?" the Surgeon General interrupted.

"I have been on the phone with some of the Emergency Rooms in the impacted areas of this nerve agent. The people infected are experiencing the following symptoms: muscle convulsions, runny nose, crying, drooling, release of bowels and bladder, even some temporary paralysis. Those that will die are doing so in about ten minutes post exposure. Everyone else will recover, and all we must do for the moment is to keep them comfortable and well hydrated. This could be an indication that more than one type of public health related attack is taking place. The hospitals in the area surrounding the nuclear strike are over run in the same way we experienced last time, only this strike was larger, and that must be our priority," said the Medical Professional.

"Mr. President, this bio-agent attack may have been a test of some new capability. If they use those weapons on our troops while we are in contact, they will be slaughtered as they won't be able to offer any kind of resistance thanks to the associated symptoms. Everyone must wear protective gas masks, whenever they are about to make contact with the enemy," the

Vice President said.

"General, issue that order, and Doctor, you better figure out if whatever it is that is happening is highly contagious or not, and if it is more than one type of attack, we don't need a fucking pandemic on top of everything else. If the people who survive are carriers, I don't even want to think about the growing problems we will face in the days to come," said the President.

"Frank, get here and get to work, we will be at your old stomping grounds over at Fort Bragg. If we work together, we might just get through this mess and make the world a safer place in the end," the President said, then walked out of the room to see the pilots.

***

"We up yet?" Phil asked.

"Yeah, but YouTube isn't going to allow this to post because of their damn 'standards' or some shit," Sam said.

"Fuck, ok load it on our website, and we'll just link it to Twitter, and we'll see how long the Tweet stays up," Phil instructed.

"Ok, we can go anytime then."

"Go dude! Do you think our server can handle the traffic?" Phil said as Sam tapped on the keyboard.

"Sure, our plan adjusts with traffic dynamically, so it

may get expensive, but we will stay up."

They had a pretty solid following and knew how to hashtag tweets for maximum exposure. It was less than a minute before people started re-tweeting and commenting. They were even picking up new followers quickly.

"It is getting out. Let's see anyone deny what is really going on. If it weren't for people like us someone on the news would start to claim our guys all lived through the attack, or that it was staged, or something. We have to be the beacon of truth. Maybe we should pack a bag and follow the attacks as they go down the coast?" Sam asked.

"Dude, that sounds like a plan. Citizen journalists are going to be needed. We are at war, and we need to be on it," Phil said not sure how he was going to explain this to his boss, and only partially caring if he got fired.

"How long before you can be packed for say maybe a week?"

"Shit man, an hour? This matters, let's get on the road today. Be sure to grab all your chargers, we are going to have to stay ready," Phil said.

<AP NEWS FLASH> Hospitals in some of the southern states are being overrun with citizens suffering from the effects of a currently unknown biological agent. Many people around the nation are nervous they might be showing signs. There will be an upcoming press release

showing what symptoms to be watchful of, however if symptoms being experienced are not acute, the malady is likely not related. Hospitals are asking that people think before jamming local emergency rooms with false alarms.

So far between the attacks in Los Angeles, the invasion in Maine and the biological attacks as many as a million Americans may have perished. No official numbers are known at this time. The CDC has asked those in the areas experiencing a biological attack do not travel outside the area. There is a need to keep the situation contained.

<AP ECONOMICS NEWS FLASH> Prices of day-to-day items are rising by the hour, and in some places hoarding of non-perishables is happening. Governors of all fifty States have issued statements that price gouging will not be tolerating and urging people against hoarding. There have also been sporadic statements that are unconfirmed of certain consumer goods starting to appear on an online underground market of sorts.

Middle Eastern nations have stated they will no longer be exporting oil; however, the United States has been a net exporter of oil for a number of years due to extensive use of fracking. While environmental groups may not be in favor of the practice it is thought that these changes in the oil market will not impact the availability of oil in the United States. This has not changed the rapid rise in prices across the nation. Energy futures are leading the pace for the entire market for which they are rapidly rising.

Chapter Eight
Where will the War be fought?

The war was only forty-eight hours old and already much had happened. The Unified Islamic Forces were winning, that much was obvious from the intelligence briefing that had just ended. Hopefully, the reports weren't overstated and therefore not reflective of reality.

For the second time in as many days General Farwad marveled at the overall size of the forces he had under his command. The challenges left to face in this phase of the war effort were far greater than the those required wipe Israel off the map, and that battle had resulted in greater numbers of people killed than he had ever dreamed would happen in a single day by conventional means. It was as if equipment and men he needed to achieve these military goals were appearing magically from nowhere. He supposed they were just being transferred to his command from all of the newly allied nations. Where these things came from didn't matter and at the moment he did not really care. They were here, and that was what mattered. Hopefully the growing and highly complex supply chains could keep up. The number of rifle rounds, the amount of fuel, and just fucking meals he would need in the coming months for the operations to come was shocking.

After the previous invasion by the Americans had destroyed significant portions of each of the individual militaries in the region the only way to remain relevant had been to unite and form one unified Islamic force against the Westerners. If that had not become possible, they would continue to have small fights and continued skirmishes with one another until nothing was left.

Well, that and the work done by the Chinese cyber assault teams had proved to be enough of a force multiplier that all the pieces of the puzzle were now in place to allow these newly expanded forces a chance at success. The Chinese had certainly put his men in a position to be able to slaughter the Israelis, removing that annoyance of a nation from the surface of the planet once and for all. Without the cyber capabilities they brought to the battle, an invasion of the American homeland would be useless, and far less than a glorious suicide. He just hoped the Chinese could stay in front of the American's technologically. This enemy had an annoying habit of fixing their weaknesses with surprising speed and agility. He intended to keep quickly pushing the advantage as long as he could before that happened.

Finally, at long last, the dream of uniting every person on the planet under rule of Islamic law was within their grasp. Those who would not covert willingly would simply be killed or become indentured servants if they were easily held in compliance. It was an easy choice, and it was theirs to make. Convert, become a compliant slave, or die.

He had defeated Israel by using some of the very tanks which were lined up in front of him. Thankfully the losses had been minimal. His men, all true believers, had performed their jobs against non-believers admirably. But that was Israel, a nation of less than fifteen million people when the war began, and far fewer after a successful nuclear attack that had been strategically placed to miss the important religious sites, but still do massive damage to infrastructure and defense services. Even with all of that prep work it was still hard.

Now they were going to have to fight a much larger enemy, both in a geographic sense and from the military strength perspective. A full on invasion of the United States had never been done with any measure of success, even when that Nation was an infant. The British tried it twice without success. During World War II, the Japanese tried attacking them at home, to a very limited success and they weren't foolish enough to attempt a land invasion. Even then, without today's modern military technology available to the Americans it was considered just too difficult. Perhaps if their technology, which they were very dependent upon, was taken out of the equation there was a chance at victory.

It was a much more challenging task, and much less easy to achieve problem than the flea speck that used to be Israel. There were some men already inside the U.S. borders securing an easier to defeat region of that massive nation. That would ensure there would be an easy landing point for the larger force to follow, and there were many more men on the way.

Sadly, one flotilla had been destroyed, but some losses were to be expected. At least now the U.S. nuclear arsenal had been taken out of the equation due to the Chinese ability to take control of the ICBMs.

His troops, especially this tank armada, was going to be the key on the ground. The air battle was another matter, and one that concerned him greatly.

Surprise could have been what allowed the soldiers already there to gain a foothold. Infantry could even hold a position for a period of time. The combination of tanks and infantry would become key to gaining ground once the invasion was known, which it already was, therefore the clock was ticking. Their window of opportunity was not large.

All in all, he had more men than the enemy did from a pure soldier count perspective. His infantry alone was ten times the size of theirs. The mandatory conscription the leadership put in place had seen to that. The enemy training was much better and even without their smart weapons they were formidable, but his forces did have the numbers, and the passion. Allah was also on their side, and he was confident that would be the deciding factor.

The leadership of the new Unified Islamic State, whom he did not fully trust yet, had told him there was another new capability that might render very well trained, and highly effective United States troops they did encounter less effective in the fight. When he had asked questions about what this new capability was all they would say was that he would be briefed on all of the details while on the way to the United States. There were assurances given that the enemy had no way to counter this capability, which made him nervous. That was a sign of arrogance, and arrogance had a way of being exploited by the enemy.

He watched for a few minutes as troops, weapons, food, and other essential supplies were loaded into every available boat and airplane. The boats ranged from commandeered luxury cruise vessels to cargo ships. The airplanes were a mix of commercial and military cargo types, with a rare private luxury jet thrown in that would be used for the higher-ranking officers.

This would be the war to end all wars. The industrial, military, and civilian resources of the entire Islamic world were being used for this singular purpose.

He spoke with as many officers under his command as possible before boarding his assigned jet. He was needed on the ground far away as quickly as possible now that the Israeli threat had been eliminated. The U.S. would not go down as easily. He knew their citizenry had more privately owned weapons than anywhere in the world. More weapons in fact than Israel had once had citizens, and many of their civilians were known to be shockingly proficient in their use. Some were even known to stockpile ammunition.

That was on top of the United States and its massive industrial capabilities. This was a far more complicated enemy.

The military of any nation had a defined size and known tactics, all of which could be planned for. It was the civilians which would be an unpredictable challenge and may cause the end of large numbers of his poorly trained, but highly motivated soldiers. That was, unless his tank divisions could get there, and get there quickly. Some limited numbers were already nearing their coast, but he needed all of them and a robust supply chain that would not fail if this was going to work.

He walked up the steps of the Gulfstream luxury jet that had been reserved for him and his leadership team. There had been an extra intelligence officer added to the passenger list at the last moment.

"I suppose you are the one that will tell me how things are progressing in the fight against the Americans and all about this new set of capabilities that is supposed to make this whole thing work?" the General asked the strange man.

"Yes, General, I will. You will find our new chemical and biological capabilities impressive. I will also show you some video evidence of how well our special capabilities will work at rendering their troops completely unable to fight or even put up any kind of reasonable resistance if used properly. We have already run a series of tests using these capabilities against a portion of their civilian population," the man said with a grin.

So, this was the big secret, he should have guessed, "That will help, but what of their citizenry who will mount a massive militia resistance in every town? Do you have a solution for this? Are these biological capabilities really going to hold those civilians back? Not to mention there had better be a way to keep our men healthy while we are killing theirs if this weapon is contagious like any normal virus," the General rattled off, not really expecting a response.

"I have a few suggestions that will aid in reaching our ultimate goal."

***

"Frank, are you telling me everything that scientist briefed me on is real and can be either moved to the field, or produced in enough quantity, fast enough to make a difference in a useful period of time?" President Press asked his Vice President, not really believing what he was hearing.

"Yes Mr. President, it appears that way. No one here is a manufacturing expert, but the claim is that these devices aren't that complicated. If I was the one who got to choose what we did first, I would say we build five more, potentially larger versions of those faster than light travel gizmos and dozens of those hand-held plasma weapons. That would allow our special operations teams to get in anywhere on the planet undetected. Even if the teams were detected they could fight off just about anything for a short period of time. We can go after their leadership, their planning teams, critical military infrastructure, you name it. It would allow us to hit quickly without warning and be back out of the area before they can really figure out what is going on. That capability can really be what saves us. We can take the fight to them in ways they would never be able to see coming, or plan for.

"If we chose to go a more substantial way, we could even get our people in, allow them to place a nuke, or some other type of massive explosive, and be gone before a five second or even ten second countdown timer could reach zero, thus removing the need for missiles or bombers," the Vice President explained.

"Well, that would be useful if we can figure out where to send them. We know who did this, but thanks to their cyber teams we can't figure out where the hell they are. I don't suppose they have a 'where's waldo' locating magic trick hiding in a lab someplace," the President told the video image of the Vice President. The entire team was growing more frustrated with the lack of actionable intelligence.

"So far, we know of their soldiers in New England, and from what the latest briefing has told me, we have lost all satellite tracking capability. But I do have a suggestion that might help us get some C-cubed-I," the Vice President offered.

"Go ahead, and we will get some manufacturing experts to you to see just how long that whole process will take."

"A while back we retired a large number of U2 spy planes. These are the high-altitude glider-jet hybrids. They get up high enough so that if we retrofit a few with different cameras we can get some wide area looks from an altitude that will make it almost like we have satellite coverage. However, we must take them fully off the network, which we can't do with drones. The images can't be live feeds, and we can't use any kind of automated navigation, not with all these viruses eating into our computer networks. These flights will have to be done the old fashion way, hands on, because even our modern auto-pilot systems are GPS dependent, and honestly, I wouldn't trust that right now," Vice President Banner suggested.

"Sounds like a reasonable plan, but scary that we are so dependent on technology," the President said. "We need to know where they are. If we can't figure that much out, I don't know how we stop them without resorting to World War II tactics. We won't even know what they are sending our way from overseas right now, making it very challenging to mount any kind of meaningful defense. Not to mention this U2 retrofit has to take place much quicker than we normally do these sorts of things," the President was starting to sound desperate while naming things to do off as they came to his mind in no particular order.

"Mr. President, I keep getting more and more calls from Congresspeople who want us to launch a full-scale nuclear attack of our own. They seem to think our small strike was merely a good start, and that the entire Middle East region of the world should be turned to ash. When I mention the damage to their civilian population no one on the other end of the line seems to care," the VP said.

"I know. So far, we have managed to keep secret the fact that they can take control of our missiles and change our target packages. I don't want that to get out. If the news gets this information the public panic would be something we just can't have at this point, as I am sure that there is, or soon will be far more widespread panic," the President was obviously having trouble keeping control of his emotions.

***

Susan had been an executive secretary at the White House for almost nine years. Usually her job was answering phone calls from people all over the country who would call and ask to speak to the President. She would politely explain that he was busy, but if they could explain their problem to her she would see that the message got through, and then she would pass it along to the right department who would probably just add it to one of the many piles of things the President would never see.

Normally there was a small staff of two or maybe three people performing this task. Today something was different. No matter how controversial the topic making its way through the news cycle the phone calls had never come in this fast. Even when the Vice President had been killed on his way to being sworn in, not even when Dallas and Detroit had been hit with nuclear weapons had the number of phone calls and emails remotely approached this level.

There was another difference. In every previous one of these mad rush sessions there was a difference of opinion in the callers. This time it was consistent.

Everyone wanted a massive nuclear attack against anyone they even suspected of being involved in this madness. People were pissed off, people were scared, and wanted payback, on a scale that has not been seen in the history of the world.

***

Texas Senator Sanchez stepped up to the microphone, in front of a huge crowd at the State of Texas Capital building, "I have come here today to tell you that I am going to introduce new legislation with a singular goal. These new mass casualty attacks and now invasion is being done purely in the name of religion. The enemy is intent to destroy anyone who does not follow their religious belief system. That religion is Islam. They will kill to ensure theirs is the only belief system left on the planet, and they will not stop until that goal is reached.

"We must respond to these acts of violence with violence. Some say we must take an eye for an eye. However, I fear this will not be enough. We must expel anyone currently in the United States, who believes as these aggressors do, each one of them are potential allies who could be compelled to give intelligence to those who are attacking us. They must get outside of our borders immediately, or be thrown in jail, even if they are citizens."

There was a thunderous applause from the crowd.

***

"Oh, that's fucking helpful," the President whispered sarcastically as he muted the feed from the Senator.

He turned back to his computer and wrote an email to the head of DHS.

Find out if we have vigilante organizations attacking citizens based on a religious litmus test and stop them if we do. – POTUS

***

Matt struggled, but finally managed to open his eyes. It took him a minute to realize he was in a hospital and that his father was asleep in the chair next to him.

"Dad," he managed to say softly.

"Dad," he said a little louder when his father didn't respond.

The man sat up abruptly, "Matt! You are awake!"

He ran to the door and shouted down the hall, "Nurse! He's awake! And talking!"

He leapt back to the bedside, "Matt, they said you may never wake up! I'm so sorry for what happened to you, I am so very sorry."

"Shelly?" Matt asked.

"Oh Matt. I'm so sorry, I thought you would know.

They found her body, or what was left of it. I thought you knew that already. We assumed the two of you were together when she was killed."

"Dad, what happened?"

"We've been invaded, son. We are at war."

Tears started to flow down Matt's face as medical people and a man in a military uniform crowded around his bed. He wasn't sure how, but he knew he wanted revenge upon whomever did this. Enough was enough, first his brother and now this.

***

"Mr. President," Chairman Jackson said as he opened the door to the office. "There is a video breaking on Social Media you need to be made aware of as I believe it is going to contribute to that vigilante problem we have been talking about."

"Do I need to see it, or can we just skip to the part that is going to cause problems," the President said wearily.

"Well sir, two guys who fancy themselves independent journalists went into the aftermath of the National Guard unit that was destroyed before anyone could get there to clean it up and broadcast everything, every gory detail. The video is authentic, and they must have lived locally, or we would have had it secured. If we look at the comments on Twitter and the new Reddit thread there are people organizing, and about to go out looking for payback, and a using language that indicates they are likely going to be seeking revenge which may cause the enemy to do the same and become far more brutal in their techniques."

"Well, we knew that was going to happen sooner or later. Let's get word out to all of the commanders in the field to be careful and as they encounter these citizens to work with them and find them ways to contribute to the effort."

"Yes Mr. President."

<AP NEWS FLASH> There has been widespread vandalism at Mosques all over the country. While these have been condemned, it is not difficult for anyone to understand the frustration of those involved in perpetrating these crimes. Police have asked for anyone who feels they want to do these things to dial their local mental health hotlines. No one can fault them for desire, but those perpetrating such actions will be brought to justice.

There has been a rush on specific consumer goods. Toilet paper, hand sanitizer and bottled water are all in very short supply.

Hospitals are being overwhelmed outside the Los Angeles area. Medical supplies are running out, millions of people have been killed. Many people are leaving the area so quickly that gasoline is becoming hard to find. It is hoped that shipping will not be disrupted for long by this fuel shortage, and to prevent such a challenge the sale of diesel fuel is being limited to vehicles involved in shipping goods only. No consumer use of diesel fuel will occur until further notice.

Prices of food in the area around Los Angeles have skyrocketed, and the Governor of California has asked for calm as several grocery stores have been raided by large groups of people stealing food items.

<AP ECONOMIC NEWS FLASH> Oil prices per barrel have increased so quickly that domestic producers have made moves to bring people back out of retirement and have asked for anyone even interested in the field to apply immediately. These companies have vowed to increase supply as quickly as possible to bring prices back down to something resembling their normal range. The stock futures on these domestic producers are one of the very few positive areas on the futures market.

Stock markets all over the world continue to decline. Automatic trading halts have been put in place, however as people need to free up capital from these investments the markets are expected to be forced to open.

There are calls by investors and large investment banks all over the world for government intervention in the form of cash infusions into the market. They claim liquidity will be the key to markets not crashing.

Chapter Nine
London

Nigel was reflecting on the hundreds of hours he had spent in helicopters reporting the news throughout his career. He had gotten his start as a traffic reporter before that job had been taken over by internet-based cameras mounted high atop buildings. Even that technology was now obsolete and tracking available through smart phones now showed real time traffic patterns and delays all over world, and they did it for every street simultaneously. Even traffic accident images could be quickly found on social media, effectively eliminating the need for the expense of operating a helicopter randomly flying around town looking for the trouble spots.

He was always looking for an excuse to get back in the passenger's seat above the London rooftops. The view from here was not one that many people got to see first-hand. People flew over London every day, but they were in the passenger seats on a jet moving at hundreds of miles an hour, thousands of feet in the air. Not very many people got to do it at a few hundred feet above the rooftops at the much slower air speeds of a chopper.

The news from America and the Middle East was horrifying. By comparison London was still festive, and so far, remained untouched. The older he got the more he liked these types of public celebration events. As a young reporter he raced toward the most dramatic situations he could find. The more tragic, the more graphic, the faster he would be sure to get there. Those sorts of things were always good for ratings, and ratings were good for the career. Approaching retirement, he was not as interested in ratings as much as he used to be. These days he wanted to find ways to make people feel better about the world around them.

The day's event was the Queen's Birthday, and it was always a time for a celebration across the entire nation. The Queen would come down the road, sometimes in a limousine, other times in a more traditional type of transportation involving a horse, or team of horses and lavishly decorated buggy. This year was one of the years she was planning to be in the latter.

He believed her majesty decided to go that way in order to give a sense of normalcy, or a sense of tradition in a world rapidly descending into international chaos.

During a production meeting for the day's events the Executive Producer was very specific in her explanation of the tone the coverage was going to take. There would be no mention of the growing global war. So far England had been spared. This would be a day of jubilation, and nothing else would be broadcast. The national focus deserved to be on something pleasant.

The helicopter team was almost in position. He could see the famous Ferris Wheel near the even more famous river. Big Ben stood tall, still giving time, just at it had since the 1800s.

His headphones came to life with voices from the broadcast control room, "Nigel, can you hear us?" came the voice of Rose, the Deputy Executive Producer.

"Loud and clear, Rose."

"Great, we are going to throw to you in ninety seconds. We will be flipping between the exterior and interior cameras. You should always assume you are being seen by the audience as we will change that without warning. You ready?" she asked, as professional as always.

"Ready when you are," he replied, sitting up a little straighter, and positioning himself for the camera mounted inside the chopper.

His headset crackled a bit, then he could hear the in-studio anchor.

"We have our news helicopter in the skies over London to bring you the best view of the festivities. Nigel, what can you see? How does the crowd look from up there?"

"The crowd size is far beyond anything we have seen in recent years. Everyone is here to honor the Queen's big day and…"

A deafening static filled his headset. It stopped as abruptly as it started and was replaced by a voice speaking in heavily accented English.

"We are now in control of your broadcast. Your control room is useless. If you do not point your camera toward the tower known as Big Ben and back off two kilometers from that area, we will take over your onboard computers and crash your helicopter into the densest part of the crowd."

The pilot had a look of confusion. "What should we do?" he asked of Nigel.

Nigel tried to use the radio several times and got no response from anyone, not even from regional air control on the emergency frequency.

"Let's do what they said, something isn't right if we can't get a single return from the ground that can't be good news," Nigel suggested, not sure what was going on.

He started thinking about the news reports concerning the American computer networks being hacked, and his heart began to race, threating to pound out of his chest. He thought about his newly born grand-daughter and how much he wanted to watch her grow up.

He wiped perspiration from his forehead before it flowed into his eyes.

Neither he nor the pilot were sure if someone outside the helicopter really could take control and crash it, much less hit a specific target, but hackers were learning new tricks every single day, and the request seemed harmless to everything except the news coverage for the moment. It was what might come next that was the concern.

What was it they wanted the cameras to see?

The pilot swung them around to put the requested

distance between the tower and aircraft while keeping the camera directly on Big Ben the entire time.

The crowd was becoming frantic. He didn't know what caused the change that happened slowly at first, but the mass of people was no longer peaceful and cheery. They were all running, away from Big Ben, as if trying to escape something.

He wanted to know what could cause things to change this quickly.

Some old news reporter habits die hard.

Then, if he looked carefully, he could see some puffs of black smoke start to rise from the area around Big Ben.

He wasn't sure if he was on the air, but he began narrating the scene, "Oh, no, I think Big Ben is about to be the target of a terror..."

His headphones made a horrible, deafening noise.

"Nigel," said the heavily accented voice, "they can't hear you. Let us take care of filling silent air with the voice track that matters. Your thoughts are neither needed nor welcome at the moment."

A few seconds passed before the voice started speaking to the television audience, "People of London and the world. We are in charge now. The world order has changed. We are the leaders now, and Islamic rule will be instituted worldwide, or you will perish. You get to decide your future. The power of *Allah* will not be defeated. As we know you will not believe this without more than mere words, we will give you a demonstration of our power."

The voice stopped, and Big Ben exploded.

It was deafening, even at two kilometers, so loud it made Nigel involuntarily push against the safety belts.

The helicopter was blown around, but the pilot kept it under reasonable control. That two-kilometer instruction had been well thought out by whomever had given the instruction.

Bricks were thrown for hundreds of yards in every direction.

Nigel stared on in silence with his mouth open. As the sound of the explosion died down, and the ringing in his ears subsided the screams of the crowd could be heard, even over the noisy helicopter engines rotating a few feet above his head.

"News helicopter BBC-1. You will now cover the slaughter as it happens. Climb to 1.5 kilometers and slowly follow the natural flow of the river."

The pilot did as the voice instructed without asking questions, but neither of the newsmen wanted to know what was coming next. This was one new story Nigel would really rather not be reporting.

Nigel's headset came alive again, "Nigel, can you hear me?" came the pissed off, static filled voice of his Executive Producer.

"Yes," he said, not sure what was coming next. Nothing in his career had prepared him for this moment.

"There was an explosion in the executive offices here at the station. We don't know whom we have lost. We are under instruction from somewhere to broadcast whatever you send us. So, do whatever you think is best, but we think we can manage to keep your audio going out now instead of theirs," said the Executive Producer.

As the Producer finished speaking, the broadcast light came on, indicating Nigel was going out to the world, live. It also seemed that the EP had managed to throw a kill switch on the voices that had come across his radio somehow.

"Ladies and Gentlemen, Britain has now been pulled into this War. This one isn't being fought across the channel in Europe, or in some far away land, but right here in London. Big Ben is gone, spread all across London in small bits.

"We are moving into position to get a better view. I hope we can help find safe routes for people to get out of the city."

The helicopter quickly flew across the rooftops and climbed to 1.5 kilometers in altitude.

"We will bring you details and video from the destruction, and aftermath of the clock tower attack once we get people out of the area. We must do this in case there are more bombs. No one has any measure of protection down there, and we don't know how many of our fellow countrymen have been lost, or what might be coming next!"

The pilot had almost gotten to the front of the running crowd below, the screams could be easily heard over the beating blades of the chopper when more explosions began.

"Oh my God!" Nigel exclaimed. "They wanted people to run this way. They have car bombs in place. Once a dense crowd is close to one of their pre-positioned vehicle IEDs they trigger a detonation. These things are large enough that people are being thrown high into the air! Oh my God! Stop! Everyone stay where you are! If a bomb hasn't gone off maybe there isn't one in place where you are! STOP RUNNING!"

Nigel continued shouting instructions at the crowd to no avail, then he saw a new problem. They looked like insects against the sky. There had to be hundreds of them.

Small drones.

He knew before the first of them detonated, somehow, he knew.

"Ladies and Gentlemen, it looks like a swarm of drones is coming this way. You must avoid them at all costs."

The drones swept down. Smaller explosions were being placed with laser-like precision among the crowd.

"I don't understand why anyone would want to slaughter innocent civilians like this. There are children in this crowd. What have they done for someone to want to take their lives? This is…"

Nigel suddenly realized the camera outside the chopper was feeding the enemy all the information they needed to aim the attacks. He stopped narrating and unbuckled himself, determined to cut the power cable that ran through the cockpit to the camera.

As he wriggled out of his seat his headphones came to life, "If you cut that camera feed, we will crash your aircraft into..."

Nigel cut the cable going to the camera mounted on the exterior of the helicopter.

It took only a few seconds, but despite the pilot's best efforts the helicopter was driven into the crowd sending bits of rotary blades and body parts flying in all directions. There was no more broadcast of the attack, and Nigel would never know if he saved any lives.

***

President Press interrupted the meeting when his phone rang, and the caller ID displayed "You know who."

He put it on speaker, "President Press here, who is this?"

"Mr. President, this is General Farwad. We have just destroyed large parts of London and killed more than thirty thousand people in a conventional attack. You can't win this. Are you prepared to surrender? Or shall we bring destruction upon every single American city?"

"Go fuck yourself," the President said and cut the

line.

"Someone, find out what the hell he's talking about," he ordered the room.

***

Tony had been watching the news from London on a BBC internet site, when the feed was cut, he knew he and Josh had to get to work on this and everything else happening for their social media accounts.

He texted Josh.

Tony: Dude WTF is going on in the world?

Josh: IDK.

Tony: Does your sister still work at the ER in Chicago?

Josh: Yes, why?

Tony: See if she'll let us record a video call about these attacks, including this biological one for our YouTube channel. We can break this shit wide open cuz the media is just going to hide it or filter it so the public won't know the whole truth. Like this thing in London, they cut the feed. They don't want the truth out.

Josh: I'll get her dude. Let's do it. Come over now.

Tony: I'm on my way. See if you can find any webcam feeds from London that aren't broadcast news.

Josh: Already on it! There are a crap ton of them.

Tony: Great, start recording whatever you can.

<AP NEWS FLASH> London was celebrating the Queen's Birthday when they were attacked. This was a conventional attack but was targeting civilians as they gathered for the celebration. The famed clock "Big Ben" no longer exists. Some video footage of the attack is available through our web portal but was cut off as the pilot realized the enemy was using his feed to direct the attack. As more verifiable video become available, we will provide links on our website and social media feeds.

More details will be available on all outlets as soon as they can be verified. The world is definitely at war. World War III is here, we hope that the civilized nations of the world can prevail in this conflict. London has not seen this level of destruction since World War II. A modern war on the same scale could lead to far more global destruction due to advances in weapons technology. *<STORY DEVELOPING>*

<AP ECONOMIC NEWS FLASH> The European and London exchanges were open when London was attacked, causing the markets to go into a tailspin. Trading has been halted and will not resume today. Out of concern for runs on the banks all European nations are imposing strict limits on cash withdrawals. The limits vary from nation to nation, see our website for more specific detailed information.

We are in uncharted economic territory. The last time the world was at war global markets were not as dependent upon one another as they are today. Conflict on a global scale has the potential to cause a depression on a scale *never before considered possible.*

Chapter Ten
Allies Needed

President Press finally had access to enough functional communications equipment to have a video conference with some of the officially allied nations of the world. On the line were the leadership from England, France, Germany, Italy, Japan, South Korea, and Russia and while not an official ally had an interest in seeing the conflict end. There were others he would have liked to have on the line, but this would have to do for the moment. There were still parts of the world that secure communications couldn't be guaranteed.

"Thank you all for agreeing to this meeting on such short notice, but you must agree we are faced with a unique and unprecedented set of challenges. Let me start with a point-by-point briefing of the information that isn't the in the public eye that we know for certain," President Press said after everyone introduced themselves, which was needless considering the attendee list had either all met in the past or at minimum knew exactly who each other were.

"The majority of middle eastern nations of the world have united as one, and apparently been joined by China to declare war on what appears to be every other nation on the planet not declaring itself and their citizens to be followers of Islam. We do not yet understand why China is working with them, or exactly what role they play here, but we have a team working to answer this question as they don't seem to fit the religious litmus test but are on the side of the Middle East anyway. Perhaps it is economic, we are working through several hypothesis at the moment.

"Next, the nation of Israel along with an unknown, but very large number of its citizens, no longer exists," the President paused as there was an uncomfortable shifting in the chairs among the leadership. It was obvious that this was either news to some people in the room, or it was something they were still trying to come to terms with.

"Their unified military is being led, at least in part, by a General named Bijan Farwad. Everything we know about him, and his career is in the files we have sent out to everyone in the last half hour. If you have more information on this individual or his leadership team, please have your intelligence organizations forward that information to everyone here.

"They have also managed to land troops in the United States Homeland, they hit Los Angeles, a purely civilian target, with a thermonuclear weapon, and they managed to release a biological weapon in the form of at least one if not multiple strains of a deadly virus on our civilians. We are still working on details concerning this biological threat situation, which we will share as they become available. If you have any intelligence on a development program that may have been in the works, please forward that information to everyone as quickly as possible.

"In London they have destroyed Big Ben and used armed commercial drones as well as car bombs to kill around thirty thousand people, wounding many more, almost entirely civilians.

"We have used two ICBMs from our own nuclear arsenal to attack the two separate flotillas of troops that were underway to reinforce the troops already on the ground here. We destroyed one of those flotillas and were forced to destroy the other missile in flight as we had lost positive control, despite the nature of those networks," there were audible gasps from almost everyone in the meeting except those from the United States as they realized the implication of this statement. That sort of thing was supposed to be impossible.

President Press held up his hand. "As near as we can determine, this new alliance of nations has developed a capability in breaking through any cyber defense we, and I assume anyone in this meeting, has. This includes, and some your nations have experienced a few of these at least: banking, communications, in a more limited sense utility companies, and even our most secure military and intelligence systems. This means that use of unconventional and even smart weapons will not be as straightforward as we would normally take for granted. We assume this was the point to the timing of the attack as they finally cracked a way to turn our smart weapons stupid. Therefore, a force multiplier we have spent decades building up and depending upon, may not be useful in this conflict."

The President knew he had to get unanimous agreement on this next point before revealing the new capabilities which were hopefully going to be the key to victory.

"I believe," the President said slowly, "if our nations do not work together, and at minimum share every bit of information available, we may not survive. It is clear by their actions as well as their words that they intend to kill anyone they deem unwilling or unworthy of converting to the ways they interpret the teachings of Islam. Ladies and Gentlemen, we are faced with a new religion-based World War and despite our differences, which we must put aside, we must work together if we are going to defeat our common enemy.

"I ask everyone here, is anyone against this proposed alliance? We may not be able to afford for anyone to sit on the sidelines this time," President Press said.

He was met with resoundingly positive responses.

"Excellent. I will work with my staff to get all the details we have that haven't already been transmitted sent out to everyone. We did hold a few details back to ensure agreement before divulging these strategic data points, I am sure you understand. I expect the same has happened in return.

"We will also be sending an envoy to each of you to give an in-person briefing on some new advanced capabilities we have at our disposal as I fear this means of communication is not fully secure. These new capabilities are things we will be using, and as such you need to know about them and understand them. If your teams come up with methods to use these devices we are still in the planning phases ourselves, any suggestions are welcome.

He secretly wondered who would believe how soon those briefings would take place.

"In just a moment there will be a strange glow on a wall in whatever room you are in. Do not fear, and do not allow your security teams to harm the person who steps through that eerie glow. They will explain everything you need to know about these new capabilities," the President smiled. He had only seen the equipment work once, but he really wanted to see the look on everyone's face.

They didn't have enough of this capability to get to everyone at once, but they could be retargeted rapidly. The screen displaying the Russian President was the first to see action. On the wall directly behind him a glowing orange circle appeared. The light seemed to extend out of the wall. Then, the light intensified and a Lieutenant General wearing a U.S. Army uniform stepped calmly into the room.

The General spoke in perfect Russian, "Hello Mr. President, I am Lieutenant General Sosa. I am here to brief the Russian Federation on faster the light travel and handheld plasma weapons."

The conversation was repeated by a different military officer on every screen. The Russian President was the only one who spoke, and in perfect English he said, "What the, how the fuck?"

"Ladies and Gentlemen, I will leave you to it, and we will all speak again in a few hours. I suggest you take everything these officers say seriously," the President said as he closed the connection with a smirk.

***

Doctor Claudia Hernandez had been a medical doctor for more than two decades and could not recall ever having been this tired.

For the last ten years she had split her time between the Center for Disease Control and various hospital emergency rooms in Atlanta. But this virus, whatever it was, she just couldn't figure out what to even call it. Her team couldn't determine what virus it might be related to much less how to treat it with success beyond basic fluids and rest.

It wasn't SARS or even Ebola, although it could be related to either of them. It was too fast and too severe to be anything seen before. This thing had to have been designed in a lab someplace. Somebody somewhere built this bug to cause Chaos.

Every patient was the same, assuming they managed to make it to the hospital alive. Their symptoms were severe, debilitating muscle cramps, bleeding from multiple orifices, diarrhea, vomiting, and high fever. As near as she could tell the cause of death was always one of two things. A loss of involuntary and voluntary muscle control. The challenge with the loss of involuntary muscles is that some of the patients just stopped breathing. Then there was the severe fluid loss. One of those two challenges seemed to be killing people faster than the fever, but by pumping in enough fluids and anti-biotics there were few improvements to be seen. It required hospitalization, and as a result was time consuming and labor intensive, but it appeared to be slowly working. The real problem was the extreme contagiousness, and how many patients were coming in. They were just a few days into fighting this thing, and no one knew much for sure, but based on years of dealing with infectious diseases led her to believe this one was particularly nasty.

From the reports she had seen, some people were dead within an hour of exposure. Based on how fast the samples grew in the lab that made sense. It was unprecedented, and the lab result was not in dispute.

Could there be two different viruses? Why did some people expire so quickly, and others did not? It made no sense.

There were so many people waiting to be treated, and her moment of rest was over. She forced herself to her feet. She hadn't slept in almost thirty hours, but duty called. If she could just isolate what this damn bug was modern medicine could beat it. Right now, the only thing she knew for certain was that despite the contagious nature if people made it to medical help, most of them could survive, as long as supplies and medical staff could be found. How many would expire if care was not available, she had no idea and didn't even want to give herself time to consider. It seemed extremely unlikely that anyone could survive without help.

How was it that some died, and others just needed

basic yet intense and continuous care? There had to be two variants, maybe?

She made sure her mask was secure before entering the treatment room. This one had three middle aged men with I-V drips. They had recovered enough that they could finally spare some good-sized blood samples. These were not the first samples she had gathered from this type of patient, but with enough different samples from a large enough patient population at different phases of the disease, the CDC might figure out a solution.

"Am I going to be ok doctor?" one of them asked.

"You are definitely improving. Just rest, don't worry, and let us work," she said as pleasantly as she could manage through the gas mask. Research had also been her medical preference as bedside manner had never been something that came naturally.

"Thanks, I just hurt so much. Every muscle aches. It even hurts when I blink," he said as he fell back asleep.

She hurriedly left the room, taking the samples and headed back to the lab.

***

Chad Ryan had been setting broken bones for ten years. But he felt that he had done more casts in the last few days than in the rest of his career combined.

At first, it had been people who had been too close to

the nuclear blast to escape collapsed buildings, but far enough away to not suffer from any significant radiation poisoning.

That first day had been a gruesome one. He had been called in to help in the ER, despite his lack of experience there. His schooling technically qualified him for the work at least on bones, although there wasn't nearly the level of doctor or nurse practitioner involvement one would normally expect.

He even lent a hand doing some triage.

The number of people bleeding from open sores, eye sockets, gum line, any number of other body parts had been staggering.

The images going through his memory bothered him, but not as much as the smell. The smell had been unlike anything he had ever experienced. It was like some combination of rotting meat and open sewage.

Just thinking about it made him want to lose his lunch. He had forced himself to focus on the x-ray in front of him and move forward with the next patient.

Unlike that first day, now all the patients seemed to be people who were trying to clean up the mess. The claims were that they were looking for survivors but after a week, with his medical training he knew there wouldn't be any of those.

Bodies still needed to be recovered, and identified, not to mention counted and cleaned up before diseases started to spread. However, the people doing the cleanup needed to stay safe, and protect themselves rather than try to rush at this point.

He had lost more than one friend in this attack. He watched the list of identified bodies that were released hour by hour for names he recognized and so far, two of his friends were on that list. He knew a lot more would follow. There were still so many people he couldn't get in touch with.

He knew his story was not unique, and when he finally got off work, he promised himself he would figure out a way to start a support group for those who had lost family and friends. People needed to help one another, even emotionally. He would ensure they had a place to gather, at least some small number of people. There was no way he could convince himself he was alone in these feelings, at least he hoped not.

***

"Sharon, thanks for joining me us for this webcast, in these confusing days the network news just brings us poll tested statements from politicians. What we are looking for is the truth," Tony said.

"I'll answer what I can," she said.

"That's all we ask. In the nuclear blast we all knew what to expect, but what can you tell us about the biological attack we are starting to hear bullshit reports about?" Tony asked.

"Well, from what we are being told in the information flowing from the CDC, it is an infectious disease or diseases that for some reason kills some large number of people quickly. But those that survive the first hour, if they make it to medical treatment, and medical supplies hold out, the majority of patients are expected to survive?" she explained.

"What do you mean if supplies hold out?"

"Well, our medical systems, hospitals, supply houses, manufacturers are used to a specific patient load and if things go beyond that normal state, plus some margin for an unexpected surge, we could run out of supplies or hospital beds." Sharon said.

"How much margin is there in the system," Tony asked.

"Not as much as it will take to clear this problem if this thing is as virulent as we are being told," she explained vaguely.

"What does that mean? Can you explain it for the layperson to understand?" he asked.

"Well, you can expect at some point, we will have to make choices about who gets treated and who doesn't. This will likely be based on age, or general health, but some people are saying it could be first come first served," the nurse explained without emotion.

"So, wait, are you telling me that some people will die because they won't be able to get help, and the only reason they won't be able to is that we won't have enough equipment or people to treat them?" Tony asked, not seeming to believe what he was hearing.

"Well, yes, we could surpass the breaking point if patient count ramps up too quickly," she said.

"Is there a way to prevent that from happening?"

"Unfortunately, from what we are being told, no there isn't. At this point between the nuclear blast and the diseases it isn't a matter of if it happens, it is only a matter of when," she explained, without apology.

<AP NEWS FLASH> The number of lives lost in Los Angeles is now verified to be more than one million and that number is rising. Hospitals are still overwhelmed, but relief supplies have been getting in since shortly after the attacks. Unfortunately, the United States Office of Emergency Management is all too familiar with how to respond to a crisis such as this. The stockpiles of supplies they keep have certainly saved lives.

The biological attack has killed at least a half a million people and counting. No one knows what the deadly disease is, but word from the CDC is that no one should attempt to travel in or out of the quarantined areas. That means approximately thirty million Americans are stuck in those areas.

The enemy invasion force in Maine is finally being held in place by the National Guard. No word on how large this force is available to the press yet.

The President has reportedly been meeting with world leaders to obtain assistance from our allies in defending our way of life.

There is a YouTube video of an emergency room nurse that is going viral at this time. No comment from the CDC on the validity of the nurse's statements on the biological agent working its way through parts of the population of the United States.

<AP ECONOMIC NEWS FLASH> The U.S. Stock Markets are trending downward quickly. The loss of value has been astounding. Automatic halts have been put in place at a 10% daily loss. The loss is expected to deepen when trading resumes. This was anticipated by many, and according to some economists is necessary so that companies can understand their actual financial positions and plans can be made for the future.

The only market segment escaping these uniformly downward trends are defense stocks which are quickly trending up. There is so much downward momentum even this sector of the economy could feel the pressure at some point. This is despite the situation we are currently facing. The prevailing thought is that their products will soon be in wide demand and these corporations would be expanding rapidly due to increased demand.

Chapter Eleven
The United States Fights Back

President Press stood in front of one of the bizarre transport devices which he had started referring to as the magic door. It was smaller than he would have imagined when he first saw the video presentation. Despite multiple people explaining how it worked, he really didn't understand the process and wasn't sure he was going to try to do much other than accept that it did indeed work.

There were a dozen scientists and engineers tapping away on keyboards doing whatever it was they did to prepare this crazy system to send some armed troops and equipment to the exact location where General Farwad was suspected of being bunkered down with his leadership team. That location had only become known through cooperation of the new allied nations. They had all gone deep into their intelligence sources and found a location that had been confirmed so many ways it had to be at least close.

At that location, the General and his officers were supposedly planning a new offensive at this very moment, and the intent of this operation was to eliminate that team, which would aid in at the very least disrupting the tempo of their organized attacks.

"Men," the President said as he went down the line shaking hands with the SEAL team, "This mission could take out the top layer of their military leadership and at the same time disrupt their planning session. Surprise will certainly be on our side, and with your combined skills I am confident this mission will be successful. I wish you luck, not that you will need it."

The unit known as SEAL Team One was led by a Lieutenant Commander named Jack Anderson who saluted the Commander in Chief and crisply said, "We will do our best Mr. President."

"Now, go get them!" President Press said.

The young officer gave his men one last quick equipment check. Everyone gave a thumbs up.

"Good to go!" Lieutenant Commander Anderson shouted to the engineers running the equipment.

The President and his secret service detail stepped back to the far side of the room. If all went well, these men would be gone for less than ten minutes.

The President wasn't sure, but once the gateway opened up if enemy troops were organized, and in the right place they might come pouring through the opening. He hoped that wouldn't happen, and he had been assured the gateway could be closed quickly.

One of the machines started spitting out a beam of energy towards an elevated platform in the center of the room. Within seconds it formed a swirling circle of light letting out an orange glow from the edges and a purple glow from the center.

"Ready when you are Commander," one of the

scientists on the left side of the room shouted over the noise of the equipment.

"SEAL TEAM ONE, MOVE OUT!" The young officer shouted as he stepped quickly onto the platform.

One by one, all sixteen SEALs followed him and disappeared from sight. They were all there one second and gone the next.

***

General Farwad and his primary staff of seven officers were using the tops of shipping containers as a makeshift table in the back of a warehouse in the central part of Maine.

Milling around were a dozen or so conscripted soldiers fetching whatever items or information one of the officers requested as quickly as they could manage.

In a part of the warehouse blocked from their view by stacks of civilian shipping on pallets, sixteen men silently entered the warehouse without needing to open a door, or breakthrough any kind of security.

The helmeted men, rifles at the ready, rapidly made their way toward the rear of the building. As they got to the end of a row of shipping crates the lead SEAL put up the "hold" hand signal.

The men stacked up and prepared to attack.

The point man gave the hand signals, 3, 2, 1, GO.

The SEALs rapidly came around the corner and opened fire.

The first man to be hit was a newly conscripted soldier with an AK-47 slung over his shoulder that he had probably never fired. He was hit with a short burst of rounds which entered and exited his head in rapid succession, leaving a red mist and some tissue with the consistency of cottage cheese sprayed across the backs of some officers who up until that point were still focused on the conference table.

The sound of the weapons fire sent the more disciplined officers diving for cover. The remaining conscripts, and one of the more junior officers turned to look at what was happening rather than moving for cover. They were quickly dispatched, dead before they hit the ground, all within seconds of the first rounds being fired.

The officers on the other hand were a slight challenge, but only slight. They were trained and experienced. They found cover and weapons then started to return fire, but they weren't SEALs.

The Navy men were ready for this, had surprise on their side, and were much better trained.

Bullets went in both directions as the SEALs also found cover, none wounded.

One of the SEAL team members started launching grenades over the piles of equipment hiding the officers, practically landing the explosive devices in their laps. One by one they stopped firing until only two remained, and both were out of ammunition.

General Farwad watched as the only other remaining officer dropped his weapon, threw up his hands and surrendered.

He cursed to himself watching the act of cowardice.

He couldn't understand how this group of enemy soldiers made it past all the guards, and into the secured facility without being stopped. This situation should not have been possible.

How had the Americans done this?

It appeared to be magic, but he knew better. This was some new technology they hadn't accounted for.

He cursed, loudly.

He had no rounds left, no ability to do much but try to hide.

There was a small office in the front of the warehouse. If he could get there it had an exit door that would allow him to get outside and rally some men to fight back against this small team of enemy soldiers.

Before he could get to his feet he was dragged down from behind, his hands were bound, and two large men were dragging him past his fallen soldiers, leaving a trail of blood that was swept up from the rapidly expanding red pool on the ground. He only had one option left to fight back, but he had to choose exactly the right time for the maximum impact before he used that.

***

It took less than five minutes before the SEALs started coming back through the portal. The first pair were enlisted soldiers, one helping the other to walk as he had blood on his uniform from what looked like a minor leg wound. The facility medical staff had been standing by to deal with any wounded. They grabbed the wounded SEAL and whisked him away.

One by one the rest of the team returned.

The last group through the gate were Lieutenant Commander Anderson along with a senior enlisted soldier, and they were dragging General Bijan Farwad with his hands tied behind his back.

"General Farwad," the President whispered as he quickly made his way across the room to meet this man.

"President Press, it is so good to make your acquaintance. What is this place?" the General asked in heavily accented English, in shock from the attack as much as the technology he had never imagined could exist, but somehow still somewhat in control of himself. His eyes kept moving around the room, trying to figure out how he had gotten here.

"How did you get me here? Where are we?" General Farwad asked.

"You may have been able to beat some of our cyber defenses, but our scientists and engineers are the best the world has ever seen, and they produce capabilities beyond anything you and your allies can imagine, much less put into the field," the President bragged.

General Farwad laughed, loudly.

"You can have all the technology in the universe, Allah will always show us a way," the imprisoned General said as he slammed the heel of his boot on the floor.

Everyone who noticed that action was confused, then panicked as a small cloud of mist accompanied by a hissing sound could be heard.

"In case you are curious, I have just released a concentrated form of biological weapon into this room. Everyone here, including me, will be dead in five or six minutes," he said between fits of laughter.

Three secret service agents grabbed the President and began running for the door. Within five steps they began tripping over their own feet as heavy coughing fits and muscle spasms began taking bodily control away.

The President managed to keep walking, slowly for a few more steps. He almost made it to the door before hitting the ground with red foam coming from his mouth and nose. His entire body went into violent convulsions as red bodily fluids started to flow from every orifice.

***

"General Jackson!" said Major Pierce. "The mission was successful, but, um, we have a problem, sir, I'm not sure how to say this."

"Take a deep breath and tell me what happened," the Chairman of the Joint Chiefs said to the Major seeming to have trouble forming sentences.

"The President has been killed," the young officer said.

"*What?* How?" was all the normally unflappable senior officer could say.

"The SEAL team brought back General Farad as a prisoner, who is also dead. As near as we can determine he had a hidden suicide device in the heel of a boot that released a highly concentrated dose of virus that killed everyone in the room, it is unclear why the secret service permitted the President to be there, in such closer proximity to the prisoner."

"Holy shit. Get the Vice President on the line," The Chairman ordered wondering what else could possibly go wrong.

***

Vice President Banner was sitting at a conference table at his official residence inside Naval Observatory when his cell phone rang. Most of his calls came through someone who would come bring him the news of the call, as a result it rang infrequently enough that he was startled, "Hello, this is the Vice President."

"Mr. Vice President, this is General Jackson," the

obviously stressed-out voice of the Chairman of the Joint Chiefs said.

"General, you know you can call me Frank," he said.

"Not this time. Mr. Vice President, it is my unfortunate duty to report that the President of the United States is dead, and you are to be sworn in as the President as soon as possible," the General said.

Frank had no idea what to say. He wasn't sure he believed it, but right then the door to his room burst open and three members of his secret service detail entered.

"Mr. Vice President, we have to get you to the White House where you will be met by your fiancé and the Chief Justice of the Supreme Court, where you will be sworn in as President of the United States," Angela Cook said. She was one of the younger agents, but very good at her job.

"Mr. Chairman, I will have to call you back," he said as he disconnected the line. In the distance he heard a helicopter coming in for a landing.

"What the hell happened," Frank asked.

"All I know is that the President is dead, and you will be sworn in and immediately assume the office of the President," Angela replied.

"Let's go," he said hoping this was a drill, but somehow knowing that it wasn't.

<AP NEWS FLASH> *It has become known in the last few*

minutes that the President has been killed. The Vice President is on the way to the White House to be sworn in and is expected to make a statement within the hour. <STORY DEVELOPING>

<AP ECONOMIC NEWS FLASH> The stock market had closed for the day when the news of President Press being killed was released. All of the futures markets, and any international market conducting business instantly turned negative so quickly that trading was automatically halted. Vice President Banner will be sworn in shortly and the economic community believes that he must include economic statements in any remarks, or the markets will continue to tumble even farther due to uncertainty.

Chapter Twelve
A Change in Leadership

"Mr. Vice President, if you could place your left hand on the bible, raise your right hand and repeat after me," Chief Justice of the Supreme Court Claremont said.

Frank did as he was instructed. He didn't need to hear the words but listened carefully anyway. When the man was finished, he spoke carefully, knowing he was being recorded from multiple angles and didn't want to make any mistake, "I, Frank Banner, do solemnly swear that I will faithfully execute the Office of President of the United States, and to the best of my ability, preserve, protect and defend the Constitution of the United States, so help me God."

"Mr. President let me be the first to shake your hand," said the Chief Justice.

"I appreciate you getting here so fast under these conditions," said now President Frank Banner.

Frank checked to make sure the cameras were off, "Well, honey, looks like we have to move again," the President said to his fiancé, trying to lighten the somber mood in the room not really sure what else to say or do.

"Mr. President, your personal items will be here by the end of the day, you don't need to be concerned," a stressed looking staffer said somberly from a few rows of people back from where Frank stood in front of the Resolute Desk in the Oval Office.

Everyone was in state of shock or disbelief and unsure what to do next. Frank resorted to his ingrained military discipline and took charge.

"Ok, in this order, I want five minutes with the speech writer, then the Joint Chiefs down in the Situation Room, then with the Cabinet," President Banner said, getting down to work, not really sure what else to do. His military discipline was forcing him to leap into action, and to keep things moving forward. A rapid pace of action typically helped everyone stay focused on the tasks at hand instead of the tragic and sudden loss they had just suffered. If the staff kept working hard enough, they might not become overwhelmed with an avalanche of emotions. Unfortunately, Frank had a great deal of experience dealing with unexpected and sudden death.

The unnecessary staff members in the room took the cue and made their way out of the room, while a small group stayed. The President's fiancé, a man and a woman stayed in front of the President, looking directly at him, both had notebooks and pens.

"Please, have a seat, and let's get started" Frank said, directing them to a couch, he stayed standing. He sometimes found it easier to think while walking around a room.

"Mr. President, I am the White House Director of Communications, Jessica Maxim. This is my deputy

Mr. Ricardo Sanchez. We are the primary speech writers, or were, for President Press," the woman said.

"Ok. I am sure you are going to have to tell me those names several times, and for that I apologize up front. I have some speech writers, but we are all going to have to work together, and quickly for a while. We need to address the nation as quickly as possible. People are going to be frightened, now more than ever. The world is at war in a way that has never happened before, it is time we call it what it is, and it is going to result in public madness, chaos and panic if we don't start being more open with the American citizenry. This war is different, and that doesn't seem likely to go back to being a normal war everyone knows how to emotionally cope with as the use of unconventional weapons has happened, and seems likely to continue," Frank said.

Jessica was scribbling notes on a pad, "Go on Mr. President. What do you have in mind to say? Just give us generalities and we can get a draft, then we can focus it in for you after you give it a read. This one is going to get a lot of attention."

"We need to let people know we are focused on the crisis facing the world, both the physical and the economic threat. We need to state emphatically that these horrible and tragic events are something the enemy will never be able to repeat, and in the coming days we will release whatever details we can without giving away national security related information, and lastly that I will personally be making a weekly television appearance to give updates until the war is over. Daily is too much, and I want to set a regular tempo. I'm not a great public speaker, and remember, until less than a year ago I was a soldier, so don't try to make me out to be something that I'm not. I want to come off as genuine."

"Frank," his fiancé, now the soon to be First Lady of the United States said from her position standing behind him. "I can stay here and work with them. Make sure you sound like you."

"Honey, thanks, I forgot you were even here. Forget I just admitted that about my fiancé. If you would help them, I would really appreciate it. Also, let's have somebody get your family, and mine on some airplanes to get them here. I hate to pull some privilege associate with rank, but let's keep everyone together here in the residence for the moment, I don't want someone taking a shot at them, or taking them hostage, and I really don't want them swarmed by the media without help. I love you!" the new President said, kissing her as he gathered a notepad intending to make his way to the door.

Frank took a deep breath.

How the hell had he become the President? That was a question to answer later.

He looked around the Oval Office and had no idea which door led where.

"Ok, so here is a slightly embarrassing question that stays between us, but how do I get to the Situation Room from here?" he asked the closest member of his protective detail.

"Follow me, Mr. President," Angela said.

"Lead the way," he said with a hand gesture toward the wrong door which he shrugged off as he followed her out the opposite side of the room.

They left the Oval Office and walked past a group of assistants' desks, then they turned the corner and made their way through an area full of cubicles. Frank noticed that anytime he entered an area everyone stood up.

"Why do they stand like that?" he asked the half dozen people walking with him.

"Sir, when the President is in the area, until he sits, or says otherwise no one sits. It has been a policy here for decades and is done as a sign of respect, not just for the person but for the office," some man in a nice suit responded. Frank didn't know his name, or his job function, but had seen him around few times when he had been in the building to meet with President Press.

They reached an elevator he recognized, and he finally felt comfortable they were headed in the right direction.

Half of the group was not needed in the next meeting, and as a result didn't board the elevator.

As Frank entered the Situation room he found the Chairman of the Joint Chiefs of Staff, as well as a few other members of the team standing at attention, "At ease, please take your seats," he said knowing that this was going to take some getting used to.

Less than a year ago, he had been just a recently

promoted Major in the Army, and now these much more senior officers were looking to him for direction.

"Generals, this isn't meant with any disrespect, and I don't think anyone here, or anywhere else in or out of uniform is at fault, but what the *hell* happened, seriously the President has been killed? How in the name of God did that happen?" President Banner asked.

The Chairman was, per protocol, the one who would answer whenever possible in these situations, "Mr. President as near as we can determine, upon returning from a successful mission with a POW in the form of one General Farwad, the prisoner killed everyone in the room. In short, he committed suicide and took our men, as well as President Press with him as he departed this world. The thing that is sticking in our head is that he had no immunity to the biological weapon so it appears they are prepared to fight to the last man if even the most senior leaders are ready to die like this."

"How the hell did he hide this device. The SEALs didn't find it when they disarmed him?" President Banner asked.

"We will have more information shortly, but we believe it was in a boot heel, and triggered when he banged it on the floor hard enough at a weird angle, which means that many of their troops will be similarly equipped. It acted amazingly fast, and killed everyone within minutes, which is far different from some of the other biological agent attacks we are seeing. Also, as you well know that isn't a standard part of our prisoner search protocol when in the middle of an extraction, so this isn't something we trained the SEALs to look for," Chairman Jackson said.

"Get that information to all of our commanders as well as first responders all over New England by secure, unsecure, nightly news, Twitter, or even carrier pigeon form of communication if you have to," the President said.

"Yes, Mr. President," the Chairman pointed to a Major who left the briefing to carry out the order.

"How long before we get that information verified," President Banner asked.

"An hour or so before we can get in the room, then it shouldn't take very long. It is fairly obvious from the security video what happened. At present I have an 80-90% confidence in this information," the Chairman explained.

"Ok, that's about as good as it gets. What happened on the mission? How much of their key military leadership did we manage to take out of the equation?" the President asked.

"Everyone we set out to get, their top eight officers on the ground here in the United States, are out of the picture. One thing we have not seen and are looking for is any movement by the Chinese military. They appear to have moved a carrier group, but we can't locate it at the present time. However, they are not near our shorelines, but it is a big Ocean, and without Satellites we are dependent upon aircraft search patterns," Chairman Jackson reported.

"Well, keep looking, they have to be out there somewhere I doubt their involvement is just the cyber-attack, if they were going to get involved I can't imagine they would be that limited. Is there a plan to press our advantage on the ground?" Frank asked, starting to feel like he was in his element.

"Of course, Mr. President, we will take you through that now. May I first say I don't like the circumstances that put you in that chair, but for the problems we face you are exactly the right type of person at exactly the right time. If they asked me to construct a war-time President you would be the result," the General said.

"Thank you, Mr. Chairman, I hope I can live up to your expectations, and find the right person to deal with the economic challenges we face because that is going to be a big part of this. I was in enough briefings to understand that we have to pay for the war somehow," President Banner said.

"Now, if you will look at the screen on the right," Chairman Jackson began as he dove into their plan of action.

***

President Banner was seated at the Resolute Desk in the Oval Office. His fiancé was standing next to the camera which had a screen mounted below it for him to read his speech.

"Mr. President, you are live in 5...4...3...2," the

cameraman did the rest of the countdown with his fingers.

"My fellow Americans. President Scott Press has become a casualty of war.

"In an operation that took place in the last few hours, we captured a high value target who was here on American soil. President Press was speaking with the POW, who then killed himself and everyone else in the room, which included our President, with a biological agent. This was a one in a billion situation that will never happen again.

"I'd like to offer my prayers to his family and ask that everyone within the sound of my voice keep them in your thoughts as they struggle through this difficult time.

"I have been sworn in as President of the United States for approximately two hours. During that time, I met with our military leadership, and though it may not seem like it, I can tell you that we have struck a serious blow to the enemy. In the coming hours, a member of the Joint Chiefs of Staff will be holding a press conference to give you as many details as possible.

"I'd like to remind everyone, that until relatively recently I was a soldier in the United States Army Special Operations Command and served in combat during the earliest parts of this war.

"I want to make something clear. Given the scope of this operation, and the actions being taken place against us, I am going to start to refer to this conflict as World War III.

"I call it that because this Unified Islamic State clearly intends to kill anyone unwilling, or that they deem unworthy, of converting to Islam. These have been their words. Given their operations in Israel, and London that does not mean these actions are merely being taken against the United States, so we are not in this alone.

"I will not let this forced conversion or extermination happen. The peace-loving people of the world will not be exterminated.

"Economically speaking we face challenges that may surpass the military threats facing our nation. In the next twenty-four hours I will be releasing the names of a task force whose only concern will be working to ensure we minimize the economic problems facing our nation. I know there will be hard times ahead, but we will do everything we can to limit the impact.

"I realize some of you are saying that I have never run for any office, that I was appointed to the office of the Vice President, therefore I shouldn't be President.

"I understand your concerns. I also vow to work hard for you each and every day. I will conduct myself and my administration with as much transparency as possible, but keep in mind that we are at War.

"Given the amount of data that can flow in the modern age, and the nature of social media, there may be confusion in the coming days and weeks. We will do everything in our power to limit these challenges.

"I will personally be giving an address every week until this war is over. We will get to know one another, and I will, with the help of the men and women in uniform, protect and defend the United States of America. We will not fail.

<AP NEWS FLASH> The new President has confirmed that President Scott Press has been murdered. Former Vice President Banner is now the President of the United States.

Some kind of military operation has taken place, and according to the new President the United States has experienced some kind of victory in battle. There will be a Pentagon briefing with additional details in the next few hours.

Since the nuclear attack in Los Angeles, the invasion, and the biological attacks have started the economy has been suffering, in some cases staggeringly so, depending upon the region of the country being discussed. There is a concern that the new President may be too focused on military operations and too economically inexperienced to effective policies to get the economy moving again. <STORY DEVELOPING>

<AP ECONOMIC NEWS FLASH> President Banner has stated that in the next day a special economic team of advisors will be assembled to help determine the best policies to rescue the flailing economy <STORY DEVELOPING>

Chapter Thirteen
Targeting Paris

General Hashem Rahbar took a deep breath as he set down the satellite phone. He had been saddened to hear of the capture, and martyrdom of General Farwad. The elimination of the U.S. President meant that the situation was not a complete loss. A considerable blow had been landed on the greater Satan, and every military leader on the planet knew that you couldn't possibly win every battle. So, while the Americans did land a blow, it had not been a victory without a cost.

His orders were simple. Finish the upcoming attack in France, then quickly relocate himself and as much of his team as possible to the United States and take over for his long-time mentor. Hopefully keeping things under control until additional reinforcements arrive.

He climbed into the SUV and started the drive to their command post, which was nothing more than a small, generic, hard to notice, warehouse filled with electronics and other equipment. This mission would be simple and, if successful, would devastate the Parisian economy because no one would want to go back into that city to work or for tourism for a long time. He knew some people would call this a terrorist tactic, and he didn't care. It had the potential of damaging, not just the French economy, but all the economies of Western Europe. Economic impact was just as important as military impact in this conflict. If the Western nations could not fund a prolonged war that would aid in the long-term strategy the Islamic Nations were executing. This was not a short-term fight. It was going to take time achieve total victory. The Americans had a notoriously short attention span.

The warehouse was a short distance from Paris. It was just like hundreds of other old worn-down warehouses that dotted the outsides of any major metropolitan city. It had been rented for years in the name of a corporation that did a small, but legitimate and barely noticed business. Inside the facility were a dozen or so older computers and hundreds of commercially available semi-autonomous drones with reasonable range and payload capacity. The team had spent days preparing these devices for this operation.

General Rahbar had no intention of repeating the mistakes of the London operation. He didn't care about a television audience, the desire for which had resulted in the London not being as large of a success as they had hoped. His only concern was a successful mission. The need for an audience was not a winning military strategy in his mind. A dead or surrendering enemy was all that mattered.

He wanted to let the victory drive the hearts and minds of the followers of Allah. The non-believers were starting to get organized, and he must thrust some additional confusion into the equation at the higher levels of governments around the world. Of course, some good old-fashioned extreme level of fear injected into their citizens couldn't hurt the situation.

Car bombs were one thing, but the world had become used to that. This was new, and would be shocking, and difficult to stop for any nation.

He gave the order to begin and watched as his soldiers carried out their tasks. His leadership style was to observe until he had to step in. He wouldn't micro-manage. It wasn't possible on larger, more complicated missions such as this. Especially when his team consisted of so few soldiers.

The first to take flight was a single mid-altitude drone capable of staying in the air longer than most and had been equipped with telephoto lenses for the digital cameras so they could track progress of, as well as guide the smaller drones to specific targets, if need be. Why that fool in London insisted on using a co-opted helicopter was beyond him. It would be important to see the success of various attacks waves, so on the second wave they could assign or change targeting priorities as needed, not to broadcast the event live to the world. The propaganda war could be fought when the battle was over. The fool had even failed in the propaganda war when the pilot crashed the aircraft instead of being part of the show.

The first wave was away. No car bombs would be used here. Not in Paris. He had insisted on having a very small number of men so this team could stay completely covert, and car bombs could be noticed in a city where things were always moving, especially after that had just been done in London.

This attack would be achieved by a total of fifteen men and approximately seven hundred and fifty drones with pre-programmed targets and flight routes that could be shifted in flight if needed. As soon as the final wave took off, he and his men could evacuate the warehouse destroying all the computers and vanish thanks to the automation available in this commercial technology. Once they disappeared each would make their way either to immediate transportation or back to one of the safehouses located around southern France and as far as Spain where they would wait until it was safe to move.

All would eventually meet him in North America. This was a special team of drone experts. They would be necessary in the near future, and vital along with the re-enforcements currently at sea. The mission in the United States would be impossible without them.

This entire attack would not take very long. The first, and most important two targets were to be the Eiffel Tower followed by the Notre Dame Cathedral.

Both were world renowned structures, and always full of tourists. If all they could achieve on this day was the destruction of these two structures he would be pleased, and it would strike fear into the city that depended on people feeling safe and conducting business to keep the economy of the nation moving. Without that sense of safety and security the tourists wouldn't come.

Economies were easier to destroy than militaries, but militaries needed economies to function. Therefore, this was just one in a series of strategic moves aimed at militarily crippling the western world. Economic destruction was an important step in military domination.

The tower would be the first strike. He sat on a crate and watched the monitor as the drones started to close in. To those on the ground they would look like a flock of birds from this angle and distance. Just little black dots flying in some random cloud formation. This time of day the target area was sure to be full of tourists and people working to serve those who came in from all over the world. The time for this attack had been specifically chosen to ensure the maximum loss of life along with enough wounded to clog local hospitals beyond their breaking point.

Through the video feed, people on the ground could be seen pointing at the drone swarm. The crowd did not make any indication of leaving the area. Some of them began pointing cameras at the incoming swarm, obviously not understanding what was about to happen.

General Rahbar laughed to himself. This would be easier than he thought, these people didn't think any threat to their day was even possible. He knew the excuses they would use; it wouldn't happen to *them*. They certainly didn't see these drones as danger. They may even consider them something designed for their amusement.

Did they learn nothing from London?

Based on some of the behaviors in the United States resulting from the attacks, these people may even be thinking it would help their social media accounts gain notoriety.

The fools, was fame and attention from people they would never meet on some website really all that mattered to them?

The drone swarm was broken into three groups. Some would go after the crowd, some would hit the first of two observation platforms, others would hit the second of the visitor platforms of the world-famous tower. Some engineer had determined that if enough explosive was detonated in the right spot, it might just be enough to cause the entire rough iron structure to come crumbling down.

The first drones to dive were programmed to find large clusters of humans. The commercially available object recognition software was amazing and had been developed largely by the Americans. There was fun bit of irony using their own technology against them. With this type of software if you paid your fee, they asked no questions. You could also train it to home in on any object for which you could supply a few images.

Each drone carried makeshift bombs. Less than a pound of explosive packed with small bits of random metal were all they needed to turn this peaceful Paris morning into the most horrifying day imaginable for those lucky enough to survive.

The flying bombs would be at an altitude of a mere five meters above the ground when they detonated. The micro-cameras and on-board computers would automatically search for groups of people clustered together, then explode when relatively close to the center of that group as seen from above.

The drones were zeroing in. The software deciding on where to go.

He was astounded at how inexpensive this campaign was to pull together. It was far less expensive than some military training exercises he had been part of during his career. Ah, the wonders of modern technology.

The first of the drones detonated. Shrapnel was directed downward, not with a great deal of velocity, but the range would still ensure lots of injuries and some lethality. People were quickly, and in some cases repeatedly, hit with these blasts from different angles.

The targets were being partially turned into a red soup, thick, chunky and mixed into a pool of blood. Their bodies, below the neck, remained largely intact. It was their heads that took most of the damage. The lethality was going to be much higher than the General had imagined. The planning team hadn't taken into account the angle of attack.

So much the better.

Heads were blown to pieces. Bone, blood, and brain went everywhere, like a chunky rain. Bodies would flop to the ground, their nervous systems confused by the sudden trauma causing random muscle spasms. Arms and legs were moving, a few bodies were twitching so much they looked more like fish pulled abruptly from the water than humans. Those who were not hit started to run, often not looking where they were going. Others who were on the sides of blast zones and only suffered minor wounds, turned to run but tripped over the headless corpses or slipped on the slick brain matter and blood covering the ground more and more with each passing moment. The panicked human herd did not care who fell, they just kept running, many times stepping on those who might have survived except for the dozens of people crushing them in a stampede.

The second part of the swarm moved in as per the plan. The first level on the Eiffel Tower was a restaurant, and important structurally for the towering metallic structure above. These drones were packed with as much high explosive as possible in small metal cylinders. This would release a massive amount of pressure, heat, some shrapnel, and hopefully destroy one or more of the vital support beams.

A cloud of drones formed a fuzzy line and headed for the same location. It was a conga line of explosives, one after the other, in rapid succession. The targeting worked perfectly and pounded into the vital support structure that the engineers had decided to go after. A steady drumbeat of detonations kept going and going until finally one explosion sent more, and much-larger shards metal flying out from the damaged point of impact.

The top two thirds of the Eiffel Tower slowly tilted and twisted. General Rahbar watched a wide area shot of the attack and was pleased to see that the crowd, the parts of it that were still alive, were in fear, and scrambling for their lives. Some were doing so while attempting to capture the event on video with a smartphone.

He rolled his eyes at those idiotic infidels and refocused on the tower. It kept tilting a little more every second. Then, all the sudden, it moved much more quickly and came crashing to the ground. The steel beams fragmented and went flying in all directions.

The third wave would not be needed for the original intent, and their batteries would be getting low, "Send all the extra drones into the crowd," he ordered the men in control of the swarm.

The second major swarm was finally approaching Notre Dame. The ancient church was a gathering place for people who believed in a false profit. It was a symbol that had to be erased from the planet as it was being prepared for Islamic rule.

The attack on Notre Dame was organized a little differently. The drones hit all at once. Some went through stained glass windows, others hit doors, some just plowed into walls and detonated on contact. Within seconds stone had been blown out, centuries old artistic stained-glass windows were shattered or melting, and smoke was billowing from every possible opening.

Moments later fire began bellowing out of the roof as a raging inferno grew into what the Christians would probably call a vision of Hell itself.

He heard multiple helicopters pass over their location and decided that the moment the last drones left the hangar the location of the perpetrators of this attack would be known. They had to go with one of the backup plans.

"Put all remaining drones on a twenty-minute timer for launch and set them to strike any emergency vehicles or personnel anywhere throughout the city," the General ordered.

It wasn't the original plan, but it was one of the backups that he knew would be meaningful.

"Men, once the timers are set get to the vehicles!" his second in command shouted.

With a little luck the General hoped he would be starting his travel to the United States as the lone passenger in a small but very fast business jet before the enemy figured out where the attack had originated. His men would be following by one of several routes in the coming days.

***

Frank had been called to the situation room and this time had managed to find his own way.

"Mr. Chairman, what happened," the President asked the moment he stepped into the room, motioning for everyone to take their seats.

"Mr. President, Paris has been hit, and hit hard with a truly terrifying, yet seemingly conventional attack." Chairman Jackson said.

"Give me whatever you have so far," President

Banner said.

"They used a large number of inexpensive, commercially available drones with a reasonable range and payload capacity, they modified them with some kind of autonomous system to get them to work as swarms. They loaded them with explosives and destroyed the Eiffel Tower, and the fires they managed to get started will likely result in the complete loss of the Notre Dame Cathedral. No information is available on the number of casualties as the attack is still taking place, but it is going to be a large number. We think this attack was done for maximum psychological impact as it doesn't appear to be biological, or unconventional in any way, just flying IEDs," the General reported.

"Ok. This is new and going to be shockingly hard to counter. Is there any indication a similar attack is going to take place here in the United States?" the President asked.

"Not that we are aware of, but this kind of thing can pop up in moments, so we'll have to work up some data," the General admitted.

"I want a plan to deal with this kind of attack, and let's take a look at what we have, in whatever stage it is in, sometime in the next few hours," Frank said.

"Yes, Mr. President," the room full of Generals replied as the President left the room to go to the Oval Office to find some video, which by now would be on social media if not the news.

Frank was getting really tired of getting intelligence information from unofficial sources after the fact. He was going to have to say something to the American public and do so today. He hoped that the Generals could come up with a way to deal with this kind of a strike so that he could offer some form of confident statement that it couldn't happen here.

***

Sam and Phil were online watching the attack and doing a live voice over streaming to YouTube.

Sam took a drink of water as Phil took over, "Sorry that we have to keep switching feeds, but we are picking up what we can from people on the ground in Paris. Their cameras are being destroyed and cell towers are being overloaded with traffic, but we will keep giving you whatever we can. This is really horrifying."

One of their feeds that was somewhat stable from outside Notre Dame. They kept that one on their feed as fire leapt into the sky. Then, without warning, one of the walls collapsed.

"Holy crap," Sam said. "That was the east wall of Notre Dame, that's going to be the end of the cathedral. Whomever did this, and we have to assume Iran, or this Unified Islamic State or whatever they are calling themselves today, is behind this and getting exactly what they want.

"First the Eiffel Tower and now the Cathedral. Thousands upon thousands of dead, and any first responders that happen to come in the area are now being targeted with this new wave of drones. What the fuck is wrong with these people."

"Let's hope they don't do this kind of thing here. I don't know how anyone would defend against this. This is indiscriminate, and insane."

Secretly both of them were pleased as their follower count was skyrocketing, even during the broadcast. They were now a viral sensation, and everyone would know who they were, if they didn't already, and at least the attack wasn't here in the United States.

<AP NEWS FLASH>Paris has been attacked. The Eiffel Tower is in fragments. Notre Dame Cathedral is on fire and expected to be a total loss. Drones packed with explosives are still hitting first responders as they attempt to help the wounded. The city is in chaos. People are in panic, and there are reports of several deaths due to trampling in the fleeing crowds. We urge everyone to remain as calm as possible as while in the act of attempting to get to safety.

We will monitor the situation and release details as they can be verified. Currently reports coming from Paris are inconsistent.

So far, in this conflict it is estimated that globally two and a half million people have perished. These numbers consist of multiple nations now seeing sick people due to the spread of the virus used in the biological strike in the United States.

Once the sick people, who were barely symptomatic if at all, started getting on international flights, the patient count worldwide started to skyrocket. This is now a new global challenge. No nation is safe.

A quarantine zone around Los Angeles has been established. The hospitals in the area are running out of supplies. FEMA has requested that any medical center with supplies that can be spared reach out to them to arrange for redeployment of those supplies to where they are desperately needed.

<AP ECONOMICS NEWS FLASH> The attack in Paris is going to be economically devastating to the European economy. The economic impact could result in as much loss of life as from the military actions.

This now establishes the crash across all first world nations. The enemy appears to be attempting to destroy the world economy as part of their battle plan, and that may be working according to economists. A nation needs to step forward and be not just a military leader, but an economic leader and it is considered that the United States may be the only nation with the resources to accomplish this with any measurable success.

Chapter Fourteen
Viral Solution and a New Challenge

General Jackson had been at the podium speaking to the press for almost twenty minutes. So far, they had covered the elimination of the Iranian military leadership in a raid on U.S. soil and explained that President Press had been killed by a prisoner and managed to do so without explaining that the two events took place minutes apart, and hundreds of miles from one another. He was finishing a review of what was known of the Paris fiasco and wondered what the first question would be given all of the new events that had taken place within a very short period of time.

"Now, I will take a few questions," he said, as per his normal way of doing these conferences. When he first started doing this kind of thing he was amazed to discover that there was a civilian employee from the PR team who told him before the briefing which reporters got to ask questions, and in what order. He pointed to the first one on his list.

"Robin Holmes, CNN. Chairman Jackson, you said the Paris attacks were conducted with widely available, easily modified commercial drones. Is there known method that can be used to detect and potentially prevent this type of attack in the future?" the reporter asked.

"Remember that this information is less than an hour

old, but we already have a team at the Pentagon working on this question. They are exploring several options, all of which are viable candidates, and when the time is right, we will give you more information. Unfortunately, I can't give you more than that for security reasons," One down he thought as he pointed to the next reporter on his list.

"George Mirra, Fox News. Chairman Jackson, why was the President allowed in the room with someone who had not been searched for ways to do him harm? That seems like a huge lapse in security."

Crap, the one question he had really not wanted, but knew would come. He really wanted to answer this one, but knew he had to deflect.

"President Press was a very 'hands on' type of leader. We have to admire and respect his style of getting things done. He wanted to be there, in that room, to see with his own eyes the man who was responsible for the murders of so many of our non-combatants. We all owe President Press our eternal gratitude for his sacrifice. If you want to know more, I'll have to refer you to the Secret Service," he tap danced around the question without giving anything specific, knowing that the Secret Service would offer the classic "no comment" no matter how many times that question was asked.

He had to keep this discussion going for another twenty minutes. The plan was to attempt to keep parts of the world distracted from a military action that was supposed to happen while hoping that there would be so much focus on his briefing things might stay covert. The mission had been planned for later but, had to be moved forward in hopes of accelerating the fight against the madness facing the world.

***

During the Press Conference President Frank Banner was safely tucked away deep inside the Situation Room of the White House. It wasn't that he was unwilling to risk being harmed, but the nation couldn't handle any more leadership changes at the moment. There had been enough of that, and there was currently no Vice President. There was still a known line of succession, but stability was always a good thing in times of war. The chaos needed to end.

Despite assurances to the contrary from some technology experts at Army R&D he was still not convinced that the nation was safe from the threat of a drone swarm attack. There was a plan that involved using the portal system to just transport the any drone swarm being reported out to sea where the battery power would not be nearly sufficient to make it back to shore.

His concern over that was a problem for later, there was a mission he wanted to pay attention to as it could solve one of their several widespread disasters currently killing more Americans with each passing hour.

"Mr. Choi are you and the team ready?" asked the President.

"Yes, Mr. President. Before we go, let me virtually introduce the guy we got to replace you after your decision to go all political on us. President Banner, this is Captain Louis Martin," Frank's former Warrant Officer said.

"Captain! Good to talk to you. Congratulations on getting what I consider to be the best team in the Special Forces, that job certainly elevated my career a little. You are on a pathway for sure success," said the President.

"Thank you, Mr. President. I hope I can live up to your example," said the young officer. "I know you were President Press' friend, and I would like to offer my condolences on your, and the nation's loss." The Captain was obviously nervous and speaking very quickly.

"Thank you, Captain, I am actually allowed to speak on behalf of the nation now without asking permission, and we appreciate that. I do want to give you one warning. The men in your unit really do all the work, I spent most of my time in your position trying not to get in the way. So, if you want some unsolicited advice, that is probably the best I can give you," advised Frank.

"I will do my best Mr. President. Do we have your permission to execute the mission as planned?" asked Captain Martin formally.

***

"Proceed with your mission, and good luck, and if you must change plans mid-stream based on the situation on the ground, feel free to make that decision on the ground without asking," the entire team heard the President say in their earpieces.

The team members all put on their gas masks.

A round of reports could be heard indicating the masks were sealed, and the team was ready to go.

The technicians around the lab were furiously typing on keyboards or fiddling with controls on scientific equipment. The energy gate appeared on the platform in front of Captain Martin. He and Warrant Officer Choi stepped through the circle of light with the rest of the team lined up behind them each waiting their turn.

The entire team had done this weird transport thing once before in training, but Mr. Choi wasn't sure he would ever get used to this new capability. There was almost no feeling to it. Simply step through a circle of light and you are in a room on the other side of the planet, he suspected the only reason they "trained" on it was to prove to the team that it worked without injury. It was a psychologically strange feeling, not physically. Physically there was almost no feeling, which made it all the more bizarre.

Warrant Officer Choi and Captain Martin made their way down a row of storage shelves stocked with medical equipment and supplies, but they were not in a hospital treating the sick or injured sense, this was a research facility. Ten men appeared, as if by magic, right behind them. You couldn't see through the bizarre panel of light, but when people came out of it, the only reasonable description Peter could think of for it was magic.

There were only two of those bizarre transportation devices on the planet, and one was quarantined awaiting bio-cleanup so the "portal" to get them home would be closed for safety reasons until they requested evac. Others were being built but weren't ready yet. After the last mission extra precautions would be taken whenever possible considering this was the only other functional device.

The team came to the end of the row of shelves. Luckily, the shelves weren't jam packed so they could see through for a few rows in either direction, which would be both useful and dangerous if a threat presented itself.

Warrant Officer Choi help up the "hold" hand signal, he wanted to have a bit more of a look around before stepping out into the wide-open area. It was very early in the morning here, and this was a bio-research laboratory devoid of personnel at this time of day. Had the team come in the traditional route, through facility security instead of sneaking in behind it, they would have had to defeat multiple layers of risky situations, including bad guys with guns who wouldn't hesitate to use them. That would mean the team would have to use theirs, and in the process destroying the covert nature of the mission.

This mission *had* to remain secret. If it didn't there would be no improvement in the situation on the other side of the world.

This way was better. They could show up practically on top of their target. Had they known about this transport ring's existence prior to that damn raid at the nuclear research facility where the special nuclear materials were stolen, and ultimately used inside the United States this whole war might have been prevented.

That seemed like so long ago now.

The area was supposed to be clear of any threats. Peter didn't see anything, or anyone moving and assumed that the intelligence reports were right but would keep an eye out anyway.

He gave a hand signal and the team moved as one, rifles at the ready, heads swiveling side to side searching, scanning, always on the lookout for any sign of a threat.

Peter walked across the twenty feet of open space to get to the row of walled off offices lining the far side of the space. He opened the door to the office that the intelligence briefing given by the Russians, who were acting as allies in this situation, claimed would have what they needed. Inside was a desk, a larger table, and a few shelves containing smaller storage containers, including a refrigerated medical sample storage vessel that looked like a dorm room refrigerator with a glass front.

Warrant Officer Choi and the Captain entered cautiously. This office was thought to contain some really nasty stuff. The rest of the team waited outside the office, taking a knee, each covering a pre-determined area looking for any sign of trouble.

Peter set a small, secure box designed to keep glass test tubes from breaking on the table and opened it as the Captain opened the refrigeration unit. Peter couldn't read the language on any of the labels, but Captain Martin could.

The Captain carefully handed one sample then the another across the table, then very carefully closed the refrigeration unit as Peter stored the second tube.

With the transportation case closed, Peter slung his weapon and cautiously picked up the case. The pair exited the office.

Captain Martin broke silence as he pushed the transmit button on the radio mounted to his neck, "Alpha team ready to extract. Cargo intact," he said quickly and quietly.

The team reversed their path. By time they got down the aisle the gateway was ready. The team was transported home, and the gateway closed as soon as the last man, a Sergeant by the name of Fisher re-appeared safely back in the United States.

Scientists in full bio-containment suits descended on the team. One of them took the case from Warrant Officer Choi who was relieved to be rid of the thing knowing what it contained. A number of scientists with some weird type of instruments were scanning the team of Green Berets. After a few tense moments they were declared free of any trace of the deadly virus on their clothing, which apparently was a possibility with the bug they were carrying tucked away in that hand-held plastic case. Just plastic, that was it. That was all that kept widespread death and destruction at bay. It was theoretically sealed but given what was in it, distance seemed like a the best idea.

"All clear," one of them shouted.

"Mr. President if you are still listening, we have what we went for and no one caught wind of us being there. Just like walking down the hall and coming back," said Captain Martin.

"Congratulations men, you may have just saved millions of lives, and given us what we may need to immediately turn this fight back on our enemy," the President's voice said as it filled everyone's earpiece.

***

Just thirty-six hours later President Banner was sitting at the desk in the Oval Office watching numbers counting down on the screen below the camera.

"My fellow Americans, thank you for giving me your time this evening.

"By now you know about the Paris attacks. I can now tell you that the Pentagon has a plan to ensure these types of attacks can be dealt with quickly should they occur virtually anywhere in the United States, or the world for that matter. I can't give out any details for security reasons, but I have personally reviewed these plans and I am confident in our ability to prevent this horrendous type of attack from happening ever again. That's right, Paris was their one chance to use that threat, and we can now make that a thing of history.

"That is not only piece of good news I have for you tonight.

Frank paused, knowing the next part of his speech could drive the enemy leadership crazy, and that may cause them to make mistakes.

"A little more than twenty-four hours ago the United States Special Forces successfully acquired an original sample of at least one of the virus strains used in the attacks here in the United States, and we got them directly from our enemy's biological research laboratory. This has already been and will continue to be invaluable in the research effort to counter the challenges we are facing as a result of these biological attacks. It will lead us to a solution for the virus causing so much pain, suffering and death in a very short period of time as compared to the normal research cycle for this kind of disease.

"I feel safe saying that these events by themselves would represent a victory that will cause a fundamental shift in the warfighting taking place.

"I have even more for you this evening. Our soldiers captured a vaccine that, according to some recently acquired intelligence data, has been proven to work, been reproduced, and been used on their own soldiers. It is currently being tested by our scientists to verify those results and ensure it works without any side effects, especially any that would be life threatening. Under the assumption that this vaccine is going to work it will soon be going into mass production. This will be done at several different locations around the country to be sure that no single attack or accident can eliminate the capabilities. I will not go into exactly where for security reason."

Frank paused again. The speech writers told him to do so at this point, both to let the words sink in, and for dramatic effect.

"The Center for Disease Control in Atlanta will be holding a press conference in the next hour with additional details on how this vaccine will be distributed around the United States, and to our allies around the world.

"We will be speaking again after I meet with our new economic team on some steps we will be taking to get our economy back on track. That meeting will take place early tomorrow morning and information on when you can expect some action will be following shortly thereafter.

"Thank you, my fellow Americans, good night and God Bless the United States of America," the President concluded.

The camera light went off. Frank turned to look at the National Security Advisor, the Secretary of State, and the head of the Central Intelligence Agency who were clustered behind and to the right of the camera all smiling and giving him a thumbs up.

***

General Rahbar looked at his Deputy Commander, threw his folder across the room scattering paperwork everywhere, and demanded, "How the *fuck* did they get all of that without us knowing?"

***

Admiral Chao Xiao was on the bridge of the newest aircraft carrier to join the Chinese fleet. In his armada he commanded submarines, destroyers, landing craft, tens of thousands of men and some very special civilians who were ready to take over the critical infrastructure in the American technology capital known as Silicon Valley. If anywhere in the United States could find a way to defeat the Chinese cyber teams it was there, and that was a threat to their war plans that could not be allowed. Even if the Americans fielded a better firewall, it could be a problem that would not be tolerated as it would bring their smart weapons and unconventional weapons back as options on the battlefield. If that happened the Americans and their Allies would make short work of finishing the war.

Chinese spies had been in that valley for years infiltrating many of these companies as legitimate employees gaining network access. Not to mention a better understanding of how those systems worked, and access to thousands upon thousands of CPUs in cloud computing farms all over the world. Those corporations controlled virtually everything computationally relevant to the future of the planet.

They would be ready to take over those civilian computer networks the moment he was in physical control of the region. If they controlled the civilian networks, they would control large parts of the economy. Not to mention control of the companies that developed the most up to date cyber security software would limit the ability to update their military capabilities, thus ensuring defeat of the Western Nations.

They would have their finger on the pulse of everything from the most advanced banking systems to the shipping and logistics systems that kept America, and the world, moving.

It would be easy to vaporize the area and eliminate the threat, but controlling the technology would be a strategic victory that at minimum would put them on equal footing with the American's capabilities. Then they could dispatch the Unified Islamic whatever they were calling themselves, useful idiots, and take real control of the world.

"Send word to our spies that our first missiles will be on target in fifteen minutes and the first landing of our men will be mere moments afterwards. If the men aren't ready, they need to be, and quickly. It is time to execute," the Admiral ordered as the sailors around him leapt into action.

***

The sun was starting to set over the San Francisco

Bay as Li Xiu Ying and Josh Dean were sitting down for drinks in the executive conference room at the end of a long day. They were on one of the upper floors of the building, one of the taller ones in town, where they both had offices with amazing views. Josh was the CEO of an up and coming cyber security company that had as its only goal to keep the world's computer networks safe from external influence. Li was the CTO, the powerhouse behind all of their recent advances.

Josh, at five foot eight inches tall was a pure software geek turned CEO, his image was complete with pale skin, even in California sun. On the other hand, Li was an exotic beauty at five foot seven inches, raven black hair, and striking eyes. Today they were celebrating a new breakthrough the company was ready to deploy.

"This new upgrade, now that we have it fully tested, will massively increase our market share. The financial and business analysts are saying it could be by as much as twenty percent," Li said as she continued to prepare drinks for both of them. "The algorithm will make the resulting firewalls strong enough to keep anyone out. This new quantum computing capability is really the difference maker we had hoped for."

"That's good news, the board has been nervous about our cash burn rate, will you be ready to brief them before next month's meeting about the rollout plan? Maybe we can get them to come in sooner than scheduled," he was always excited to deliver good news.

Li handed Josh his drink, "Domestic rollout will come first. Then we can move into Europe and South America as well. I expect that within two years we will be able to take this global with at least half the corporate world using our system."

Josh idly swirled his drink while dreaming of the company being a global powerhouse, all based off this one idea, this one algorithm, that seemed to come out of nowhere. Li had a small smile at his dreamy look as he sat there with his drink, never noticing the small bubbles that were coming into existence at the bottom of the glass.

Kicking her shoes off and popping a button on her blouse for fun, Li moved over to the couch that was facing the window looking out into the bay and curled herself up on one end. Motioning for Josh to come and sit down next to her.

"Once we develop the cash flow this new version will provide, we can branch into other technology areas as we have always planned. This is going to be good for our early investors and employees who held onto their stock," she said.

She was toying with him, stringing him along for a few minutes, and thoroughly enjoying the process.

Josh sipped his drink as he made his way to the couch and had started to sit down when a sudden intense pain hit. Groaning, Josh dropped his drink and started coughing, struggling to breath, "Li, what's happening to me? Call 911, I need help."

He started grabbing his chest.

Sitting back with a grin, Li continued to sip her drink and casually watch as Josh gasped and coughed up blood, writhing in pain.

He could no longer maintain his balance and fell over on his side. As he rolled onto his back, he realized he was going to die.

Li slowly slid down to kneel beside Josh. She gently caressed his cheek, she bent over, whispering to in his ear, "Poor dear Josh, you sweet fool, who do you think actually gave us this development? Our employees? No. The best engineers in China did this, and it doesn't do what you think it does. The best part is your investment bankers paid for it. My real employers are steadfast and extremely dangerous. The time you have left will be spent in pain and suffering but don't worry, it will only be for an hour or maybe two."

Li sat back and watch him continue to writhe in pain, waiting for the cruise missiles that should be coming into view at any moment. This was what years of hard work had been for, finally China would take its rightful place on the world stage.

***

Tony looked at his friend, Josh as their YouTube stream went live. They had prepped some areas to talk about but didn't script these things. They had decided that a free-wheeling style would be more "genuine."

"The new President, what is that, three in less than two years? Anyway, the new President just gave a press conference whey they claim to have 'obtained' a vaccine from the enemy that is supposed to save our lives. Does this scare the crap out of anyone else? We are going to trust something captured from the people that developed a biological weapon, and used it against civilians?" Josh said trying to drive the narrative to a particular area.

"I believe they grabbed something. But it seems just a little too easy. I mean we suddenly have the ability to grab a virus sample and a vaccine really quickly, from a lab halfway around the world? All the sudden this cluster fuck is going to be turned around and we are going to start to win? Or is it more likely that the enemy left something that looks like it would be beneficial and is trying to lull is into injecting our own citizens with this disease designed to kill us? I don't trust it, or this new guy who has no experience at this level." Tony said.

"I'm with you man, this seems like a freaking disaster waiting to happen. This guy, what is his name, Frank Banner? He doesn't know anything about how to handle this job. I get that he is a war hero, and props to him for that, but this isn't anything he is ready for. Let's go to twitter and see what people are saying about this total amateur."

***

Sandra Cooper happened to see the YouTube feed

and grew angry. She went to find her chief of staff and decided to put her nursing background and position as fiancé to the President to good use and fight back on social media. It was time to stop being silent, and let the professionals answer some questions. These morons were just going to cause people to panic.

These idiots with webcams weren't experts of any kind. They had to be silenced, or at very least corrected.

"Sorry mom, I've got to go do something about this," she said to her mother who was just settling into the White House residence.

<AP NEWS FLASH>The President has attempted to give us hope. With all of the death and destruction there has been, seemingly there has been no real sense of victory for the United States and allies. However, we have now won a minor victory, but some are saying he is not ready for the challenges ahead, especially the economic and biological issues.

So far during this war, with the formal declaration passing Congress by massive margins, more than three million people have been killed between Israel, London, Paris and the United States. Most of those being civilians.

Millions more are sick, some of those will die, but now there is, according to the new President, hope for the future. The war effort may not be a lost cause, as it so recently appeared.

<AP ECONOMIC NEWS FLASH>The President gave a very brief speech from the Oval Office of the White House. He has stated that his new economic advisors have an economic plan, or at least the initial steps of a plan, which will be announced tomorrow. Market futures are holding steady, investors are waiting for the details of this new plan before making decisions. <STORY DEVELOPING>

Chapter Fifteen
From Bad to Worse

Claudia could not recall ever being as tired as she was at this moment. Between treating patients at the hospital and the work in the lab, she couldn't remember the last time she had slept for more than four continuous hours. There were scores of dead and dying littering her dreams, so many people lining the hallways covered in sheets, it was too much. A solution had to be found and found quickly or the medical system of the United States was in real danger of collapsing.

Dr. Hernandez looked at the lab results from an patient's blood draw again, and still wasn't able to be exactly sure what to make of it. The data was so confusing.

The samples gathered from local infected individuals were much different than the ones delivered by a military courier. They were similar in some ways but not identical, and they were supposed to be identical. One of these two held a secret, and she was afraid it was the hand delivered one. Was it a solution? Was it a new, and possibly an even harder to deal with genetically engineered virus?

Somehow a vaccine had also mysteriously arrived. It had quickly been tested and proven to be effective against one of the original virus strains that had been causing so much pain and suffering all over the nation. That was at least one thing to be celebrated, but not if another, potentially more dangerous bug was out there starting to be seen in the emergency wards around the Nation.

Surrounded by expensive lab equipment that currently held no answers, with her fingers fiddling with the handle on a coffee mug, she let out a sigh. While blankly staring out into space she was trying to figure out a next step that would be productive.

She was snapped back to reality when her phone chimed indicating an incoming text message. She picked up her phone and saw it was from a colleague working two floors down attacking the same problem from a different angle asking her to come down and take a look at something.

A short walk and some stairs later she walked into a room full of monkeys.

"Jack, what's going on?" Dr. Hernandez asked.

"Something is weird. I have three cages you need to take a look at. It isn't a great statistical sample, but it bothers me, a lot," Phil explained.

He was a tall man, easily 6'3" with dark hair turning to grey and glasses. His height meant that the lab coats he insisted on wearing were always short on him, which Claudia always found funny.

"Which ones?" she asked. His lab had close to a hundred monkeys in it.

He made his way to the back where all the cages were completely airtight, isolating their inhabitants from the rest of the room.

"I inoculated these three guys with the vaccine samples we manufactured from that original vaccine sample, then exposed them to the virus which was gathered from one of the deceased human patients over at Atlanta General. They never became symptomatic despite having the virus in their system. They are probably contagious but at least healthy. In other words, the inoculation worked well enough to save their lives," he explained.

"They don't look healthy at all. If you saved them, why do they look like they are about to expire?" Claudia asked, closely examining the three monkeys who were clearly about to die. They were obviously in extreme pain, and had blood flowing from every available opening, with the majority of it flowing from the eyes. These did not seem like the picture health he was describing, but he always had an odd way of making his point.

"Because after a day and a half of completely healthy living I exposed them to the new virus those army guys brought over. Claudia, it is close, but it isn't the same bug. This vaccine, while it works against what has been used on our general population is completely useless against this new thing. They have only been exposed for about three hours," Phil said, the frustration coming through in his voice.

"Fuck," was all the ever-professional Dr. Claudia Hernandez could bring herself to say as she started to rub her temples.

***

"Mr. President," one of Frank's many assistants said upon poking their head into the dining room in the Presidential Residence inside the White House.

"Yes," Frank said after swallowing as fast as he could and getting to his feet.

"Mr. President, I have the Director of the Center for Disease Control on the phone. He says it's urgent, and he called on a secure line. We have it in the office down the hall," the young man explained.

"On my way. Sandy, can you come with me just in case I need help understanding anything medical?" he asked his fiancé, hoping as a former nurse she could translate all the medical jargon to plain English.

They made their way to the office, Frank engaged the speakerphone, "This is President Banner, and Registered Nurse Sandra Cooper."

"Mr. President, I have two doctors with me, Dr. Claudia Hernandez, and Dr. Phillip Williams. They need to inform you of a critical new development. Doctors, please explain to the President what you just told me," the Director said.

Phil proceeded to explain the results of the monkey exposure, then turned the discussion over to Claudia.

"Mr. President, Ma'am, I have been treating patients as well as working here at the CDC. To date all patients who survived long enough to get to medical care have been infected with a single viral strain, and the vaccine we have been given appears to be highly effective against that original strain. However, the viral sample that the military courier delivered is a related, yet different strain, and the vaccine we have doesn't seem effective in preventing this new strain. It is like when an influenza vaccine works against some, but not all strains of the disease. It will be highly effective against the strains it is design to counter, but is virtually worthless against others," Claudia explained.

Frank rolled his eyes and pounded on the desk.

Sandra stepped closer to the phone, "Doctors, I was an ER nurse. I am not a researcher by any means, but as I understand it, with the viral sample you have it is possible to develop a vaccine. How long will that take?"

"Excellent question ma'am. In the past few years, it has gotten faster but it still is just a shade under a year if we accelerate testing, then we have to mass produce and distribute. With a crash program, maybe 18 months," Dr. Hernandez explained.

"There goes that idea," the President said aloud.

"Doctors, I'm going to need both of you to get here to Washington as fast as you can. Check on flights and let my assistant know when you will arrive," Frank said.

"Ummm...Mr. President," Christopher Gintz, the former aide to President Press, now Frank's aide said. "When the Office of the President requests someone fast, we don't wait for commercial flights."

"I really need to get used to this kind of thing,"

President Banner said.

"Ok. Doctors, we will get you here. Get yourselves packed for a few days. I'm going to bring the Army Special Operations team that brought us those samples here as well. We need some alternatives to that year and a half long timeline," the President said, not sure if his plan had any merit. But he hoped that if the enemy developed a vaccine for one of these weaponized viruses, they developed at least two. It made sense, but not much was making a lot of sense these days. Until his theory was proven out, he would hold it as a hope as one of their own Generals had succumbed to a biological weapon of some kind.

How many of these weaponized bugs did they have?

***

Captain Martin was in his office doing paperwork when he received the call. It had been succinct and to the point. Get the team, his special operations team, bring dress uniforms and get to Washington D.C. on a government jet that would be landing on the Fort Bragg airstrip within ninety minutes. Upon arrival the team would be escorted to the White House for a meeting with the President and relevant senior staff.

He stared at the phone, not sure what to do next.

The White House? He had spoken to the man, but that was one thing, this was another.

He stood up, stepped around his desk and headed

for Peter Choi's office. The Warrant Officer, and the rest of the team, had known the President since he was Captain Banner when had sat at the very desk he had just been using to file reports.

He knocked on the open office door as he entered, "Mr. Choi, I just received a call, we are going TDY for a day or so, apparently, but..."

"Don't worry sir, you'll get used to it. The President is just a man, and once you get over the address he lives at and the title he now bares you will realize it's just another building that a family lives in that has a crap ton of offices, and does some relatively important work," Peter said.

"How did you know..." was all the Captain could get out.

"I am a high and mighty Chief Warrant Officer and I know everything that happens to this team. Nah, seriously, President Banner texted me, and the rest of the team a few minutes ago. I bet he doesn't have your number, or you would have been on the list," Peter said with a smile and a slight chuckle.

"Well of course he did, why wouldn't the President do that himself," the Captain said, somewhere between sarcasm and frustration. "Is there anything else you are aware of that I should know?"

Peter stood up, came around the desk and clapped the man on the shoulder, "You'll be fully one of us after this trip. Just be yourself, he'll like you. Then I can retire and consider my career of training you upwardly mobile guys complete, and finally get some fishing done."

***

A whirlwind trip on short notice was part of life when you were part of SOCOM. Peter looked at the team, everyone waiting for the meeting to start, no one sure what was to be discussed, which wasn't all that unusual. It was just a conference room, like so many others around the world. More security than most, but other than that not much different. Well, it did have nicer chairs and a more polished table than most.

There was no knock at the door before it opened, "Atten-shun!" someone shouted.

"Oh, sit down everyone," President Banner looked at his aide. "I used to get shot at with these guys," he said as he exchanged vigorous handshakes with his former team.

"Captain Martin, it is about time we met in person," the President said approaching the nervous young officer.

"Yes, Mr. President," Louis said speaking very quickly.

"If you think *this* is awkward and makes you nervous just wait a few minutes, half the Joint Chiefs will be here," Frank said with a wink.

"Ok men. I'm not going to be in here during this briefing, but we have a problem. That last little job you did returned a fantastically useful bit of intel and if we can get lucky we can use it to save lives, but we'll let the experts explain all that. I just wanted to come say hello. I have a meeting about filling the Vice President spot, then one on how to keep the economy moving, and all in the next hour. Before you guys leave here have someone come get me. Also, I will have the kitchen send over some food," the President said and left the as fast as he had entered.

***

The soldiers had been listening to Drs. Williams and Hernandez for an hour. The problem was obvious, there had to be a second vaccine, if not more, somewhere in that research facility.

"Dr. Hernandez," Captain Martin said, "when we went in and grabbed those samples, I saw what had to be sixty different vials of stuff. I can read the language enough to tell a virus from a vaccine, but everything else on those labels was medical gibberish to me. In fact, there could have been more than one vaccine, I saw one, grabbed it and left. We didn't stick around for a long time reading every medical sample around. We wanted to leave as little trace that we had been there as possible. Two missing notebooks isn't much, emptying out the entire facility would have been another. Can you give some ideas on exactly what we should be looking for?"

"Where did you get these vials? Can I see the facility, at least some photographs?" she asked.

"You wouldn't believe it if we told you, and we only took a few photos in addition to the helmet cam video. But we could pretty easily get you in there to see it in person if you really wanted, but that would be dangerous, and more than likely out of the question I'm afraid, unless the President agreed with the idea," Sergeant Fisher said.

"More dangerous than treating hundreds of highly contagious patients, many of whom I have had to watch die with blood seeping out of their eye sockets? More dangerous than another million or more deaths we might have prevented if we get the right vaccine?!" Dr. Hernandez, her lack of sleep and frustration at watching people die getting the better of her as she shouted at the man.

"Well, Captain? Chairman Jackson? Can we take her there? If the target is just as soft as it was the last time it won't be an issue, except for maybe demonstrating the new transportation device that she isn't cleared to know about," Warrant Officer Choi asked.

"I'll be right back, I need to talk to POTUS," Chairman Jackson said as he got out of his chair and left the room.

"Doctor, can I ask you a question that is a little off topic," inquired Peter Choi.

"Sure."

"What is it like to have this virus? I know what we have seen on the news, but everyone here knows better than to trust that. I mean, what does it feel like to be the patient?" Peter asked.

"It is very very horrible. It is painful, it sets in fast, and one strain kills without mercy, the other one, if you can get to treatment is survivable, mostly, but it takes a long time, ties up beds and personnel and is very painful. There is no long incubation period which works in our favor, but you are contagious essentially from the very first moment of infection. But there is a problem that hasn't been brought to the public yet, but perhaps it should. There are now so many dead and dying that due to the nature of infectious diseases, and dead bodies that are now leaking fluids so rapidly that it will cause, if it isn't already, a massive public health hazard. This stuff could end up in the sanitation system and be transmitted without contact to an uninfected human. That means millions more infected will result as people start to die at home because not everyone is going to seek treatment. This may have already happened, I haven't been following that side of things, and hygiene isn't as good as when someone dies at a hospital. If this isn't already happening it will in the coming months if not weeks, and with the fatality rate on this thing we could lose half the population of the United States in the next six months if something doesn't change."

"What? Did you say half the nation?" asked President Banner from the doorway. He and the Chairman of the Joint Chiefs had silently re-appeared.

"Yes, Mr. President. Unless we can get in front of this, it could be at that level, if not worse," Dr. Hernandez replied.

"Captain Martin, you are going to go back, and take a civilian specialist with you. That is, if you are up for a little trip, Doctor, as I can't give you an order," the President said.

***

Tony turned on his computer and flipped to through his social media accounts. There had been a ton of growth since the interview with his sister.

Twitter seemed to be the most vibrant.

He felt it was time to send out a few more posts. The conversation had to keep going and stay focused.

So far, we have lost an unknown number of people to this disease? How many more before we act?

He had a few more, but he wanted to limit it to two so people had a chance to respond.

The second one had to really hit home, and maybe get the conspiracy theorists to take it viral. He thought for a moment and carefully typed.

You would think with modern medicine we could stop the disease. Is this U.S. Government in on this? What is the endgame and why aren't we fighting back? #popcontrol

<AP NEWS FLASH> All around the nation, new cases of the flu-like weaponized virus are being reported. Symptoms are acute and appear very quickly. There is a statement from the CDC available online urging the public to not come in contact with any bodily fluids from an infected person. It is even being said that the bodies of the deceased are contagious for an extended period of time after death making direct contact is potentially lethal.

More than three million people have been killed since the re-initiation of hostilities globally. More than two million of those are from this disease. Shortages of medical supplies have not been a problem yet but are anticipated in the near future if something doesn't change the tide of the ever-increasing number of infected persons.

<AP ECONOMIC NEWS> The U.S. Economy is crashing more every day. The parts of the nation not being ravaged by war are being hit with disease. That disease means increased spending on medical care and less economic activity in the rest of the economy. So many people are out of work we need a federal jobs program, and we need it now. If we don't get one people will not be able to purchase basic necessities much longer. Time is ticking and the President must act immediately. The military conflict isn't the only type of war facing the population of the United States.

Chapter Sixteen
From Here to There

"What the hell. No way. I don't have time for sick jokes," Claudia thought. She had never heard such insanity. Walk through an energy portal and appear on the other side of the planet instantly? To her this was just some kind of science fiction or fantasy mumbo jumbo make believe.

It couldn't be possible.

She couldn't believe it.

The human body couldn't deal with the stresses of moving that far that fast.

"If this portal system is so good, why not just open it below the sample storage vessel and let the whole thing just fall through," she asked.

Dr. Gross jumped in to explain, "It doesn't exactly work that way. The gravitational pull wouldn't send it through the portal. For some reason, we have never figured out completely why, gravity doesn't set things in motion to come through, probably because we are bending a dimension in a way that we don't normally experience to get this to work. The thing has to be accelerated from the side it is on. There is some sort of energy barrier we have yet to figure out or determine how it works that acts like a solid wall or in this case a floor. We can throw something through, but something on the same side as the thing we want has to set it in motion. It is weird and I personally suspect some kind of quantum effect, but this technology is still relatively new. Besides, with these samples that would be dangerous. What happens if we didn't catch them, and they broke?

"On top of that, our target for opening the portal is never exact. The further away the target zone the further off we are. At this distance we will probably be off by a few feet, so we have to be careful where we aim. One mistake and it ends up in a wall or splitting a person on the other side in half. Also, there is a limited amount of mass that can go through the portal at once which is proportional to the amount of power we pump in and we can only do a limited amount of power before we melt this equipment, so we have to be careful. But we are working on building a much larger version, which is just about complete and will be ready for testing in the near future."

She shook her head trying to clear the confusion, and looked at the team of soldiers in the room, "All of you have done this, multiple times?"

She was met with a room full of head nods and thumbs up.

"What does it feel like?" she asked.

"Just like walking across a room until you realize you just walked a few thousand miles, but the disorientation is psychological not physical, so don't think about it and you'll be fine," Sergeant Brown said.

"So, you want me to go with you, into an Iranian biological weapons research facility. How will we do that without getting killed? Surely there is security at such a place," Dr. Hernandez said naively.

"Because with the energy portal we show up behind their security, and within a few feet of where they store the stuff, all without them knowing," explained Captain Martin.

"All this is done with the equipment you just showed me? That was just a pile of regular lab gear, I can find most of that stuff at any major university." Claudia said, not sure she believed any of what she had been told and shown in videos.

"That's correct," said Doctor Gross with a goofy smile.

The door to the room slammed open and an enlisted soldier who had been standing guard burst in.

"Captain, there is an attack taking place in New Hampshire, you and your men need to mount up! This is going to have to wait while you execute Plan B," he said.

The team burst from the room to get their combat gear.

Doctor Hernandez couldn't understand what a small team could do to stop an attack if it was invading a state. It would have to be huge. She followed them from the room, moving more slowly than the soldiers.

***

Less than thirty minutes later the team was in body armor, gas masks, and weapons were being held at the ready. The energy portal was taking shape as Claudia and Jack were watching on a monitor in the next room. They still weren't sure exactly what was going on, but they both wanted to see this equipment in action.

They watched as the men moved through the portal in pairs and disappeared. Neither of them wanted to believe their eyes, but it had just happened.

***

Captain Martin was the first through, shoulder to shoulder with Master Sergeant Fisher.

This time it wasn't a mission to go steal some biological samples, they were going to go in and start a fight. If all went well, they would be entering in a quiet part of the enemy command and control facility.

Sergeant Fisher saw it take shape around him first. They had actually managed to show up in the heart of the enemy command and control facility, but they showed up directly in the field of view of half the enemy soldiers in facility. It wasn't what they would consider optimal, but they had surprise on their side so that was something.

He and Captain Martin opened fire as they dove for cover. The rest of the team rapidly appearing behind them, reacting as professionals.

The enemy was surprised, but some reacted quickly, they put down their comm gear or whatever they were working on and reached for weapons to return fire on the team.

***

Doctor Gross was at a computer monitor checking and rechecking the system performance when a bullet came through the portal, entered his shoulder and he fell to the ground.

***

Warrant Officer Choi was the last through the gate. He and Sergeant Brown dove to the sides behind a stack of comm gear while simultaneously firing on the enemy.

The concept of this mission was easy. Wait for an attack to start, jump in behind the lines, and take out the enemy command and control system, as well as the people operating that equipment. This would cause the larger enemy units making contact with other U.S. Soldiers in the area to become confused without orders or intelligence, and as a result be much easier to defeat.

The room held approximately thirty-five enemy soldiers with ranks ranging from low level enlisted technicians to General.

Rifle fire was going in both directions. The enemy soldiers were technicians in uniform. They didn't react well to the psychological pressure of a combat situation and were no match for the seasoned Special Operators.

It didn't take long before the enemy was down to just five soldiers, well bunkered behind larger equipment, flutily attempting to engage in a fight. There was still one General shouting orders, and three men trying to surrender. The rest were either dead or dying. So far none of the Special Operators had sustained so much as a scratch. Surprise, training and experience always worked well that way. It wasn't perfect, but it did help.

Warrant Officer Choi sent a flurry of hand signals to the rest of the team. No point shouting orders over the gunfire and taking the chance that one of those enemy asshats spoke English. Two of the men tossed hand grenades to the other side of the room which distracted those returning fire and caused them to abandon their cover. The rest of the team took it upon themselves to have those still attempting to engage to be taken down by a few well-placed high velocity rifle rounds.

The team rushed forward, grabbed the remaining enemy soldiers, none of whom had weapons, including the General who was still shouting orders, and muscled them to an area free of weapons.

The team proceeded to strip them naked. They even removed their socks and shoes. No one on the team understood this order, but as the saying goes, orders are orders. Sometimes you just have to follow 'em.

With the job done, two team members placed explosives and five-minute timers on all the electronic gear that still appeared to be functional, then called for transport and headed home.

***

Sergeant Fisher came through the gate first, with a prisoner in tow. He found a room in chaos and quickly realized no one was going to shoot him, but four people were on the ground bleeding from bullet wounds.

Being a combat medic, he quickly sprang into action. Two people were being treated by Drs. Williams and Hernandez. He handed off his prisoner and ran to the wounded person surrounded by the most blood.

It was Doctor Gross.

"Ok doc, you are in my hands now, and I have helped people hurt much worse than this, including our current President," Sergeant Fisher said, trying to calm the man and surrounding scientists who were panic stricken down as he looked at the wound.

"No arteries have been cut, bullet is still in there, probably up against a bone, but a little surgery, some rest, and you will be as good as new. It is going to hurt for a while, but we can take care of that," the Sergeant explained as he worked to get the bleeding under control.

He looked at the calmest of the scientists, "If you look in my pack there is a medical kit, please grab the pain killer, follow the instructions and inject Doctor Gross, it will get the pain under control while I work the bleeding."

The man did as he was instructed, and with reasonable speed to Sergeant Fisher's delight.

When he got the bleeding stopped and Doctor Gross stabilized, he went from one of the wounded to the next until he was convinced that everyone was being helped, and he could offer no additional assistance.

He crossed the lab to where Warrant Officer Choi was guarding the prisoners.

"Sir, if bullets can go through those gates, and we have a little bit of intel that I hope they have floating around somewhere, I have an idea," Peter said.

"Way ahead of you Sergeant," the smaller man said with a grin.

"I just heard on the radio that the enemy is on the way to counter one of our units. When we blew the facility, they seem to have lost contact with one another, our guys are really cleaning up," Captain Martin said as he stripped off his gas mask.

"So, you are thinking we figure out where all their comm trucks are and shove in 500-lb Air Force Bombs with a timer, then close the portal instead of sending troops?" Sergeant Fisher asked.

"I was thinking a little bit larger, something like starting with the 1,000-lb bomb but sure. If we can figure out where their troops are and their transportation routes out at sea as they make their way here to the United States, and we can find it while they are still out at sea, I say we drop a fucking nuke," said the Captain.

***

Dr. Hernandez stepped through the energy gate. She was the last one through.

It was exactly as they said. It felt like walking across a room, but you ended up halfway around the globe. She wondered just how far the thing could transport someone.

She found the professional soldiers spread out and guarding the area. Captain Martin was motioning for her to follow him.

Together they walked past some lab equipment and entered an office where he pointed towards a refrigeration unit full of test tubes.

She understood some of the typical labels found in medical research labs around the world, some of the labels were in symbols used in the medical profession while others were written in a language that she didn't understand but the Captain did. At least the symbols were universal. There were thirty-two vials containing what the labels claimed were original virus samples, and thirty containing vaccines. She looked again. All of the viruses appeared to be labeled uniquely, and all but two had a matching vaccine.

"There are two viruses here without a vaccine," she said quietly.

The Captain held up a hand indicating for her to remain silent.

She took them all and placed them in the case designed for safe transport. Then she grabbed the two laboratory notebooks from the desk, and the team headed home.

***

Tony looked into his webcam, "We now have confirmation that more than four million people have died since this conflict has started. The network news will try to tell you that number is much smaller, but they are not telling the truth, only we are. It is a combination of those killed by the nuclear bomb, and those killed by the virus. I don't know how much more of this we can take before the President decides to fight back and end this. They can't have that many soldiers, how hard is it with our modern technology to just kill all of them quickly."

He took a deep breath before continuing, "I am going to get in my car, drive to the White House and demand action. But on the way I hear there is an attack going on in New Hampshire and I will be going there first. I want to see for myself how big this conflict is. We see things on the nightly news, sure but is it real or is it fake. They lie so often we need to verify everything. That is what we are here for, the citizen journalists!"

<AP NEWS FLASH>*The number of people diagnosed with the super-bug is nearing one million living patients. The number deceased since the initiation of hostilities from all causes is now approaching a verified three and a half million, there are unverified reports showing it to be much higher. How many of those infected that will survive is unknown.*

Medical supplies are running low all across the country. Anyone from the non-quarantined zones around the country is urged to donate blood as often as possible.

A commercial shipping vessel, on the way to Italy spotted a cluster of ships bringing additional enemy troops towards the United States. The White House has not responded to questions on this frightening development.

An attack in New Hampshire has started. Our troops are in direct conflict with theirs. In the early parts of the attack, it was clear their side was making headway and advancing into the state. Then, for some reason, our troops managed to turn things around as the enemy troops became disorganized and our men and women in uniform pushed them back, winning the day. It is certainly a blow in the larger conflict, but far from full victory.

<AP ECONOMIC NEWS FLASH>*The United States markets and economy are falling fast, however those*

around the world are doing worse. The President has announced a new economic team that has said if we can end the conflict quickly the United States will thrive due to our technology base and ability to bounce back faster due to our superior economic resources.

We hope the President does what he can to end this conflict in days, not months, and certainly not years. If we can't, the economy is sure to collapse which could easily lead to a military defeat, and possibly be the end of the United States as we know it.

Chapter Seventeen
Calming the Public?

President Frank Banner had been listening to new suggestions on ways to kick start the economy which had fallen off a cliff since the nuclear attack in Los Angeles. This was not the first one of these meetings, and the "suggestions" weren't really getting any better, they just had more graphs now.

He was upset with himself for not understanding how bad things were out there when something someone said finally made sense. Maybe it was the way it was phrased this time.

"Wait a second," the President said. "If I understand what you just said, our economy and the health of it is not based on production of goods and is only in a minor way based on people providing services. It is instead based in large part on the velocity of money, and what that translates to in English is that the faster, and more often people have money change hands the better, even if it is changing hands for worthless crap no one really wants or needs?"

"It is a little more complicated than that, Mr. President, but you are basically correct," said the Fed Chairman.

"So, we need people to not be afraid and to go out and enjoy themselves or do some kind of retail psychological therapy, while a disgusting genetically engineered virus that has killed people numbering in the millions, which is a number I'm still having trouble wrapping my God Damn head around," Frank said.

"Yes, Mr. President," said Lester, the former President's Chief of Staff. Frank wasn't sure what to think of him yet, but there was something that always made him feel uncomfortable about the man, like there were things he didn't know.

Frank stood up, "Ok, all of you go find a conference room someplace to use as a brain pod, stick a bunch of smart people in it, and start working on a plan. That plan needs to be how to get money moving with this virus still in play because from what I am learning in other meetings, it isn't going to be gone in the near future. I'll go see what I can do to change the condition concerning the virus which could completely fix this problem should we be able to eradicate the fucking thing."

There was a round of everyone thanking Frank for his time as they left the room.

Frank knew his fiancé had been helping get medical supplies where they needed to be, "Hey Chris, where is Sandra working on that project she has going?" he asked his personal aid.

"Down in the Roosevelt Room, Mr. President. Do you remember the way?" the young man asked.

"I actually do remember that one, thanks," Frank said as he made his way out of the Oval Office closely followed by the Secret Service.

A few hallways later Frank found Sandra. She had a lot more people working than he would have anticipated. He wondered if that was a sign of the scale of the problem.

As soon as he entered everyone, except his Sandra, stood up. He motioned for them to sit. This was a protocol he didn't care much for given the circumstances of how he had been promoted, not to mention the problems these people should be focused on rather than worrying about standing up to honor some tradition, surely at this point the work mattered more and there would be time for the honorifics later.

"Honey, I need you for a few minutes, and maybe one or two of your smart people. There may be an enormous amount of help coming your way pretty fast, and I don't want to get anyone, or anything involved that gets in the way," the President said.

"It's about time," Sandra said. She was a nurse, and cared about helping people in pain, not about some protocol for speaking a particular way to the President of the United States.

***

"Come on Tony, it will be great for our vlog. Think about how many hits we will get, it will go far past anything we have ever had," Josh said.

"People in there are dying. How are we going to be sure we don't catch whatever the hell it is?" Tony asked, not for the first time.

"We have the surgical masks. We won't touch anything or anyone. We are just going to take some pictures and maybe steal some medical notes. People have a right to know what is really going on," Josh reminded him.

"Ok, but let's go fast. Just in and out."

The two put on their masks and made their way to the hospital visitor entrance. Josh had done some research and found the names of a few patients they could use to craft a story as to why they should be there. They decided to claim they wanted to visit a good friend who they were worried about. They just had to get past the reception desk and everything else would be easy.

The pair walked up to the door, it automatically opened, as did the inner door. When the second set did its job. The smell that hit them in the face was unlike anything they had ever expected, experienced or imagined. It certainly wasn't the typical hospital smell.

Rotting fish would be an improvement over whatever was causing this odor.

The only description for it was vomit crossed with maggot filled meat.

The visitor desk had a very-tired looking woman sitting behind the computer terminal.

"Who are you two here to see?" the woman asked without looking up.

"My Aunt is here, Olivia Haggard," Alex said.

"Sixth floor, room 625, up those elevators," she said as she pointed down the hall behind her. "Be sure to not rub your eyes, sanitize your hands before you leave, and do not touch anything you don't have a need to touch."

They quickly made their way to the elevator.

As the doors closed Tony asked, "What the hell is that smell?"

"I don't know," Josh admitted.

The higher the elevator went, the worse the smell became.

The door opened on the sixth floor. It was a hospital patient floor, complete with reception desk, but there were things going on that were unlike either of them would have expected. There were a dozen gurneys in the hall with bodies covered with sheets. Each of the sheets had splotches of crimson, mostly centered near the head.

Steve timidly snapped some pictures.

There were nurses, all of whom seemed beyond exhaustion. They shuffled from room to room, pushing carts full of medication, or carrying clip boards.

One doctor moved among them, mumbling to himself about the lack of cleanliness and repeatedly asking anyone who came near when someone was going to move the damn useless bodies to the morgue.

They carefully stepped down the hall. Not sure what to do. In their wildest imagination this would not have been what they expected to find. When you think of a hospital you think clean, you think sanitized, you don't think of sticky floors and dead bodies under sheets turning brown due to some kind of fluid being absorbed.

An alarm sounded in the second room on the right.

The doctor let out a sigh and plodded toward the sound.

Tony and Josh stepped forward and looked in the room. The patient in the bed was having a seizure and blood was spewing out of an eye socket like a water fountain.

"Dude let's get the hell out of here," Tony said, grabbing his friend by the arm.

The pair turned on their heels as a nurse shouted down the hall, "You two can't be here, now go before I quarantine your asses."

Josh grabbed a clipboard that was balanced on the legs of one of the deceased patients, and they bolted for the stairs. Their feet carried them faster than they had ever moved before.

Six floors later they raced past the visitor desk, the woman there started laughing, "Third time today," was all they could make out.

They didn't stop until they got to their car which was on the far side of the parking lot.

"We have to get the truth out. This isn't what we

have been told. Fucking fake news," Josh said, gasping to catch his breath.

"I'm sorry I doubted you, let's go find some Wi-Fi," Alex conceded.

***

Hours later, Frank was still working with his fiancé, but they had moved to the Oval Office when the news broke nationally.

Lester opened the door without knocking, "Mr. President, Miss Cooper, we have a problem. Someone went into a hospital, found some medical records, took some pictures, a short video and posted them to some blog."

"How widely has it been seen, and how bad is it?" the President asked.

"Six million hits so far, and bad. There is starting to be panic in every city with confirmed cases. People are leaving in droves and headed to the northern parts of the country where there are still virus free areas. But at least in New England, and with the attack in California, we are now fighting a war," Lester reported.

"Sandy, what happens next," Frank asked.

"Frank, this thing is mutating, or it is not a single bug, or even two. Some people are infected, they show symptoms, and they die within hours. Now, it appears there is a new strain where it may take somewhere between two and ten days for someone to show symptoms. One person who is sick, and doesn't realize it, but can be contagious while running around hugging people goes to the movies or the grocery store, and sneezes causing another entire city to end up like Atlanta. Where at last count one third of the population is symptomatic," the First Lady explained.

"One third? Lester, why didn't I know that, and why or how has that not been on the news," the President demanded.

"Well, uh, Mr. President we can at least, in a limited sense, control the news, and you needed to focus on the war," Lester stammered.

"You are fired, get out. We need to protect and defend the citizens, and if they don't trust us, we can't effectively do that. We have to be honest. This isn't. What you have done isn't helping us at all, get the hell out," the President shouted.

***

Warrant Officer Choi was with the team in a conference room watching YouTube.

A group of United States Citizens with hunting rifles and other improvised personal gear had taken several of the invading military captive. They had built a makeshift wooden "prison" of sorts. It was basically just a wooden fence. They had staked their prisoners to the ground on top of a mound of smaller pieces of wood and were pouring gasoline all over the area.

The largest of them came into camera view. "This one is for Matt and Shelly. Assholes like this came into our country, beat a kid almost to death, after they had raped and murdered his girlfriend. For them, and for everyone else who was killed in Los Angeles or is sick and dying because of this damn virus, we are making an example of these four."

The camera view went wide. Someone whose identity was completely hidden from view threw a zippo lighter into the pile and flames instantly erupted.

"Turn that shit off," Peter said.

"Have we got the position information we need?" Sergeant Fisher asked.

"Just waiting on the go order from the President," Peter said.

"Fuck let's call him. This vigilante shit needs to end. We are better than this."

<AP NEWS FLASH>*Conditions in Atlanta area hospitals are worse than the public has been told. We can't help but be curious, given the level of dishonestly, if the casualty numbers we are being given are accurate.*

People are fleeing the infected areas of the country and heading north, as these areas of the country are disease free to date.

With the economy grinding to a halt, it brings to question if anyone in Washington is qualified to solve the problems we face, or if we are even going to survive as a nation.

<AP ECONOMIC NEWS>The President and his economic team have announced a plan for the government to start buying goods from local businesses. This will extend across multiple business sectors starting with local restaurants who are willing to deliver food to private homes for people unable to afford food or are too sick to do any meal preperation.

It is thought this will continue into many forms of businesses, assuming they are United States owned. It was also announced that manufacturing companies can expect a new series of orders as soon as some details can be sorted out concerning what products are needed first.

Economists are hailing this as an action that could actually work to get the economy moving again.

The economic team has also asked for any company with a concept that can help determine if people are sick or not at a distance, in a non-invasive way to submit that idea to a soon to be launched website.

Chapter Eighteen
Gateway and Additional Release of Nuclear Weapons

Warrant Officer Choi knew that after this one he was going to retire. There would not be another conflict for him. These things used to make sense. You sat on an airplane for a long time, you jumped out, parachuted to the ground, you used your rifle, and the mission was either a success or failure. This new form of warfare was so different, he wasn't about to even think about what things would be like the next time.

He and Captain Martin were the only two members of the team in the room. This was not the kind of place where you wanted more people than absolutely necessary, and the two highest ranked members of the team had volunteered to handle things.

The two of them had a specific mission that could essentially end a large part of the enemy invasion of the United States. There were enemy soldiers already on the ground, but if their supply chain and replacements could be cut off or destroyed it would effectively end their invasion. At least in fairly short order. Or, at the very least, would stop it from expanding.

They had the last known location, direction and

speed of enemy troop transportation thanks to the one week turn a bunch of engineers did on re-awakening some U-2 Spy Planes. That information was going to be used along with the transportation portal to deliver nuclear weapons and destroy those troop transports and their passengers in a giant ball of fire while they were still hundreds of miles from the United States shoreline.

"You ready for this Captain?" Peter asked.

"As ready as I am ever going to be," replied the Captain.

Peter pushed a few buttons on the computer in front of him and waited. Just a few seconds later and President Banner's image appeared on the computer display covering the front of the room.

"Captain Martin, Mr. Choi are you ready?" the President asked.

"Yes, Mr. President. But I have to tell you that your face across a twenty-foot computer screen is at the same time a welcome, and frightening image. With all due respect, you should really learn to shave more carefully," the Warrant Officer chided his long-time friend, and Commander in Chief.

"Mr. Choi, someday we will have to work on your version of respect," the President said with a smile. "I get that you are trying to relieve stress for both you and me, and I appreciate that. Let's get this done then have a damn beer. I bet you twenty dollars you can't hold the jokes until the next time we see each other."

"I'll just pay you now, do you take PayPal?" the Warrant Officer replied.

"Just release the weapons," the President said.

"Yes, Mr. President. I assume you will be watching?" the Captain replied stopping the Warrant Officer from throwing out another bit of sarcasm.

"Yes Captain, I will, but I will be absolutely silent until it is done and remember only about twenty people on the planet know what we are doing and how we are doing it, so this should be easy," the President replied.

"We will just treat you like a fly on the wall," said the Warrant Officer.

"Let's work closest to farthest away," said Captain Martin.

The scientists and engineers in the room checked the coordinates and did a quick calculation on what should be the new location of one of the enemy's troop transport flotillas.

"We will have the system open in ten seconds," a technician said.

"What altitude and opening size?" Warrant Officer Choi asked.

"One mile up and approximately three feet," a technician in the back of the room shouted.

"Shit sir, they won't see this coming at all. No sensor on those ships is going to know anything," Peter said to Captain Martin.

"I hate to say it, Chief, but let's hope that you are

right," the Captain replied, less optimistic than the older man.

"Let's get to work," Peter said.

A technician picked up the controls of a smallish drone that had a decent camera with a zoom lens, and satellite communications attached. The briefing had stated emphatically they had a lot of these drones, but their batteries would only last a total of five minutes before they had to either return through the portal or they would crash into the ocean, it seemed logical at this point to just let them crash.

The two military officers had a clear view of what the drone "saw." As the engines spooled up, and the quad copter sounds filled the room the two stood and nonchalantly watched the monitor.

The drone lifted off, and it slowly approached the portal that had formed on the platform in the center of the room. The circle of light grew larger until it disappeared, and the screen was blank for a second or two before reforming as a view of open ocean. It took a moment for the drone operator to see what they were looking for. An enemy flotilla of two converted cargo vessels carrying troops and equipment towards the United States. According to the position data they were still a few hundred miles off the U.S. Coastline and far enough from anywhere inhabited that they didn't have any issues taking the next step.

"Captain Martin, Mr. Choi, they are exactly where we expected, you can release the weapon in twenty seconds and we will trigger it from here," came the voice of Sergeant Fisher across the speakers in the room.

The two picked up the, for lack of a better term, storage crate, one on each side. They grabbed the two handles closest to them took up to the edge of the portal and looked at one another.

"On three," said Warrant Officer Choi, "One...Two...Three," and they heaved the crate through.

The portal closed almost instantly the moment the crate disappeared.

Everyone in the room watched the drone feed. The crate could not be seen, the image was purely of the ships. Then, without warning, there was a bright flash and the drone feed stopped.

"We have confirmation of a detonation," said Sergeant Fisher across the speaker system in the room. It will be a while before we know exactly how much damage we did, but let's move on to the rest of them before we worry about that.

They repeated this process for the remainder of the known troop transports at sea. This would at very least limit the invasion force coming into the United States. It would mean there was still a challenge in many places in the world, but this would at least severely limit the enemy's capabilities here in the United States.

As the final bomb detonated Peter reflected on what they had just done. Many of the men who dropped the bombs in World War II had psychological issues with their actions later in life. He wasn't sure he would have issues but given what was going on in the world he was certain that at the moment his actions were justified.

"How long before the air clears and we can see the results?" Peter asked.

"Mr. Choi, we have it on our side, let me get someone to feed you some video," came the voice of the President.

"Thank you, Mr. President," Peter answered.

The monitors in the front of the room came up for all to see. It flipped between every detonation site. The ships that "survived" were burning, most of them in pieces that would be rapidly heading for the bottom of the ocean.

"These video feeds are from very high-altitude U-2 aircraft at long range. We can't necessarily see which ships are still above water and which aren't but what the Navy team is telling me none of them will be above water for long. It appears as though we have a shockingly high success rate," explained the President.

"If there is nothing above water, I don't understand how we can't claim absolute dominance," the Warrant Officer said.

"According to intelligence reports, there were some submarines escorting these ships. We are not sure if those have been destroyed or not," explained the President.

"Oh, fuck, well that is a problem," Warrant Officer

Choi said with a sigh.

"They can't contain too many soldiers," said Chairman of the Joint Chiefs Jackson.

"Any chance any of those vessels are missile boats? I mean, the Chinese Navy just hit the West Coast and we haven't hit them back at all," Warrant Officer Choi reminded everyone.

"Unfortunately, there are a number of missile boats likely, and as for California, that is our next target package, Chief. Our current tactical situation is a bit of a problem. We have enemy troops on both coasts. Some have landed, some are still at sea, at least on the West Coast. However, they are too close for us to nuke them. We know for a fact the Middle East didn't have any missile boats, but we can't locate a few of the Chinese boats, and they may have loaned them out, so this is still a concern," the President explained to his friend.

"Peter, I want you and the rest of the team to get your butts here to the White House and lend a hand. I have great strategists here, but you guys and I speak the same language and we need tactical help. Messages are getting lost. Captain, I should have addressed you and I apologize I have known the Chief for what seems like forever," the President apologized suddenly realizing he had just breached protocol.

"Absolutely no issue Mr. President. I have learned quickly and taken some advice from a smart guy that my job is just to stay out of the way and enable them to do their job," replied Captain Martin, starting to get more comfortable directly interacting with the President.

"Captain, I appreciate that, but Mr. Choi is the one who taught me that lesson," the President said with a smile. "Now I have like five other meetings people want me in, but damn good work gentlemen."

***

"Mr. President the economy is not rebounding in any fashion. It is getting worse by the day," said Doctor of Economics Ronald Chelser.

"Mr. Chelser, I completely agree with you, and we don't need to review the situation. I don't have time in my day for that. For sake of this discussion let's assume it is on life support, and the life support is about to have the battery die and there is a power outage estimated to last days. Now, someone told me that our economy is based on money changing hands often and everywhere. The more often it changes hands the more robust the growth. That growth is what will give us a rebound. Do I have this basically correct?" asked the President, trying to cut to the heart of the matter and jump to the solution part of the discussion.

"You are basically correct, Mr. President," the dangerously skinny man in the rumpled suit said.

"Now, I put out a statement that we would be putting together a plan to try to get things moving by pumping in cash. What parts of the economy are going to cause the most job losses if we don't get things moving?" the President asked.

"Overwhelmingly the people that will be the most hurt by this situation are those that earn the least. And shockingly large numbers of those people work for smaller or local businesses. These are typically service industry workers," the man explained.

"Things like waiters, store clerks, warehouse workers, maids, and so on?" the President asked.

"Yes, Mr. President," the man said.

"Now, how do we get those industries to survive?" the President asked, really not sure how to execute the plan, but ideas were starting to form.

"Let's find the easiest ones we can. Start with restaurants. Don't worry about if they are chains or not because many chain restaurants are actually owned by franchisees, and it is really the employees we need to be sure stay employees rather than being laid off. People are afraid to leave their homes. We can institute health checks for food service workers, and since no one is working and people are showing up at food banks is becoming increasingly difficult for some due to the gas prices. As a potential solution we could offer gas vouchers and even pay some if not all of the cost of restaurants to deliver food to people who would otherwise visit foodbanks or use government EBT cards to purchase food but are now having problems with the budget provided due to massive spikes in food costs. I heard that idea floating around, and it really isn't bad at all. It gives a lift to everything from farming to energy to the delivery guy," Doctor Chelser said.

"Ok, that's one, but that isn't going to keep things moving. What else can we do? What is next?" the President asked.

"No one who would normally use a maid is going to permit them into their home. We could do a government service job with many of these workers to help clean homes for the elderly, and also to help clean up the less bio-active regions of hospitals, and heck for that matter the homes of the deceased that are now becoming a real problem around the nation," the economist suggested.

"Now we are on a roll," the President said. "You are now in charge of the recovery plans. Get these two moving, call whomever you need to call in Congress and the Senate to appropriate the money and get this moving towards becoming reality today. We don't have time to wait. Once these are functioning, we will worry about what is next, but it has to be an all fifty-state solution. This has to help everyone, everywhere, not just some areas," the President said.

"Yes, Mr. President," the man said as he was ushered out of the room by the President's personal aid.

Frank stood up to work the muscles in his legs. He was a former soldier and used to running a lot, he didn't have the opportunity in his current job, and there was no time for the gym given the challenges facing the nation.

"Where to, Mr. President," the nearest Secret Service agent asked, knowing the President well enough now to pick up on the signal he was headed for a walk around the White House.

"Let's get back to the Situation Room, if I know my old team, they used that transport portal to get here and are already at work, I want to see what they came up with for the problems in and around Silicon Valley."

***

As Frank opened the door to the Situation Room Captain Martin called, "Attention!"

"At ease everyone, welcome to the party. If I know you guys, there is already a concept going here. What do you and the men have Captain Martin?" the President asked.

"Well, Mr. President. Unlike the East Coast which is full of Jihadis the West Coast is more of a formal military force. The Chinese landed regular soldiers in the form of Marines, and some Army. That means we have a known method to screw with their unit cohesion, and at the same time, I think, get them to give up and go home," the Captain explained.

"Some variant of shooting the highest-ranking officers first?" the President asked.

"Captain, may I?" Warrant Officer Choi asked formally.

"It's your concept Chief, knock it out," the Captain replied.

"The concept is a little more elegant than that, but

that was our first concept. We learned more about this portal system. The closer you are to the point of origin, or the more time you have to do some calculations, the more accurate your delivery point on the other side. Silicon Valley being what it is there are webcams everywhere. Those nerds love free flow of information. We have tapped into a butt ton of those, some of them are even publicly open on a 24/7 basis. There are moments when we know where these higher-ranking officers are within a few inches. I am suggesting we take some of those handheld plasma weapons jump in, grab the highest-ranking officer in the area and get back out. We would be on the ground something like sixty seconds. Maybe we even try to get some intel about what else is coming if we happen to see anything laying around. If not, maybe if you get enough POWs we can get someone to give up some intel. If they come easily great, if there is a fight, we won't have enough men on the ground to deal with a fight, so we need an edge to get out intact, thus the plasma weapons," Warrant Officer Choi explained.

"Damn Chief, that's not bad," the President said. "Chairman Jackson, your thoughts?"

"It is the best idea I have heard, turns out your old team is full of a bunch of sneaky bastards, and I think that might be just what we need right now," the Chairman of the Joint Chiefs said.

"How long before a team is ready to execute?" the President asked.

"We have a SEAL team standing by, if you trust the Navy," said Warrant Officer Choi sarcastically. The

Army and Navy had a "friendly" rivalry that would never die, but in the end it was just sarcasm, and they were all on the same team.

"Which team?" the President asked.

"SEAL team Six, Mr. President," said Chairman Jackson.

"When you say standing by, do you mean in gear and ready?" the President asked.

"Yes, we are set Mr. President," came a voice from a television monitor.

"Ahh, Mr. Tyler, I didn't see you there," the President said to the SEAL team leader whom he had met on a number of occasions before leaving his time in uniform for a career shift to politics.

"We are ready to go when you give the order, the NAVY can deliver since your army guys are getting a little tired, Mr. President," the SEAL said bluntly.

"Do we have a location?" Frank asked.

"Yes we do, Mr. President. We know where their 'on the ground' commander is right now. An officer that is their equivalent of a Lieutenant General," the Chairman explained.

"Gas masks required and keep the tech team out of the bullet path from those portals and go anytime you are ready," the President said.

"You have it Mr. Tyler, and Mr. President we now have ballistic glass in place between the portal and the technicians," Chairman Jackson explained.

Frank watched the screen as the now familiar portal

turned on, the glow started and SEAL Team Six poured through.

The screen shifted to a helmet cam view of a conference room. It looked like a typical conference room of medium quality that could have been anywhere in the world.

The President saw the back of an officer sitting through a briefing. The other people in the room with the man all looked surprised, but no one reacted in a violent way. They all stood up and shouted, no one expected this and had any idea what was going on or how to respond.

One of the SEALs grabbed the officer, and his laptop and stepped back through the portal.

The moment they stepped back through the portal it closed. The entire thing lasted about thirty seconds.

"That was almost too easy," the President said.

"This new gear is going to change the way we fight wars forever," Peter responded, "Especially now that we have worked out a few kinks and really learned the ins and outs. We are also taking a small chance that the Chinese won't have the suicide devices as they are more of an organized, professional military and less religious zealot driven. But, if this keeps working this well, we may do quite a few of these in short order."

"You read my mind Chief," Frank told his old teammate.

***

General Rahbar picked up his satellite phone on the first ring, "Yes?"

"General, we have some bad news. All of our surface vessels on their way to the Continental United States have been destroyed. We have heard from some of the submarines, but not all, so we assume some of them are lost as well. We are not sure what happened, but once we have that information it will be relayed to you," the intelligence officer on the other end reported.

"How certain is this information. That seems unbelievable," the General said.

"It is without a doubt, General," the voice said.

General Rahbar disconnected his phone, threw it at the wall and destroyed the device in frustration.

***

The President had taken off his tie and was sitting down to eat with all the men from his old team when an idea hit him.

"Hey Chief, who was that research scientist we jumped in and grabbed from Iran?" Frank asked his former Warrant Officer.

"Dr. Joba I think?" Peter said.

"Shit, that's it, we need someone to get on that guy.

Maybe he knows something about their capability set. Maybe there is something we need to know about those subs that are still on their way here that he can tell us about. Those things have me concerned given their predilection for use of unconventional weapons," the President said hoping those silent, hidden ships didn't have an as yet unseen trick on board.

"Put him with that officer we just grabbed, shake them, and maybe something will fall out? I like it," Peter agreed.

<AP NEWS FLASH>There has been a U.S. counterattack that has, according to sources, caused some shifts in the war effort. The President is planning to address the nation tomorrow evening with details. No word yet if the operation is concluded or still ongoing. <STORY DEVELOPING>

<AP ECONOMICS NEWS FLASH>The President's economic recovery advisor has released some documentation of a proposal sent to the House of Representatives and the Senate. This proposal is being referred to by members of both parties as a good start. It is hoped that the economy can start to get moving once this is enacted into law. <STORY DEVELOPING>

Chapter Nineteen
The Tide Has Turned, Maybe

President Banner stood at the podium having just finished briefing the press on the use of nuclear weapons being used in the destruction of the incoming enemy fleet, as well as a review of the economic plan that had miraculously passed Congress and the Senate in less than twenty four hours. The economic plan was being called a good start by many, and would result in additional U.S. debt, but one or two problems at a time were all they could handle at the moment, and debt loads were for later.

The staff had attempted to prepare him to take questions, and he just wanted to keep one thought in mind, if he was not absolutely certain of the correct answer defer the question to someone else. Better to not answer than to allow stories to be written about the President being incorrect or worse, misinformed, or even worse than that, incompetent. He was a newcomer to politics at any level and was focused on not just being competent but making sure people got that perception.

"Now, I will take a few questions," the President said. "Given that I am not necessarily new at talking to the press, but am new to this job, which comes with a lot more of you fine folks than I am used to, I will call outlets rather than people. I promise I will learn your names, but my brain has been focused on other issues. NBC," President Banner said.

"Percy Williams, NBC news. Mr. President, I congratulate you on the progress, we all hope that these steps result in a permanent change of momentum in this conflict. The economic policies are being heralded as something that couldn't have been done by a career politician with a specific party affiliation. I must ask, do you consider yourself a Republican or a Democrat," the tall man with impossibly perfect hair asked.

"I have never declared a party affiliation, and that may sound like a line intended to gather support from both sides of the political aisle, but I have voted for members of both parties. I consider myself center and depending on the issue I sometimes sit center right, and I sometimes sit center left. Not that any of this is a direct answer to your question," the President said with a smile knowing that question had been planted by the White House Press Secretary. "CBS, you're up."

"Mr. President," started the tall brunette woman he recognized but was so terrible with names he cursed himself for not remembering, "Stephanie Williams, CBS news, we have seen social media posts and new online personalities emerging during this conflict that are releasing videos from inside hospitals, others from the aftermath of battles, and one that showed the burning of some prisoners a militia group had taken. Do you support these kinds of what people are referring to as citizen journalism or patriotic activities where people are putting out unedited and unvetted reports?"

That wasn't a plant, and a question he had been hoping for, "Let me answer that in two parts. First, I do not condone the torture or murder of anyone that has been taken prisoner. If we have an enemy combatant under our, or even under militia control, the intelligence information we might be able to obtain from that individual is important and could aid in the larger war effort. Not to mention murder is murder. I don't care which side you are on."

The room nodded along with him.

"Second, citizen journalists and their right to free speech or to broadcast information they obtain without violating any kind of security protocols is a Constitutional Right and not one I am going to trample. While the things they broadcast, or say may not be pleasant, as long as it is true and not a fabrication, I am fine with it. However, I urge people in the strongest terms possible, if you want to help with the war effort there are ways to do that, militia is your right, but communicate with the local or state governments and work with us. Don't go out on your own. Organized responses to this threat will win the day. Everyone running around their own direction will result in chaos and friendly fire accidents, which is something we don't ever want to see happen.

"Someone out there is about to say that I am taking these citizen journalists or social media 'influencers' above the media, and I'm not. Each plays an important role. However, I heard a story about a pair that went into a hospital and were exposed to the deadly virus we are trying to deal with. This is dangerous. If they are now sick, they could be running around gathering information to post and infecting people in the process, and they did it to get a story. I want people to exercise caution, above all things. The enemy will shoot you and the disease can kill you. Make no mistake about it. If you go into the hazard zone, we may not be able to protect you. While I respect the role being played, I also think that some people are allowing their zeal for fame to overcome common sense. Especially given that this war, and our recovery from it is going to be marathon, not a sprint."

Frank took a deep breath.

"Ok, onto Fox," President Banner said, wanting to give equal time knowing just a few more networks, all the cable guys, and then he could pass this Q&A session on to someone else.

"Natalie Martin, Fox News. Mr. President, there have been many, and varied numbers in reports concerning the number of dead. These come from the impact zone in Los Angeles, the disease-ridden areas in an increasing area of the nation, the attacks in New England and now this new one in Silicon Valley. Do you have a death total that is reliable?"

"Yes, unfortunately I do. Before I get into that, I want to say something. I was a professional soldier most of my adult life. I have been around death and destruction for far too long and lost too many people that I considered friends, close friends. That was back when we measured these things in ones and twos. I know the name of every soldier I lost under my command. I know all their faces, met all their families. Now when I hear totals, they are so large it sounds abstract. I had to come up with a way to give the numbers meaning. We are a large nation, with hundreds of millions of citizens. When you hear ten thousand dead, twenty thousand dead it is very abstract. Some people will try to compare it to the flu or traffic accidents or cancer, and I don't care about any of that."

Frank took a deep breath before continuing, "We are now at a stage where we have lost more than five million people in this country, or put another way one person in seventy-one has been killed or is so sick they will not survive the week. One in seventy-one. Put another way, there are around a hundred people in a restaurant on a normal night. That works out to at least one of them would have been killed. And, that number is going to grow.

"Someone earlier asked what political party I associate with. I don't want to sound like that question doesn't matter to me, but right now it doesn't. I want to stop that number from getting to one in seventy. I don't know if I can, but I can tell you this. We are going to do everything we can militarily to stop this crap, while we are doing everything we can about this disease, and whatever we can to get the economy going because poverty kills, and we are going to do all of that as fast as we can."

"Now, CNN," Frank said, not allowing time for the inevitable follow up.

***

Admiral Zheng was reflecting on his thirty-five years of military service to China. He had seen technology in his Navy and in military forces around the world advance greatly. Never had he imagined a capability that would allow someone to walk through a wall, grab him, and be gone before anyone understood what had happened. Ten years ago, this would have been called witchcraft. Now it appeared that the Americans had developed this without anyone realizing they had it, or that it could even be possible. There were discussions in universities about teleportation, but they were always theoretical. This was the kind of thing that had only existed in movies, until now. Apparently, those discussions, and movies led scientists to think about how to do this, then to achieve something, and he couldn't think of a way to defeat an enemy who had this capability at their disposal.

He could think of many military uses for it, but no method of countering this new capability.

He sat looking at the non-descript prison interrogation room and wasn't sure if he even wanted to try to lie to them. If they had this kind of power, what else could they do. Could they extract thoughts directly from his brain?

He shook his head and sighed.

There appeared to be no limit to technology, and China was way behind the enemy.

The door opened without warning, "Admiral, I hope you are being kept comfortable. I am Mr. Smith, and I am the head of security at this facility. It is here that our scientists developed the technology used to take you as a prisoner of war. It is not our only new capability, although it is one of the more exotic, and certainly one of the flashier. I won't go into much more detail than that. I am told that you are fluent in English, is this correct?"

"Yes," was all he would say.

"Wonderful, then I won't have to have the computers translate and this will go a lot faster," Mr. Smith explained.

"As you wish, but can I ask you a question?" the Admiral inquired.

"You can ask, but I may not answer."

"How did you get me here? Was this some kind of new technology, or is this office closer than I think to where I was? Most importantly, where am I?" Admiral Zheng asked, hoping his mind was just playing tricks on him and there was some kind of outpost or forward unit in a nearby building close to where he and his team had been planning the next operation.

"Ha ha," Mr. Smith chuckled, knowing some forms of those questions were coming. "While I can't explain how the portal works, because I honestly don't understand it, I can tell you a few things. It is one of many things we have been working on for a while and had that particular one functioning for longer than you would think.

"The facts I can tell you about are that you were transported in microseconds to a facility more than eight hundred miles from where we grabbed you. Our men left here, got there, grabbed you, and were back in less than one-minute, total operation time."

"How is this possible," the Admiral asked with his mouth open in disbelief.

"I wish I understood it, but however it works, I have to admit, it is pretty cool," Mr. Smith said. "And, we have other bits of technology here that puts that to shame with regard to operational military capabilities that leapfrog anything else on the modern battlefield. Now, on to my questions."

"We have a man named Joba in the next room. He was someone we took prisoner during the last war. Until recently he was the lead scientist on the Iranian nuclear program as I understand it. However, it seems they have made some advances since he has become our guest. They have also decided to work with your country in attempting to defeat us, which I'm not sure how that happened, but apparently it has.

"They have also, perhaps with your help who knows, and honestly, who cares, released one if not more biological weapons into the United States and Europe. As you are likely aware the international death toll continues to rise.

"Your fleet came into range of Silicon Valley, we assume to try to take control of our publicly known technology, and communication centers. We want to know troop locations, we want to know threats, and most importantly exactly how many bioweapons have been released, and what can be done to counter these weapons."

"I'm not going to answer much of that. I don't know who Dr. Joba is by anything other than reputation. I can tell you that if you have this technology the answers you seek will not be hard to find if you can grab the right computers, files and paper documents from certain command centers. But you already knew that, which is why you brought me here instead of killing me," the Admiral said.

"Admiral, you can save us all a lot of time, and save a significant number of lives in the long run by helping us to end this war quickly. You and I are both soldiers. The number of civilians being slaughtered in this war makes no sense. For some reason your government, the government of a nation that you dedicated your life to, has decided to partner up with a group of nations that will turn on you as soon as they are done with this current extermination quest they have started."

"That is not what I have been told, not at all," the Admiral said.

Mr. Smith pushed a button on his tablet, "Please send in Doctor Joba."

The interrogator mindlessly tapped the interrogation desk, waiting.

An older man walked through the door. He was escorted by two soldiers.

"Dr. Joba I want you to meet Admiral Zheng. I

would like you to tell him how you have been treated since becoming our prisoner."

"I have been treated with respect and dignity. The Americans are not what I have been told. They have allowed me access to books, periodic visits with my son, and have spent the last few hours showing me technology I just would have never imagined possible," the nuclear scientist said.

"I know they adhere to all of the conventions. They are honorable soldiers. That does not change my loyalties, and it should not change yours" the Admiral said.

"Admiral, I know how you feel. But we can't win, not against their technology base. This nation is willing to let our religious beliefs live in peace, but if we push them this gets worse. They will win, but many upon many on both sides will needlessly die. My religion is ok with this in some ways, but not in a war you can't win, not when they are willing to live in peace and let us do the same. Some in my nation have misinterpreted things for many years. This technology center of theirs is so far beyond anything else on the planet, that even in my wildest dreams I would have never considered much of this to be possible, and as a result we can't win. Not even with your nation by our side," Dr. Joba said.

"What have they told you?" the Admiral asked.

"Many things, and we are willing to show you as well," Mr. Smith broke in. "But we don't have time. We have a virus killing people, an invasion on two coasts and time is short. We will handle the troops the same way we decimated the incoming re-enforcements coming for the East Coast."

"What do you mean decimated," the Admiral asked.

"Oh, you haven't heard. Not surprising I suppose considering what we have been doing in the background on your communication network. We have jammed some communications, and we will soon get to all of it, selectively. What I mean by decimated is that the incoming fleets of troops ships headed for the East Coast of the United States no longer exist. We dropped a series of nuclear weapons on them and sent them to the bottom of the ocean. We are still looking for some of the submarines, but we will find them, and we will deal with that threat as well. There will be no incoming troops from that side.

"You are probably thinking that it is irrelevant because we can't nuke your troops already inside our borders, and you would be right. But let me ask you, what do you know of plasma weapons?" Mr. Smith asked.

"Enough to know that they will never properly work due to the need of a power source that is small enough, and high enough energy density to make them viable," the Admiral stated.

"Really?" Mr. Smith touched his tablet device a few times. "Watch this for a moment."

The Admiral looked at the screen. He saw a man carrying a device that was handheld, larger than a normal rifle, looked a bit heavier, but still transportable by a single person without causing too much of a burden. The man walked on screen, pointed the device at a large brick structure, pulled the trigger, the device spewed forth something and the brick structure fell to the ground, having partially melted.

"This device falls in a similar category to flame thrower or other weapons permitted under international treaty. We can mass produce these weapons. They are accurate at huge distances, and there is nothing your troops can duck behind that can protect them. Every known form of armor can be defeated with these devices due to the extreme temperatures," explained Mr. Smith.

"This device and power source are not nuclear in nature?" the Admiral asked.

"There is no radioactive signature, and that isn't the most advanced device we have," Mr. Smith explained.

"You have non-nuclear means to eliminate my soldiers? Vaporize them?" the Admiral asked in disbelief.

"Yes, they do," said Dr. Joba.

"Yes, we do," agreed Mr. Smith.

"How many of these weapons do you have?" the Admiral asked, not really expecting an answer beyond the prototype.

"Nine thousand of them stored at this facility alone," Mr. Smith said.

"I need to call my superiors," the Admiral said.

"We won't let you give away intelligence information," said Mr. Smith.

"Between this, and your transportation technology, I need to tell them to surrender," the Admiral explained.

"Then you will cooperate?" Mr. Smith asked.

"I will cooperate, but I need to get word back to the Chinese Homeland to end this folly, they will listen to me," he explained.

"Record what you want, and we will transmit it," Mr. Smith said.

"I agree," the Admiral said.

"Did you hear that Mr. President?" Mr. Smith asked the room, which was obviously wired for sound.

"Yes, thank you Admiral, we want to try to save lives. Please tell him anything you can once this recording is done, and please tell us anything you can about the submarines you loaned to your allies," the President said.

"I will cooperate as much as I can, we need to lay down arms, this is a suicide mission," the Admiral said.

***

Chairman Jackson stood waiting for the President. He liked this one, mostly because he knew that the man could fight a war. This was a war, a big one.

The door opened and before he came in, President Banner could be heard shouting, "Keep your seats!"

Upon entering the man was obviously tired, but keeping up the pace, "Chairman Jackson, what is happening?"

"Mr. President, the invasion in California is surrendering. They want to go home peacefully, and we are going to let them. The rules of war dictate this," the Chairman said.

"I agree, let them go home, but we need to monitor their progress carefully," the President agreed.

"Those on the East Coast are not going to be so easy. They are zealots and are refusing to surrender. They are going to fight to the last, but without any kind of incoming assistance they won't last long. We have a plan for them that will cause this effort to end quickly. We will review that for you now," he said as the screen behind him started to show the details and troop movements required.

<AP NEWS FLASH>*The Invasion Force of Chinese military in California has surrendered. The press has not been told what caused this to happen. The military briefing concerning the destruction of the fleet of troops coming from the Middle East should not have been enough to cause the Chinese to lay down arms. Something else must have happened and the White House as well as Pentagon representatives have refused to comment on this merely saying that details will be "forthcoming."*

There are new details that claim the President's report of fatalities counts is not high enough. However, there is no concrete evidence to argue against them.

There is also new evidence coming from the Center for Disease Control that there are far more viral strains infecting United States citizens than previously identified. The vaccines that have been discussed are only effective against some. Details on the path forward are pending.

The President has addressed the issue of social media "influencers" using the war to attempt to gain notoriety. While he won't speak out against their actions, he has said that they should exercise caution in getting their stories, for their own safety.

<AP ECONOMIC NEWS>The President has outlined the start of a recovery plan. The Congress and Senate have passed the plan more rapidly than expected. The President has signed this into law and money flow has started. It is expected that the loss of jobs will slow down if not come to an end, and some may even recover. This plan is being heralded as a great step forward in ending the economic freefall facing the United States. <STORY DEVELOPING>

Chapter Twenty
Ups and Downs

Frank had finally managed to get some sleep. It had been a few days since he managed a full night's sleep. This was only four hours, but he felt much better, at least so far. It was more than he'd had before he started, so it was progress. He walked into the Oval Office in shorts and a sweatshirt to find the Chairman of the Joint Chiefs.

"Mr. Chairman, you sent for me?" the President said.

"Yes, Mr. President we have information flow from the Chinese. They loaned out some missile boats and a few attack subs to the United Islamic Forces. Those missile boats have Chinese sailors as well as Islamic forces on board. Some of them have surrendered. We have intelligence suggesting that others have had the Chinese sailors killed and are now under the total control of religious zealots within the United Islamic Forces," Chairman Jackson reported.

"Well, that's not good," Frank said, not sure what the next move was. "Mr. Chairman, I was a mid-ranking field soldier. This is far above any kind of warfare I was training for, what do we do with this?"

"This is why we have advisors. So, don't think of it like you aren't ready, just give us guidance and ask questions. But I think the next step is that we look for them with every sonar set we have. Go all in," the

Chairman explained. "I have already given these orders. But this is the kind of information I couldn't keep from you."

"Thank you, Mr. Chairman. I'm not going to get back to sleep tonight," Frank sighed, and sat down behind the desk. "Given their last known locations, how long before they can be in a position to cause problems for us?"

"Sometime in the next 24 hours, Mr. President."

"Well, at least this will be over soon. How much warning will we get when missiles fly, and I assume that is their plan," the President asked.

"Not much. A trained crew can get it done fast and before we detect them prepping for launch. With the Chinese sailors out of the picture it will be a little better for us, but not a lot unless they have issues. Unfortunately," the Chairman reported.

"I'm not overly familiar with our missile defense systems, is it capable of doing this?" Frank asked.

"No, not the traditional one, but there might be an alternative. Let's take a walk down to the situation room and look at a concept they are working up," the Chairman said, motioning for the door.

"Great, another new, never before tried trick, that really bothers me. When I was active duty we practiced, then practiced some more, and then practiced again. Training was life, but this, this is crazy," the President said as he made his way to the door.

"While I would agree with you sir, but the insane

thing was them coming after us in this fashion. The nukes aren't what has me worried anymore, it is all the diseases, all the different strains killing people not to mention putting a strain on our economy," the Chairman said.

"Chairman Jackson, I'm confused. These devices can vaporize millions of people instantly. They aren't just going after the military, this is a civilian attack that we know is coming, and we can't stop it. How does that make you more concerned about the virus than losing a few more cities?" the Frank asked, honestly curious wondering if he missed something.

"When a nuclear weapon hits, it is over. All we have to do is cleanup, and we know they have a limited number of them, and we have a plan to deal with the threat. With the virus we don't know exactly how to treat it, we don't know who is contagious, and all we do know that it is really really contagious, and deadly depending on the case. That thing could spend years killing us off. Maybe it's because I have had longer to think about nuclear devices, but this viral stuff isn't what I ever wanted to consider being a reality. Yet, here it is, running around, not on a battlefield, oh no, this thing is running through our civilian population, whom I am supposed to keep safe," General Jackson said, obviously tired and annoyed that he couldn't solve the problem.

As the elevator came to a stop and the doors opened the President could hear sounds from inside the situation room but couldn't hear what they were saying. The room was too well built for that, but he had never heard anything from inside that room at this distance. It had to be a rather heated discussion.

General Jackson opened the door and announced the President, causing the room to go silent.

Frank saw that half his old Special Ops team was in the room helping do some planning. Sometimes Generals needed some innovation. Special Operators were known for this sort of thing.

"Good evening, everyone. I hear there could be a plan that saves our collective bacon?" the President said.

"Yes, Mr. President, there certainly is," said Secretary of Defense Martin. "But I want to caveat this with the fact that it is experimental, and we only have a single test run to prove it works. That test was successful but under very carefully controlled conditions."

"Ok, I get that. Show me what you are talking about," Frank said.

A Captain in the back of the room typed furiously on his keyboard for a few seconds and clicked a few things with a mouse before the screen in the front of the room changed.

It was a video of a Tomahawk Missile flying through the countryside. It was somewhere in New Mexico according to the information on the screen.

"Great, I see a Tomahawk. I have seen those before, what am I looking for?" the President asked impatiently.

The disembodied voice of Doctor Gross came on the speakers in the room, "Mr. President I think you will like what happens here in a few seconds. If I may. Our transportation system is just a giant way to rearrange things in space. Big or small, we can move them around. We have another, larger device that you will just love. Here coming on the left side of the image you will notice things start to change."

"Great, how are you recovering Doctor?" the President asked. He had been briefed on the scientist's injuries, and while they didn't seem life threatening, he was probably in pain, even while recovering.

"I'm recovering nicely, thank you, Mr. President, and they are keeping me on a pain killer that works, and allows me to keep working without clouding my brain," the scientist said. "Now, right there," the man said.

The screen froze for a second. A section was highlighted as Doctor Gross started narrating, "Now you will see the familiar transportation gateway, just in the sky instead of on a platform, and larger than we normally use. Now, as the video goes forward you will see what happens when we get a large enough gateway."

The video proceeded in slow motion. The missile disappeared into the gateway.

"Well, that sends it off track, but where is the missile now?" the President asked.

"Mars," Doctor Gross said matter of factly.

"Excuse me?" Frank said choking on a sip of coffee.

"Mars, we sent it to Mars. With this portal system the

farther away our point of destination is, the less accurately we can place the thing being transported. But in this case, we really don't care, because when it explodes on Mars no one is around to be hurt," the scientist explained.

"Well, that's one way to go. Why Mars? Why not just in space?" Frank asked.

"We need a set of known coordinates to send it to and Mars is really well known, and it seemed kind of fun," Doctor Gross explained.

"Ok, well great, send it to Mars. Long term if we could send those missiles back to their launching point I might prefer that, but for the moment let's just keep with the Mars thing if we know that works. What happens if the missile doesn't completely go through the center part of the portal? What does a miss look like?" Frank asked.

"That's a great question, Mr. President. We don't have data on what happens with a missile, but metal is metal, and we tried that a few times. So, we have a video that shows this. Captain, can you pull that one up?" the scientist asked.

"Yes, give me a second."

A moment later the screen changed to show a Ford F-150 rolling towards a portal. The test looked to be a few years old. The truck wasn't lined up properly and only half of it would enter the portal. Once reaching the point where it would normally disappear, half of the truck entered the portal, the other half didn't. The truck was sliced cleanly in half.

"So, you see Mr. President, if we miss, we still win. Chop one of these missiles in half and it can't go nuclear. Worst thing that happens is a pile of nuclear material falls to the ground and we have to go pick it up, or in this case send divers down into the water to find the material. It should stay in one piece, but it is easier than cleaning up a detonation," General Jackson explained.

"How long after detection is needed to get a gateway in place?" Frank asked.

"Thirty seconds, and to answer your next question as long as we have thirty seconds between transports, we can do this to every missile they can launch," Doctor Gross explained.

"How many missiles do we think they have?" Frank asked wanting to do some quick math in his head.

"A total of three subs with a potential of twelve missiles each. A maximum of thirty-six," General Jackson explained.

"We need eighteen minutes. So as long as they don't coordinate an attack or launch all twelve missiles from a single submarine while too close to the coast we have a chance," the President said.

"You have it, and we can also catch some in flight so, really we have a little bit longer than that," General Jackson said.

"He always was good at math," Warrant Officer Choi chided.

"You still owe me twenty bucks Chief," Frank told the man.

"They took all my stuff when I came through the door, something about security for some important guy who lives here," Peter joked.

"Gotta love it. Let's get some food brought in while we wait around to see if we are going to be nuked. Since we can do classified work almost anywhere in this part of the building, let's go upstairs so there is more space. I found out this place has 24/7 food service and a hell of a list of always available dessert options," Frank said.

"I thought you were getting a little soft around the midsection, all due respect, Mr. President," Sergeant Fisher said.

"Well that's true," the President admitted. "But damn, the cheesecake defies explanation."

***

The men were eating and talking about old missions when the alarm bells rang.

"Mr. President we have detected a sub but have no launch. It does look like they are preparing," said a Captain who burst into the room, out of breath after the sprint across the building.

"Let's get to work," Frank said.

As they got back to the situation room there was an image of a sub on the surface of the water. It had a single missile tube open, but the missile was clearly still in the tube.

"Do those guys realize they can launch from just below the surface, and we wouldn't know anything until it hit the air?" asked Warrant Officer Choi.

"Apparently not," said Captain Martin.

"Well, that's at least one thing breaking our direction. Nothing like an untrained enemy to make our lives easier," President Banner said, secretly hoping the situation didn't change. Nothing made a soldier's job easier than a poorly trained enemy.

"Mr. President, a few things. If they are going to launch a single weapon, we do know exactly where that vessel is, we have had plenty of time to do calculations on this situation, and we can throw it right back at them. They are pretty far from any coast, so any detonation would have zero effect on our territory or population," came the voice of Doctor Gross.

"Do it," Frank instructed.

The entire room sat, waiting, staring at the screen.

"Where are we getting the feed?" the President asked, realizing satellites were still questionable.

"We have some satellite coverage back, but this is coming from a drone with laser comm through a few hops to other drones back to the United States, then by fiber optic on the secure military network," General Jackson explained.

"Well, I'll take that as good," the President explained.

They stood another few moments and smoke started

to plume out of the sub. The missile launched into the air; a gateway appeared at what appeared to be a few hundred feet above the vessel. Then, the missile made its way back down and collided with the ship. It didn't go nuclear, but the ship was taking on water through the open hatch, and quickly as a result of the damage done by the collision. The hatch closed as the sub went into what had to be an emergency dive.

The missile was in pieces, the motor still spewing forth flame, but that wasn't the only source of fire. No one could tell if the warhead was intact, but everything involved was headed below water.

They watched for a few minutes as bubbles came up from below the surface. Strange things started to float.

Then, without warning, there was a massive, underwater explosion. The drone wobbled, and the feed was lost.

"Mr. President, that's one down, two to go," Chairman Jackson said with a smile.

***

Frank had showered, shaved, put on a suit, and was ready to brief the press. He wanted to deliver this news himself.

"Ladies and Gentlemen, the President of the United States," said the Press Secretary.

"Thank you, take your seats," Frank said as he came

in. "I have some information to share. Since their formal surrender, we have the Chinese giving information to us to help in the war effort against their former ally the United Islamic Forces, which is going to help greatly.

"Prior to their surrender, we managed to destroy the UIF troops coming into the United States, along with their flotillas. You know all of that. But what hasn't been public until now in any specific form, is that there was still danger lurking in the form of nuclear subs headed for our coast. Well, now we know specifically where they are. The bottom of the Atlantic Ocean. We know exactly how many they had, and we have destroyed them all. Their nuclear weapons, at least those on subs, are no longer a concern.

"Now, we do have additional information on the virus, and while I wanted to come out and deliver the information on this latest military victory myself, the details will be following. We even have some video which will demonstrate a new technology that we have used in this conflict. Believe it or not, this technology does everything they are about to tell you it does, and up until now has been classified. We have decided that making this capability known to those around the world may cause more of our enemy to lay down arms. So, to finish this briefing while I go talk to people about the virus challenges that we all face, I give you the Chairman of the Joint Chiefs of Staff," Frank said his bit, exited that he wouldn't have to explain this technology to anyone.

<AP NEWS FLASH>The President kicked off the most bizarre press conference ever witnessed in the history of mankind. There were technologies displayed that would have only shown up in science fiction movies prior to today. There are many questions left to answer, but it appears as though the United States has developed a type of technology, if not more than one, that will make the war end quicker than anyone could have imagined.

There are also, potentially, new details forthcoming on the fight against the biological weapon.

<AP ECONOMIC NEWS FLASH>After the press conference kicked off by the President and finished by the Chairman of the Joint Chiefs of Staff the stock market futures went up in ways that haven't happened since the end of the previous phase of this war. The President has given investors hope, and the economic stimulus plan appears to be working. If the virus can be kept at bay there could be hope on the horizon and investors have taken note <STORY DEVELOPING>

Chapter Twenty-One
The Virus and a Vice President

President Banner entered the Oval Office and Congressman Tom Cole, the current Speaker of the House, was waiting for him. "Congressman Cole, how are you today?"

"Just fine, Mr. President, interesting presser," the Congressman said. Tom Cole had been in Congress for decades, and Frank had seen him on the news many times, but he didn't realize just how tall the man was. He was shockingly well dressed, and even shook hands like a pro.

"Well, we managed to have a bit of success," the President said.

"What the hell is that new technology? Where did it come from? Or are we just throwing a fake out there to confuse the enemy?" Mr. Cole asked as he and the President took their seats.

"I assure you it is very real. It is something I didn't even know about until just after they hit Los Angeles. Honestly, how they kept it and a number of other things under wraps is beyond me," Frank admitted.

"What department did the money come from?" the Congressman asked.

"No clue, but we will find out at some point," the President said. "We have been a bit busy around here lately if you haven't noticed, and we haven't had time to be concerned about that type of question."

"I have noticed you were busy. New President, fired the Chief of Staff, haven't replaced him yet, and it seems like things are a little chaotic around here," The Congressman said.

This was not the meeting Frank had anticipated.

"Have I done something to offend you?" Frank asked.

"No, but with your approval rating, thanks to your status as a war hero when you were still with SOCOM, and now this victory, I can't let you carry on like some kind of emperor," the Congressman warned.

"Have I done that in some fashion?" Frank asked politely.

"Not yet, but a man in your position, that came to power this quickly, let's just say I have been in this town a long time. You see things and learn from experience," the Speaker jabbed back.

"I never wanted this job, I really never considered making a career change into politics, and when they asked me to be the Vice President it was so we could rebuild the military. I had no intention of being the guy in the hot seat for all of this. So far, the only help we have gotten from you guys down the street was passing an economic stimulus bill, thanks for that by the way. Now, do you have something constructive to do here today or are you here to tell me why you should be the Vice President and no one else in town should be. If that's the case, I have already had that phone call from exactly one hundred Senators," Frank rattled off.

"I would never ask you to put me as your second," the man said, unflapped.

"What? Why is that?" Frank asked, making an attempt at seeming surprised, and he hoped succeeding.

"You have never declared a party, I don't know your position on anything, you are a political rookie meaning your re-election chances are virtually non-existent, you have no real policy experience or positions that aren't fly by the seat of your pants kinds of things on many of the challenges facing our nation. On top of that, I might consider running against you," the Congressman rattled off.

"So, when you come down to this office for the meeting you intend to come out, run off and tell the press all kinds of things about me being incompetent and how you could do a better job," Frank explained, taking a stab at a sit-guess.

"I wouldn't put it like that, but I wouldn't be doing my job if I didn't score political points from time to time," he said with a smirk.

"I wouldn't be doing my job if I let you do so at my expense. So, why don't you let me explain why I wanted you to come here today?" the President asked.

"Go ahead, Mr. President," the man said.

"I asked you here because we need your help. I have a Warrant Officer and a team of special operators I used to work with that have been in and around here lately, some of whom are political junkies and have been for years. After you replaced my previous boss at his old job you were a great supporter of his. President Press believed in me, and I had hoped you would as well. You know the ins and outs in Washington. Before running for office, you were an economist. Now, I had asked you here to come on board and be the Vice President for that very reason. Also, I will tell you a secret, we are the same political party," Frank explained.

"Why should I do this? It could be career suicide," the Congressman stated.

"Well, there it is. The what's in it for me. Think about this for a second. You come on, you help me fix everything, you take credit for it, then you run for office after I'm gone. I have a few years left in this term, and I do plan on running again just for continuity's sake, then, I'm done. You are young and won't have an age issue when I am done, and if we can fix this together, you can go ahead and take credit for it. If we fail you can come out and claim that you attempted to save a sinking ship and despite every effort you put forward, I was an egomaniac, and you couldn't save the ship from me. So, you can't lose."

"Well, that is a thought. How do I know you aren't just saying this to try to get me to not walk outside and tell the press that you and I can't see eye to eye on the next economic stimulus package?"

"We'll get to that in a minute. Now, I want to tell you something. That transportation device you saw has been used for more than just moving missiles around."

"What else have we done, hopefully something helpful," the Congressman asked.

"We sent my old team, along with a medical expert, into the Iranian biological research institute to steal samples of any biologically engineered viruses and vaccines they have developed to keep their troops safe. We have a briefing coming up that you should be in so that you can really understand where things are. As it turns out they developed thirty-two different viruses and only had thirty vaccines, apparently with two still in the works, but we are still working on verifying this. Then there is the challenge that these viruses may or may not be mutating. We still aren't sure, but we know they may," the President explained.

"Well, that's not a good thing," the Congressman said with a sigh.

"Now, this is something we need a political pro to help us with while we go off and solve these problems. I never know when I'm about to step on one of those political landmines as I tend to just be brutally honest and always tend to say exactly what I mean. Which apparently doesn't go all that great in this town," Frank said.

"You are serious about this," the Congressman said.

"Come with me," Frank commanded. He was going to draft the man against his will if he had to.

***

The President and the Speaker of the House made their way back to the Press Room. The press was still asking question after question about the war effort and attempting to get answers about the virus attack.

The virus situation was confusing, no one knew what to do about it, and still weren't even sure what to call it. The situation was spiraling out of control.

The Chairman was still explaining something to the press.

"What we have is a unique situation. The Chinese have agreed to have their military out of our nation. We have their allies refusing to give up the fight. We have stopped the flow of their troops into the nation, perhaps for all time. But they do still have a good number of troops inside our borders.

"Some of those troops have laid down arms and disappeared. Due to the number of dead and dying thanks to the virus running around the nation there is a lot of chaos. People can disappear without warning. We have always had a problem enforcing immigration laws and we have a lot of people becoming transient due to nuclear detonations and now viral infected areas. It will be easier for these men to don civilian clothes and blend in. While we do not want anyone just assuming anyone is dangerous and taking matters into their own hands, we do want people to exercise caution. We believe they are forming terror cells and planning future attacks, and this must be handled with care.

The Chairman looked off to the side and saw President Banner give him the signal to introduce him.

"Ladies and Gentlemen of the press this is a little unusual to bring him back out as he already spoke during this press conference, but I give you The President of the United States."

Everyone in the room stood.

"Take your seats, this will be fast," Frank said as he settled in behind the podium. "We have had real issues with continuity persons in the leadership offices of our government. As a result, I do not want to leave one empty any longer than practical. I want to send a name to fill the vacancy in the Office of Vice President right now. I ask the Senate to immediately take up the confirmation of Speaker of the House Tom Cole. Now, to answer your economic questions on this I give you the Speaker of the House and next Vice President of the United States."

The room stood, cameras flashed, and they started shouting questions before he reached the podium.

<AP NEWS FLASH>The war effort appears to have taken a massive swing but isn't over yet. We have a massive challenge ahead with increased terrorist activity, and a virus for which there still appears to be no solution.

President Banner has lived up to his reputation as a military officer by instantly turning the tide of the war. He was always a good soldier and has had a career of defeating the enemy whenever called upon. He has not failed the nation, or the world in that regard.

These new military capabilities are in question as to how they work, and some on social media are calling it fake news. However, there is no mistaking that the Chinese Military is leaving California quickly, and many of the troops involved in the invasion on the East Coast have disappeared. Military hostilities appear to have all but ceased, but the virus threat is still very real. <STORY DEVELOPING>

<AP ECONOMIC NEWS FLASH>The economy is showing a few signs of life. This is thought to be in large part due to the stimulus package recently passed by the Federal Government. Currently stocks are improving, however due to the ever-increasing death toll it is thought that the economy is going to have challenges going forward. <STORY DEVELOPING>

Chapter Twenty-Two
The Research Effort

Doctors Claudia Hernandez and Jack Hetterick had just cleared security at the White House when someone appeared to escort them to the meeting. They had a lot of briefing material to cover, some of it good, some of it not.

The President had a lot on his plate, and they wanted to be able to bring forward nothing but good news, but that just wasn't possible.

"The President has been asking about this meeting. I think he wants to give all his focus to this problem now that we have a few other things at least somewhat under control," Chris Gintz, personal aid to the President said as he walked them to the appropriate room.

"How long have you known him?" Claudia asked.

"Since he first showed up here before he was even nominated him for Vice President."

"Wow, so you worked for the previous President," Claudia observed.

"And the one before him," Chris said. "It sounds like I have been here a long time, but remember we seem to change Commander in Chief a lot lately."

"Sadly, far too often," Claudia said.

"Yep, first political madness, then the former VP was killed, which thrust President Press into office, now this. So far, this one seems to be doing pretty well. He knows how to delegate, and most importantly he knows what he doesn't know, and he knows how to ask questions, and he knows when decisions need to be made fast."

"All of those sounds like good things," Doctor Hetterick said. "Is that unique among Presidents?"

"They all approach the job differently. This one was shoved into it. He, from what I can tell, approaches it just like he did the military unit he commanded. To hear him tell it, he wants to empower those around him to solve the problem, and then just get out of their way. Honestly, there are so many things a President has to do in a day that no one who has that job can possibly really know how to do it all. They just need to know enough to set the direction, set the goals and just trust that the experts in the room will get them there," Chris explained as they reached their conference room. "He'll be here in a few minutes, if you need help connecting to the projection equipment let the people outside here know, they'll call IT for you."

"Thanks," Claudia said.

The two setup their laptop, connected to the displays in the room, and waited for the meeting to begin. It was a relatively short wait.

"Doctors, please sit," the President said as he entered. "I think you know everyone here, Warrant Officer Choi, Captain Martin, and I want to introduce

Congressman Cole who I just nominated to fill the vacant slot as Vice President. I asked the officers here in case we must go back into that research facility. Now, let's just dive right in, what do you have for us?"

"Congressman Cole, good to meet you, Mr. President, I know you don't have a lot of time, so we tried to just stick with high level information," Doctor Hernandez said.

"I cleared the rest of the day for this so go into as much detail as you want and let us know what we can do to help," Frank said.

"Ok, wow, well, then we can probably go further than I had planned, but let's just dive right in," she motioned to her colleague.

The screen lit up with a list of names of different virus strains.

"Ok, I can't pronounce any of those, much less understand what any of them are without some kind of context," the President said.

"On the left is a list of virus strains, on the right is a list of vaccines. You will notice there are four missing on the right-hand side," she said.

"So, we are missing four vaccines when we thought we were only missing two, but can we assume those exist in the lab? Can we just go back in and get them?" the President asked.

"Mr. President, do you recall that we brought back a few laboratory notebooks on that particular mission?" asked Captain Martin.

"No, but I'll trust you," the President said.

"We were grabbing the samples, and on the desk were a few handwritten lab notebooks. For some reason these seemed like they were worth grabbing. In this particular case they covered the development of the virus strains. It described a brick wall they hit on developing the missing vaccines," Dr. Hernandez explained.

"Wonderful," the President said. "If we know how the virus was developed can we pick up the trail where they left off and maybe develop one?"

"In time, probably," answered Doctor Hetterick.

"How much time, and what do you mean probably?"

"There is no way to know how long. The trouble with these sorts of things is that viruses are known to mutate, and we don't know enough about these yet to see just how long it will take them to mutate into something new, and potentially even harder to fight."

"Ok, so let's move on through this presentation and I'm sure I'll come up with more questions," the President said with a sigh.

"Yes, Mr. President. We were going to cover injury statistics with you, and we can go into that if you like, but what you really need to know goes beyond the mathematical which merely proves some of the problems we face. These viruses were designed to be difficult to treat. They were designed specifically to put extreme strains on our medical treatment facilities.

"These notebooks have informed us as to their goals. They wanted something hard to detect, expensive to treat, and deadly. Some strains they wanted to have cause fatalities quickly, others they wanted the infected to die, but they wanted that process to take as long and be as painful as possible," Claudia said and paused before continuing. Anticipating that someone in the room would have a question.

"Doctor Hernandez," said Congressman Cole, "Are you telling me they developed more than thirty different strains of essentially the same virus?"

"They aren't all the same base virus," said Doctor Hernandez. "Some aren't even related."

"Ok, so they aren't the same virus, which makes it harder for us to handle because we will have to have multiple research programs figuring out how to fight this thing? And those research programs may have absolutely no synergies?"

"Yes," said Doctor Hetterick bluntly.

"They did this to, according to the notes, cause as much economic, and psychological damage as possible?" Congressman Cole asked.

"It appears as though that is the case from their notes. It doesn't spell that out, but their research notes included estimated cost to treat, and eventual economic impact of hospital overruns and strains on medical equipment manufacturing facilities," Doctor Hernandez explained.

"Are there any notes in there on how to treat these things?" the President asked.

"Not exactly. There are notes on what they tried to treat it, and some of it was moderately successful. It does give us ideas on a lot of things not to do," Doctor Hernandez explained.

"Well, that is something," Frank said.

"That is about the only bit of good news we have, Mr. President," Doctor Hernandez said.

"Mr. President, if I may," Congressman Cole said. "There is some politics to play here. We need global support to go after this. We will absolutely need the allies, some of whom aren't happy that we pulled out of the Middle East after the fall of Israel. However, we did make some points back with all the new technology that we have promised to use to keep the world safe. That doesn't change our need to get our global popularity back up."

"Yes, but what does that have to do with this?" the President asked.

"Well, everywhere from Great Britain to Europe, to parts of Africa are dealing with these same viruses. It turns out international travel caused this thing to make its way around the globe. And while we have been focused on the war here inside the United States, they have been facing down a virus and terrorist attacks of their own. How many times have we all seen the footage of London and Paris?" the politician explained.

"You are right, I was so focused I didn't even think about the rest of the globe," Frank admitted.

"Well, we could play politics, we could release some

of the details, if not everything from these laboratory notebooks to the public, after we call the allies and let them know, and that will get public sentiment to fall even more in our favor, because people want to support someone. While this isn't necessarily a net positive for us, it is a net negative for the enemy, and we look like the good guys for sharing the information and not trying to keep some kind of 'deep state' secret. We have to have that positive sentiment at a global scale if we are going to find a solution to this. Because I am going to take a stab at this, Doctor Hernandez, those strains with missing vaccines are some of the hardest to treat? The ones that will cost us a ton, financially speaking, to treat anyone who gets sick with these strains?" the Congressman asked.

"You are in the ballpark. If they aren't the most expensive, but they are really close. We have also learned that they originally had no intention of releasing those without a vaccine but somehow that did happen," Doctor Hernandez said.

"They really did a number on us," the President observed.

"Yes, let's go public. Peter, you have been quiet, but you always have interesting solutions to problems, what have you got?" Frank asked his former Warrant Officer.

"Nothing, this goes so far beyond my normal work area. If we could go back into that research facility and get something useful, I'd be the first to volunteer, but it doesn't seem like that's going to be useful."

"Doctor Hernandez is he right?" the President asked.

"Most likely, Mr. President." Doctor Hernandez said.

"So, we don't have a chance to get this done with anything other than a massive research effort. Can you give us an idea of what those four viruses are like for the patient?" asked the President.

"Before we get to that it is important to know that the patient may be contagious days before they are symptomatic in any fashion. But the patient will be in store for high fevers, which are high enough to make them delusional, severe headache that will be so bad it can be debilitating. The muscle aches and pains will be far worse than anything experienced with a typical influenza strain. Ludicrously severe diarrhea, abdominal pain, nausea and vomiting.

"If the patient doesn't recover after the first seven or so days it takes a turn for the worse. They will bleed, often from many areas. The fresh blood in the vomit and feces will be accompanied by bleeding from the nose, and gums. In the final stages the patient will be highly confused, irritable, and even turn aggressive. Patients may not die until somewhere between day fourteen and twenty post infection.

"Sounds like a nightmare of a disease," observed the President.

"It is not pleasant," Doctor Hernandez said.

"How is it treated?" Congressman Cole asked.

"A range of treatments are potentially helpful. These include such things as blood products: plasma, immune therapies and several experimental drugs.

Mostly it is supportive care, rehydration, and symptomatic treatment."

"So, a lot of 'hands on nursing' in hospital beds," said Captain Martin.

"Yes, sir," replied Claudia.

"Ok, we are certainly going to release this information. Peter, I want you to be the face of that," the President said.

"Me?" Peter asked.

"Yep, I heard you are putting in your retirement papers, you went in and helped get these viruses and you can say that publicly, so let's get you retired, move up here to Washington, and you are going to head up this task force. I need someone who speaks my language. In other words, you work for me, again," Frank said. He had been saying that he wanted familiar people around, that would help him adjust to the new role. Peter knew how to problem solve and make decisions.

"Do I get a choice?" he complained.

"Nope, I talked to your wife about an hour before this meeting, her one and only question was about salary, which is more than you make now, so you have been outvoted," Frank chided.

"Well, crap sir, fine, Doctor Hernandez you and I are going to be working together I suppose."

"Claudia this doesn't minimize your role. Peter is here to take administrative tasks off your hands. I need you solving the medical problems, not playing politics and wrangling people to get their job done. That is what Peter is going to do and is something he is better at than he will ever admit," Frank explained.

"I didn't think that I was being minimized for a second, Mr. President," she said.

"Great, now who gets to talk to the press first," Frank asked.

"Why don't I take that task," Congressman Cole offered.

"You got it, now let's get back to how we stop this disease from being transmitted," the President instructed the room.

***

It took a few hours to get things organized. But Congressman Cole had given many press conferences in his time in office. He had never given one like this, but he felt comfortable with the room. Telling people how to stop the spread of a disease was not his forte, but it was his new mission. He was more comfortable with the military announcements.

He was listening to the Press Secretary give instructions to the reporters who could probably recite the rules from memory.

"Now, I give you the Vice-Presidential Nominee and the Speaker of the House Congressman Cole."

He stepped out and motioned for the room to take their seats.

"Before I get to your questions, I have a few statements. First, we have verified that the flow of troops into our nation has stopped. The Chinese soldiers are starting their trek home.

"Now, on the East Coast we a different situation. It appears everyone has laid down arms. However, they haven't given up. We can now confirm the earlier assumption that they have donned civilian clothing and are attempting to become part of society. We believe they are going to bide time and plan a series of terror attacks. We have a team working on a response for this, and we ask anyone in the nation who finds someone without identification that they suspect of being one of these people, be cautious and do not attempt to take matters into your own hands. They are to be considered dangerous when provoked but are likely to stay peaceful until receiving orders or being provoked.

"The situations in Europe and Africa are atrocious. The strains of the virus have hit there as hard if not harder than they have here. They also have challenges in that their medical treatment facilities are not, in many cases, as advanced as ours. We are hearing fatality levels that meet or exceed our own. Once we get the situation under control here at home, we plan on reaching out to attempt to help those nations we can as soon as we are able.

"We have one remaining challenge we face, not as a nation, but as a globe, and this includes our enemy. This conflict was started by one nation, or more accurately, one collection of nations in the name of religion. But before I get into the challenge, I want to make a statement about this.

"I believe in God. I believe in an afterlife. The way I hold those beliefs is mine. In a free world you are free to choose the way you believe in God, or not. I will never and have never pushed my beliefs on anyone.

"I would certainly never do so by force. This war could have been prevented by people being tolerant of one other's views. The same can be said for many wars in the past. It is not unique in the reason for it, it is unique in that it has killed roughly ten percent of the global population, so far. That number is likely to grow. I urge all nations on the planet to work together to stop this conflict and solve the medical challenges we all face.

He held up two laboratory notebooks.

"These notebooks were obtained by members of our military from a biological research facility deep inside the borders of Iran. It outlines how they developed these viruses to cause the most damage to our populations and economies possible. Not to our military but to anyone that got in the way. At the start of hostilities, they stated that they wanted people to convert or die and they would give people that choice. This virus, and this act on their part indicates they had no intention of giving anyone that choice.

The reporters in the room were silent, cameras could be heard clicking.

"Much of the contents of these notebooks will be released to anyone and everyone who wants to read them. They will be translated into all languages. We beg anyone who is involved in medical research with any knowledge at all to pay attention to what is in these pages.

"In particular there is one area I need to point out.

"There are more than thirty strains of viral infections that have been released and are currently infecting or killing people around the world. Some of these they developed vaccines for, in order to keep their soldiers safe inside these viral hot zones.

"Some of these do not have vaccines. We believe they did not intend to release those as it would likely kill them as well as us, but they have been released. If that was accidental, I do not know. But it has happened.

"This has caused the situation in the Middle East to become bizarre to say the least. Many of the nations in this part of the world were united. They have, for lack of a better term, destroyed Israel. We believe they were attempting to form one nation across the entire planet. Our technology and this virus appear to have brought that process to a halt, but we do not believe it ended the desire.

"We are going to watch carefully, but we are not going to commit troops to that area at the moment. Not while this virus is running rampant. The virus is our primary focus for the time being.

"Now, I will take your questions."

They all came at once. He thought he heard some about the nomination process, others about the submarines that had been destroyed, some about the virus and one about being a seasoned politician among amateurs, he let them all shout for a moment.

"How about we do this. One person at a time. Mellissa, CNN, go ahead."

"Mellissa Foster, CNN, Congressman Cole, do you have any information on how Americans can protect themselves against this virus?"

"Just exactly what we have been saying for days. Wash your hands often, don't come in close contact with anyone if you can help it. When shopping for food wear gloves, wash everything, often, basic preventative measures. Unfortunately, there isn't a silver bullet. This is going to take a lot of effort on behalf of everyone to get through the road ahead. Now, there are a lot of people out there offering a magic solution if you just buy some product. I wish I had somethings that I could say that was a 'do this and you are 100% safe' but I don't, and to my knowledge neither does anyone else.

"From what Doctor Hernandez has told me there is one strain of this thing that does not discriminate by age, it doesn't care about pre-existing conditions, it takes a very healthy person and makes them very unhealthy. If you start out unhealthy, it does its job even faster. Almost no one has a natural immunity to it that we have found.

"Now, next question," he said pointing to the reporter from CBS.

<AP NEWS FLASH>The Vice Presidential Nominee and current Speaker of the House held a press conference to inform the nation of the virus situation. It was informative in regard to the war effort winding down, but he warned us that the war could flare up at any time in the form of terror attacks.

What was previously thought to be one or two different viral strains is now known to be more than thirty. The Congressman did distribute to the press a plan to deal with most of them. There are a few that do not have solutions. It is not known how many of those viruses with no solution are infecting a large number of people and how many of those are more isolated in nature. <STORY DEVELOPING>

<AP ECONOMIC NEWS FLASH>Upon hearing the news of the war winding to a halt, but with an increased threat of terrorist attacks, coupled with the announcements of the situation with the biological attacks facing the nation the markets are surprisingly up. Investors are saying that the President and his Vice-Presidential nominee are facing challenges but appear to have a plan to get the situation under control and allow the world to see a promising future again. This is across the board from individual investors to institutions.

Chapter Twenty-Three
Technology Goes Public

Doctor Gross had been in the shadows doing his work for so many years he wasn't sure what to think of the potential for public attention. As a result, a compromise was made. He would record a series of two-minute videos for the White House social media accounts explaining some of his technology, and in the process making certain parts of it public knowledge. Some would be held back for security reasons but parts of it could be fantastically useful for both intimidating the enemies of the United States to a point where they would refuse to attack, and others could help revitalize the economy while keeping people from spreading the viruses all over the world.

He had already demonstrated the transportation equipment, which was not the most technologically interesting, or so he thought.

When the camera came on, he worked from memory, he didn't need a script.

"We have developed a power source that is unlike any other. The enabling technology behind it is the ability to manage and contain heat. This power source is both long lasting and portable. It emits no harmful radiation and runs on a gaseous material. To refuel you just take one of these cans," he picked up a can of compressed gas.

"And insert it here. That reloads the gaseous fuel the internal equipment uses to generate electricity. How the equipment works isn't important, what is important to know is that the device functions like a normal battery. It puts out a known voltage and current, and they can be chained together. By chaining them together it works like any other electrical system.

"The energy density is beyond any other known energy source meaning that for the weight of what you see here more electrical energy comes out the other side than with any other device.

"Watch how this works.

He put the device down, wired it up to a long series of electrical devices across the top of the table. The coffee cup sized device made them all come to life.

"As you see from this one fuel cell we can power a computer, a cell phone, two desk lamps, a television, the printer, and two different pieces of lab equipment. It will power these devices for the next three weeks, and costs pennies to refuel. Until recently this device has been experimental but it now possible to mass manufacture.

"This could cause the average electric bill in the world to drop by a factor of one hundred. The average cost of purchasing many different goods throughout the world will also decline. Think about it, it costs money, some of which is based on electricity to produce those goods. There is also an energy cost involved in shipping, with these devices and our transportation device, not only is the cost to ship reduced, but the time to ship is greatly reduced. The cost of the person to drive the truck is now gone from the equation and the overall cost of the goods we purchase everyday drops accordingly. Not to mention road accidents and traffic congestion drop."

***

The President was at his desk and preparing to sign a bill into law. It was a process he wasn't used to. His signature, making something a law.

The cameras flittered away watching the most boring event possible in his opinion. Him signing a piece of paper. But here he was signing it.

This piece of paper was now a law that would establish a new international consortium aimed at dealing with virus outbreaks and eliminating biological weapons development from taking place ever again. It also organized an international consortium to work to find a solution to the virus that was continuing to spread rapidly around the planet.

The world was watching, and it had taken a few weeks to get through Congress because of the number of international partners that had to agree prior to passage. Here it was, now a law, money would be spent, and people would be spending time on this now and getting paid, all because he had signed a piece of paper.

***

Doctor Gross had not been in his lab for a while. His team had grown, his facilities were better than ever, and he really liked this new arrangement. In Washington some of the elected officials had asked just how large of an object could be transported at once. Apparently for commercial use it had to be able to take huge amount of equipment from one place to another. He had never thought about how much commercial shipping took place every day.

The concept was simple. Take a series of smaller devices and move things to the larger depots and then from there out to final destinations. It would mean mass production of small and medium transportation units, but only a few of the larger ones like this.

It had never tried it before, never even considered one on this scale. Theoretically it could take a shockingly large amount of material from one place to another on Earth or send a small amount of equipment to the other side of the known Universe.

"Ok, are we ready?" Doctor Gross asked.

"Ready as we are ever going to be," Doctor Miller replied. "I'm not sure if we should have gotten this much bigger in one step, but it is ready to go."

"Should we try lower power?" Doctor Gross asked.

"I don't think with a device this large it would work due to the size of the aperture without massive power, but try whatever you are comfortable with," he warned.

"I think we'll be ok, let's just go for it, worst thing that can happen is some components will melt down, so let's give it a shot," Doctor Gross didn't mind the risk.

"Here we go," a technician reported.

The device came on, equipment started to make noise, keyboards were tapped.

"Where are we aiming?" Doctor Gross asked.

"We are going to send things from here to the middle of Death Valley National Park," Doctor Miller said.

"Sounds good."

They waited as things were charging up.

Suddenly there was a small smatter of sparks from the back of the room, then more, and more.

"What's that?" Doctor Gross asked.

"Nothing, diagnostics shows green. Just fresh wiring settling in. We'll chase it down later," some technician shouted.

"Wait, this isn't right," Doctor Miller said.

"What?" Doctor Gross shouted over the equipment.

"Something is coming through the gate. That can't be right. Turn it off, we must have a bug someplace."

Before anyone could act a large device came out of the portal. It hovered in the warehouse sized laboratory. It was wedge shaped and appeared to just float effortlessly in space.

"What the fuck?" Doctor Gross asked.

The portal shut down, nothing else could come through.

It hovered for a few minutes. No one was sure what to say, no one was sure what to do. There was a military guard in the room that stood there, not sure if this was a threat, something to be destroyed, or something that was supposed to happen.

"Is this one of ours?" Doctor Gross asked.

"Not anything I have ever seen," Doctor Miller said.

The floating structure landed. A door opened. A nine-foot-tall biped came out of the craft. It looked around the room. It's purple skin and two pairs of eyes one on top of the other let them know what happened.

"Remember when we said one possibility if we turned power up too high was a wormhole? I think that isn't just a possibility," said Doctor Gross unable to take his eyes off the creature that was so far not threatening anyone.

"Maybe we should get the President on the line," Doctor Miller suggested.

<AP NEWS FLASH>The President has said that a new portal has been tested and the results, while not what was expected will certainly be something that will change the future of mankind. No further information is available.

There has been a large explosion in Death Valley, the

White House has said it was related to an experiment and no one should be worried given the location of the detonation it was assumed it would go unnoticed. <STORY DEVELOPING>

<AP ECONOMIC NEWS FLASH>The market is trending flat on recent news. No one is sure what is meant by the releases from the White House and investors are waiting for additional information before making any moves.

Look for The Last World War Volume 3
Coming Soon from Imholt Press